THE VERDIGRIS PAWN

ℰ
VERDIGRIS
PAWN

ALYSA WISHINGRAD

HARPER

An Imprint of HarperCollinsPublishers

ISBN 978-0-06-290805-6

Typography by Laura Mock
21 22 23 24 25   PC/LSCH   10 9 8 7 6 5 4 3 2 1

First Edition

For DJS, OAS, and OGS
Everything and Always

Chapter One
A Game of Fist

There was a long list of things Beau should be doing. He should be studying, preparing for the day's lessons. He should be getting dressed, not lounging around in his shirt-sleeves. He should be trying to make himself into the kind of heir his father needed—no, *demanded*—him to be. But all Beau was doing was the one thing he absolutely shouldn't be doing: trying to win at a game of Fist.

He'd already lost three matches to himself, but the second peg on the candle clock hadn't burned down yet. He just might have enough time to finish this match.

Beau rotated the Fist board so that he was now playing the challenger's side, trying to remember what Fledge had taught him. When the stable master had explained the rules, it sounded so logical. Either the king knocked the verdigris pawn off the board or the pawn unseated the king.

A simple enough premise.

What wasn't simple was keeping all the rules, strategies, and exceptions to the rules straight.

By positioning the ace between the king and his front guards, Beau was certain he was setting the challenger's side up for victory. Yet as soon as he pulled his hand back, he realized his fatal mistake—the move had left his mage completely exposed to the king's yellow guards.

Game over.

"I'll never win," Beau groaned as he toppled the board in frustration. But watching the game pieces scatter only made him feel worse. The Fist set was the only thing of his mother's he had left; he'd never be able to live with himself if anything happened to it.

He'd just retrieved the king and almost all the yellow guards from under the side table when he heard the telltale *shush* and *pop* of the key at work on the door to his apartments.

Mags was early.

Beau's tutor was many things—curt, a bit lazy, and all too mercurial. The severity of his punishments varied depending on his mood. He could also be kind on the rare occasion. But he was never early.

Beau shoved everything under the cushions of his chair, then threw himself on top and started rereading Volume VII of *The Histories: The Great Battles and Their Heroes*, as if he'd been there all day.

"I'm in here," he called out. "Reading!"

But the low-pitched rumble that replied didn't belong to Mags.

"By the Goodness of Himself!" Barger, the Manor's chamberlain, proclaimed as he entered the sitting room. "Stand and await his arrival."

Beau's limbs turned cold.

An unplanned visit from his father, Himself, was completely out of the ordinary. Beau wasn't scheduled to have an audience with him for several days.

Beau dropped the book on the table and stood waiting as the waft of cloves and the shushing of long, velvet robes trailing on the floor heralded Himself's arrival.

As usual, Himself offered his only son no greeting or pleasantries while he conducted his steely-eyed inspection. Beau remained motionless as his father's pale gray eyes searched for some imperfection, real or imagined. Then came the frigid touch of those long, thin fingers as they twisted a silver button upright so that the Manor's crest stood straight or tugged at the single stray curl on Beau's head that dared to be an eighth of an inch longer than the others.

"You are surprised to see me," Himself said, his expression pinched in disgust.

"It's always a good day when you pay me a visit, Father."

"Is it?" This was neither a question nor an invitation to respond, for everything Himself said was an irrefutable statement of fact. His opinion the only one that mattered. "Your tutor will not be returning."

Beau's stomach soured.

How many tutors had Himself already fired? Beau had lost count. Yet he'd still been hoping Mags would be the last, for unlike some of his predecessors, he always allowed Beau time for a daily riding lesson with Fledge.

"I thought you'd been pleased with my progress," Beau said.

"You thought wrong."

Himself nodded to Barger, who stepped forward.

"Your tutor was found dead this morning. The fever has now spread from the guards' barracks here at the Manor to those in the Upper and Lower Middlelands," the chamberlain intoned. "A few of our outlying cottages were also affected."

Beau fought to hold steady, calm. He knew better than to show any emotion in front of his father. Still, news of his tutor's death hit hard. Underneath all his bluster and posing, Mags had been good to Beau, and Beau would miss him.

"May I attend his funeral, please?" Beau asked.

But Himself had no answer for Beau. "Bring it in," he ordered his chamberlain.

Barger summoned a footman carrying a large silver tray set with a pot of hot water, a small bowl of herbs, a single teacup, and a long-handled spoon. The servant placed the tray on the tea table, then quickly scuttled out of the apartment.

Himself adjusted the items on the tray in accordance with some measure of perfection only he understood before turning on Beau. "Pour the tea."

Beau knew what was coming next, even though he didn't understand why. Himself had already put him through this test once before and was irate when Beau failed. Yet here he was again, trying to prove that Beau was a charmer.

"Please, sir, I—"

Himself cut Beau off with a wave of his hand. "We're going to try something simpler this time. Boils. You won't mind, will you, Barger?"

"At your service as always, sir." Barger dutifully stepped up to the tea tray.

"Boils," Himself repeated. "Even the weakest charmer would have been able to raise oozing sores."

"Please, Father," Beau pressed. "You can't think me a charmer, can you?"

The vein in the center of Himself's forehead began pulsating, a warning that an explosion was close at hand. "Do you dare question me?"

"No, sir, never, sir." Beau emptied the bowl of herbs into the pot and stirred while softly repeating, "Boils, boils, boils." Although what he really wanted to say was, "Why? Why? Why?" It made no sense at all. The last of the charmers had been killed by Himself's own elite guards before Beau even was born.

Yet still he stirred.

After what he supposed might be a good amount of time, Beau poured a cup of tea and handed it to the chamberlain.

Barger downed the steaming hot brew in one go, as if to prove stupidity was a sign of loyalty.

What felt like minutes, hours, lifetimes passed, the tension in the room growing taut enough to crack glass while Himself stared at the chamberlain's face.

"Check your hands, check your legs," Himself barked as Barger readily obeyed. And yet the chamberlain remained, as he'd always been, unblemished—at least on the outside.

"Useless!" Himself shouted as he grabbed the teacup and threw it across the room. "You are unlike me in every way and far too much like *her*. Except where it would matter the most!"

Beau's stomach twisted. He knew so little about his mother, except that his likeness to her enraged his father. The only times Himself ever mentioned her was when he was berating Beau for not being strong enough, hard enough.

"It should be you!" Himself sneered. "It would be easier if it were you. At least if you were a charmer then we could stop these floods and blights from cursing us, end this fever, and quell the rumblings of revolution. Unless . . ."

Himself pulled Beau so close all he could see were the spindles of gray and yellow coloring his father's eyes. "Unless you think you're clever enough to hide your powers from me?"

"I could never do that, sir."

"That's true. You're not clever enough to deceive anyone." Himself released Beau with a disgusted sigh and began pacing back and forth. "But if it's not you, then who? I was fooled once, I will never let another charmer threaten our rule again!"

Himself kicked the table, sending the tea service clattering to the floor.

His father's anger was nothing new; it was a weight Beau was accustomed to carrying. He could withstand a season without any outside privileges or being made to recite chapters from all seven volumes of *The Histories* by heart. He'd done it before and would no doubt have to do it again. What he'd never done was doubt that Himself was always right.

Until now.

"Perhaps, Father, it's not a charmer," Beau ventured. "After all, Volume Seven says there have been none since the war."

He cleared his throat and stood a little taller. "Chapter thirty-eight. 'After killing the rebel Palus Whynde and his men, the Manor, aided by our fearless ally, Torin, Guardian of Peace from the North, handily defeated the rest of the Badem, that confederacy of charmers and villains who occupied the Bottom. The old ways and the charmers who practiced them were erased.'"

Himself stopped pacing to glare at Beau, his gaze hard enough to burn through to bone. And yet, there was also the tiniest flinch, a tell of something else boiling under the surface. But Himself said nothing to his son, turning instead to Barger, who'd just finished picking up the scattered tea things off the floor.

"Prepare for my departure. There's only one way to reinforce our guards if we are to keep the peace in the Land and extinguish any thoughts of rebellion."

"Of course, sir." Barger bowed deeply, quite unable to hide the spark of glee in his eyes. "And in which direction will you be riding out?"

"To the north."

"To the north? To see Torin?" Beau's blood fairly began fizzing at the thought of traveling that far away. The farthest afield he'd ever been was Topend. But he'd long dreamt of seeing what lay beyond the Manor, what wonders existed out past the borders of the Land. Hoping, wishing this might at long last be his chance to go somewhere, anywhere, Beau bowed to his father. "May I accompany you, please, sir? It would be my honor to assist you."

"What *assistance* could you possibly offer?" Himself scoffed. "No, you most certainly will not accompany me. In fact . . ."

Himself grabbed Volume VII of *The Histories* and threw it into the fire, causing the flames to spark and flare. "Enough reading and dreaming. Upon my return in five days' time, I will train you in the arts of war myself, make you into someone deserving of the blood in your veins, a worthy successor, no matter what it takes. Until then, you will remain in the

Manor with Barger overseeing your safety."

Beau felt as if he surely would combust right along with the pages of his book. Although Himself had made similar threats in the past, he'd always lose interest in his son and hire a new tutor. But being left in the chamberlain's care was different. The last time Himself put Barger in charge, he'd locked Beau in his apartments, depriving him of all lessons, fresh air, and even the necessity of having his chamber pots emptied. When Beau subsequently told his father how Barger had treated him, he'd been punished for lying.

The dangers of disputing his father's orders were plentiful, but what was one more penalty piled on the ever-growing mountain of trouble Beau lived atop?

"Please, sir, this isn't necessary," Beau said, mustering what he hoped was an appreciative smile. "I wouldn't want to take Barger away from his important work. Mags mapped out my studies well into next season. I can work alone."

"I decide what is necessary. You do as instructed." And with that, Himself gathered his cloak and headed out the door.

Barger moved to follow his master out but stopped in front of Beau. With his red hair pulled tightly back in a braided queue the chamberlain bore an uncanny resemblance to an equally nasty bird, the red-throated napper. Just as nappers were known to swoop in and destroy the nests of other birds, Barger was always eager to shatter Beau's world.

With a smirk blossoming on his face, the chamberlain opened his hand to reveal a flash of that unmistakable brilliant blue-green color. He then tucked it into his pocket and sauntered out of Beau's apartments.

The verdigris pawn.

Beau thought he'd stuffed the vibrant green game piece into the chair cushions with the rest of the Fist set. Yet there it was in Barger's possession.

An asset waiting to be leveraged against him.

Beau collapsed into his chair, his insides twisting and turning like a spring maelstrom.

The charge for playing Fist, a game about strategizing to overthrow the king, was nothing short of treason. Anyone caught playing it, whether the lowliest pig keeper or Himself's own heir, was considered a traitor and would pay the ultimate price for their crime.

If this were a game of Fist, Beau would try to counter Barger's move by activating his mage, the one piece that can effectively shelter the pawn from capture. Or he could try to find a way to move his ace into a position where it could knock every one of the king's guards within a two-square radius off the board. But Beau had neither a sorcerer nor a champion to help protect him in real life. He didn't even have any friends aside from Fledge.

Fledge.

It would be too easy for Barger to figure out who'd been

teaching Beau the game.

He had to warn him.

Beau cast off any worries for his own self and threw on his favorite riding coat, the one with dangling buttons and holes teasing at the elbows. Himself might have confined Beau to the Manor, but *technically* the riding stables were part of the Manor. He wasn't exactly breaking any rules, he was simply expanding their definitions.

Chapter Two

The Cordwainer's Apprentice

Beau waited until the last of Himself's elite guard rode off from the stables toward the parade grounds before dashing out from under the cover of the large weeping willow. He couldn't afford to be spotted by one of Barger's countless spies—not if he wanted to keep Fledge out of trouble.

He climbed in through the tack room window, his usual route, and landed with a thud. But what he found inside was anything but usual. The entire room was turned upside down. The tack racks were empty and what few items remained were strewn about. He'd never seen the place in such disarray.

He was too late.

Beau lunged for the door. Maybe he could somehow make Barger listen to reason or strike a bargain designed to make Barger think he'd come out on top. But just as Beau reached for the knob, the door flew open.

"Good timing, you just missed the madness." Fledge ruffled Beau's hair in greeting. "I've never had to send so many horses out at one time."

"You're here!" Beau hugged his friend tightly.

"Of course I am." The master of the stables' sunny aspect had faded, replaced now by lines of worry pleating the corners of his eyes. Even though Fledge was only ten years older than Beau, when worry creased his brow it gave him the look of a man much older than twenty-three. "What's happened? Are you all right?"

"For now, yes, but not for long."

"Come, we'll go sit down."

Fledge guided Beau into his private quarters. He placed the kettle on the fire and pulled two chairs up close to the hearth.

"Tell me what happened. Something with your tutor? Your father? Did you cross Barger again?"

"Yes," Beau said. "To all of that and more."

"Start at the beginning," Fledge counseled, his voice calm and even as usual.

"I don't know that there really is a beginning." Beau shook his head. "It's all mixed up and tangled together."

"Then begin where you can."

Beau took a deep breath and started with the least of the bad news—his father's plan to train Beau himself.

"He's threatened as much before," Fledge said. "He'll likely forget by the time he returns. What else is bothering you? It can't just be that."

"It's not." Beau's voice cracked. "It's the fever. . . . Mags is gone. His cottage is . . . was . . . next to the barracks."

"I'm so sorry, Beau," Fledge said. "Although sadly I'm not surprised. A messenger arrived this morning with word that the fever has spread to the guards in both the Upper and Lower Middlelands. The gates along the roadway are thinly guarded, there are reports of bandits overtaking carriages and wagons, and people are getting scared. Angry. But now that the rains have ended, the fever should hopefully stop spreading. Go on, tell me the rest."

Beau shifted nervously.

"I know you told me not to," Beau began. "I never thought I'd get caught. I was always so careful. But I really want to win a match against you, and so I needed to practice. Don't hate me, Fledge, please."

"You know that would never happen. Go on."

Beau tugged at his shirt collar, hoping to catch a full breath before diving in. "Barger has my verdigris pawn."

Fledge paled. "You have a Fist set?"

"It was my mother's. Hers is nearly identical to yours, except her pawn is a lot nicer, no offense."

"How did you find it?" Fledge pressed. "Where?"

"Well, back before her rooms were sealed up, I was there one day," Beau began. "I always liked the way it smelled, being surrounded by her things. Anyway, there was this chest in the far back of the wardrobe. It had all these hidden drawers and compartments you could only access by opening other doors and compartments. Like a puzzle. It took me half the day to figure out how to open up all the chambers. I found the Fist set along with some small bottles and jars in the very last one I opened."

Fledge winced.

"I swear, Fledge, I will never tell them you taught me. Never!"

Fledge rose from his chair and poked at the fire in the hearth. "I know you won't."

"What do I say?" Beau asked. "I'll have to answer for it somehow. I can tell Barger I had no idea what it was, but I'll have to admit to finding it in Mother's room."

"No," Fledge said, decisively ending the entire discussion before he softened again. "Leave your mother's memory out of it. I wish you had told me you'd found it."

"I was waiting until I knew I could win a match. I wanted you to be proud of me. Instead I put you in danger."

Fledge rested his hands on Beau's shoulders. "I'm proud of you regardless. And you don't have to worry about me. I'll be just fine."

"There is one more thing. My father tried to test me again. This time, he—" Beau began, but was interrupted by a loud rapping on the door.

A messenger from Himself's regiment.

"By the Goodness of Himself! The captain of the first regiment has requested additional blankets," the messenger announced.

Fledge sighed. "I have no more. I'll go see if there are any left of the lot that were sent from beyond the Islands. Tell him if I find any, I'll bring them immediately." Fledge waited for the messenger to leave before heading for the door himself. "Beau, saddle up your new filly and warm her up out in the paddock. I won't be long."

Though Beau's problems still loomed as large as when he'd arrived in the stables, he felt more assured as he watched Fledge walk away. His friend always had that effect on him; but sadly it always wore off as soon as Beau returned to the Manor.

The chestnut filly whinnied something between a greeting and a threat when Beau entered her stall. She'd been a challenge to train, willful and stubborn, but she was slowly getting used to him. Still, she was no replacement for Puzzle, Beau's favorite horse, who was stolen along with two of Himself's stallions more than a season ago.

"I suppose I should finally name you," Beau said. "What should it be? We need something that fits both sides of your personality."

He started to slip the bridle over the filly's head, but she shook it off with such force, it went flying out of the stall.

"Or I'll just call you Mule since you're so stubborn," Beau griped as he went to retrieve the bridle.

And that's when he saw her.

A girl with a long, brown plait running down her back slipped past, heading toward the adjoining corridor. He'd never seen a girl in the stables before, let alone one who looked to be anywhere near his own age.

"Hello!" Beau called.

The girl turned, the confusion on her face a mirror of his own.

"Are you looking for someone?" Beau asked.

"I . . . I'm looking for Master Fledge," she said, clasping her hands over her apron pocket. "I was told to bring something to him."

If that was the truth, it wasn't very convincing. Beau knew a person with a secret when he saw one.

"He'll be back soon," he said. "You should wait for him."

"No." She turned back down the corridor. "I'll come back later."

Beau had so few opportunities to ever talk to anyone his age—or at least anyone who wasn't the spawn of a pompous, snobbish Topender. He didn't want her to go.

"Stay," he insisted. "I'm sure Fledge would want you to wait for him."

The girl's look of surprise melted into a kind of skepticism.

"And how do you know what Master Fledge would or would not want? I thought a cordwainer's apprentice's job was to cobble and repair boots and tack, not keep track of the stable master."

Beau was about to correct her when he stopped short. If she knew who he was, she'd either try to impress him or flee. Any chance of a normal conversation would be gone.

"I wish!" Beau said. "I mean, I'm still just a junior apprentice."

"Well, whatever you are, count yourself lucky that at the end of the day you get to leave here."

"Why do you say that?"

The girl started back down the cobbled corridor. "The cordwainer might be fine with you stopping your work for idle chatter, but I don't have that luxury."

"Oh, come on." Beau laughed, following her. "You're too young to have to work."

The girl stopped and turned on Beau. "Is this your first time on the Manor?"

"Uh . . ." Beau had never been a very assured liar.

"I thought as much," she said. "You should watch your tongue. Your master's authority means little when you're here. Don't you know the Manor can claim anyone and keep them here to work? Even a cordwainer's junior apprentice."

"That's not true." There was no mention of anything remotely like that, in even the oldest of *The Histories*.

"It absolutely is. So unless you want to wind up working the peat bogs or in Mastery House, mind yourself while on these premises," the girl chided.

"Mastery House? What's that?"

The girl's expression flickered between disbelief and pity. "You're jesting, right? Lucky you to be so blissfully ignorant."

"I am *not* ignorant!" Beau bristled. "And who are you lucky enough to be?"

"Fourth nursemaid's assistant," the girl replied. "Otherwise known as the very bottom of the bottom."

"A nursemaid? You look too young for that," Beau replied. "But I meant what's your name."

The girl paused before replying, "Cressi."

"Named for Cressida the Bold?"

"Probably." Cressi's upper lip curled in disgust. "Though I'd take Bucket or Chair over Cressi."

"Why?" Beau asked. "She's a heroine of the first Battle for the Bottom."

"Heroine?" Cressi gave a small half laugh. "She was a traitor."

"She was not!" Beau volleyed back. "'She led the Manor forces to the cave where the knaves who blighted our fields were hiding.' She was directly responsible for Palus's capture."

Cressi squinted at him as if he'd suddenly gone out of focus. "That's definitely a jest, right?"

"It's all there in Volume Four of *The Histories*. I mean, she did use the old ways when she charmed Will Cutler into giving up their position, but she turned that information over to the Manor."

Cressi paled and stepped back, the wall the only thing stopping her from beating a full retreat.

"You're not the cordwainer's apprentice, are you?" Her voice, which had been so strong and certain, now came barely above a whisper.

Beau thought about lying, but he was terrible at it.

"Son of a Topender?" Hope raised the end of her question like a prayer.

As Beau shook his head again, all her surety and self-possession dissolved into a blank mask of subservience.

"I've made a terrible mistake, sir." Cressi dropped down into a deep curtsy. "I am at your mercy."

"Oh no! Don't do that." Beau reached out to pull her back to her feet but stopped when she flinched. "I have no mercy to give. Wait, that's not what I mean. Just . . . please stand up."

Cressi stood but refused to look at him. She looked the way he always felt when he stood in front of his father—scared to make a wrong move, yet angry enough to combust.

"See, this is why I didn't tell you who I was. You should just go on as if I truly were the cordwainer's apprentice. Can't you just make believe I'm not who I am? It's easy, I do it all the time," Beau said, but the girl remained frozen. "All right then, at least tell me what Mastery House is."

Cressi pulled her shoulders back and fixed her gaze just above Beau's head.

"Mastery House trains children for work, in accordance with their abilities," she replied, her voice cold and removed. "Once their training is completed, they're placed in service either here on the Manor, in Topend, or sometimes in the Middlelands, but that's only for those who show a talent for one of the finer crafts."

"So, if you show a talent for, say, silversmithing, you're placed as an apprentice? Is that it?"

"Apprenticeships are for children of the Lower Middlelands only. Mastery House children are destined for"—she paused to search for the right word—"lowlier work."

"You mean like fieldwork?"

"Like digging holes, crawling into mines where adults don't fit, or picking through manure to save seeds."

A lump settled in Beau's throat, making it hard to swallow. "I don't understand, why would their parents allow this?"

"It's not about what they *allow*." The way Cressi was looking at Beau now left him feeling withered and burned. "The wars stripped the people of the Bottom of everything of worth. The only currency left is bartering, theft, and bribery, yet they still have to pay their tax levy."

"But if they have no money, how do they pay?"

"With the only things they have of worth. They surrender their children."

"Surrender their children?" Beau repeated. "How can they do that?"

"You're asking the wrong question," Cressi said. "I think you mean, how can they not do it when it's the only acceptable form of payment."

"Then they should just hide them away!"

"Where? In the woods, in a cave, perhaps up a tree? You can't hide in the Bottom or anywhere else for that matter. Those who've tried have seen their homes burned to the ground, the men jailed, the women sent to work the peat bogs. And worse."

"I don't believe you," Beau said, trying to wave her words away. "This sounds like something the Badem would have done. Who would force families to give up their children?"

Cressi shook her head, her face pinched with disgust. "You."

Chapter Three
Mastery House

"Me?" The heir's eyes went wide, and his plump cheeks reddened. "I'd never force anyone to surrender their own children! Just because I was born as . . . well, me, doesn't mean I have control over anything at all. My father doesn't listen to me, ever!"

"Well, at least you'd get to keep your tongue if you dared address him," Cressi replied.

"Barely. You don't understand, it's complicated."

"Complicated?" Cressi repeated. "Is that what it is?"

There was no way the heir, a boy rumored throughout the Land to be exactly like his father, could be this simple-minded. It was all Cressi could do not to throttle him. But she'd already said way too much and risked ending the day with her head on the chopping block. Although if Nate were here and not still in Mastery House, he'd say it was her duty to run the wretch through with a blade. Then he'd try to convince her, yet again, to run away with him so they could join Doone in launching the next great revolution.

But even as Nate believed that Doone was their greatest and only hope, Cressi knew it was nothing more than wishful thinking. They didn't need a self-professed savior, they needed change—real change—in the Land.

No, she should just go back to her work tending to the sick guards out in the barracks. She'd told Friedan, the head nursemaid, she was just running to refill her pot of salve, but she'd been gone too long now. Friedan would be getting suspicious, and had possibly already sent someone to find her.

And yet . . .

The heir truly seemed to not know all that was being done in his name. This boy, born into power, just might be the Land's best chance for liberation.

"I'm sure there are facts about your life I know nothing of," Cressi said, softening her tone. "But you can't escape the fact that your family, your bloodline, are responsible for so many terrible things. Your own grandfather created the Mastery House Act."

"You have that wrong," the heir said. "My family is here to protect the people of the Land. The Battle of the Bottom, the fight for the Lower Middlelands, defeating the Badem and putting an end to the old ways were all good things. Read *The Histories*. There's no mention of a Mastery House or surrendering children in payment anywhere."

Maybe she was giving him more credit than he deserved.

"You mean the histories written by your family? Has it never occurred to you that they only wrote the parts of the story they wanted known and left out the rest?"

"History is history," Beau protested. "You can't change it. What you're saying makes no sense."

"Nothing makes any sense!" Cressi tried not to snap. "You only think destroying the Badem was a noble cause because that's what you've been told. Yet you don't even know about Mastery House, so how can you know the truth of anything?"

The heir looked as if he'd been punched in the gut. He stood there silent, his brow furrowing and twitching as if he were trying to translate her words into a language he could understand. Finally he looked up at her. "This Mastery House, can you take me there?"

Cressi knew she should say no. She'd already risked so much by even talking with him. And yet, how could she not?

"If we get caught, it will mean my head," Cressi warned as she led Beau to the farthest end of the stables.

"Mine too," he quietly replied as they turned down the fueling hall.

The dimly lit corridor was lined with half-height storage compartments holding wood for the furnace. Each compartment was locked with a heavy padlock, except for the next-to-last one.

Cressi swung the door open, revealing a low tunnel with a

small torch fixed in a holder as its only light source.

"After you, sir," she said.

"Don't do that," the heir insisted. "I'm Beau. Call me by my name."

"I can't do that."

"If you call me sir, I won't answer."

"Fine." Cressi bowed her head. "As you wish."

Beau peered into the open doorway but didn't step through. "Where does it lead?"

"To the laundry yard."

"Why are the stables and the laundry yard connected?" he asked. "And why is it so low?"

"The fires under the washing pots are fueled with dried manure," Cressi explained. "As for the height, sevens aren't usually much taller."

"What's a seven?"

"A seven-year-old." Did he truly know nothing? "Hauling fuel is one of their jobs."

Beau looked confused and horrified.

"If you want to do this, the moment is now," Cressi warned.

Beau hesitated, then shook it off and gestured for her to lead the way.

Stooped nearly in half, they slowly made their way through the tunnel in silence until another door came into view. Cressi placed the torch in a holder on the wall and, after listening for noises outside, eased the door open.

The laundry yard was empty except for the web of lines hanging thick with drying uniforms.

"Wait here for a moment." Cressi left Beau to sprint across the yard, where she grabbed a faded gray jerkin off the line before hurrying back to his side. "Put this on, you'll be less conspicuous."

But he wasn't. Even with the ragged vest over his clothes, the heir still looked far too clean and healthy.

Cressi grabbed a handful of dirt. "Here, rub it in your hair, some on your cheeks too."

"Why?"

Cressi squinted at him. "Look at me. Then look at you. Then ask that question again."

Beau looked down at himself, tugging at the misshapen jerkin. He almost seemed pleased at first, until finally she saw understanding wash over his face.

"Oh," he said meekly.

Even after he'd rubbed himself gray with dirt, he still looked far too hearty, but it would have to do.

"We're going to make a run for the hedgerow," Cressi explained, pointing to the far end of the yard. "Mastery House is on the other side."

Beau squinted at the imposing hedge. As thick and tall as three men, the barrier encircled the Manor in a nearly impenetrable wall.

"How do we get through?" he asked. "I don't see a gate."

"It's more of a path."

"A path through the hedgerow? Impossible. Have you seen the thorns that grow on it? They're deadly."

"Seen and felt their sting more times than I can count," Cressi countered. "Do you want to see Mastery House or not?"

She could easily have told him the passageway had been stripped of thorns—which it was. But then she'd have to admit that she and Nate had been the ones to cut the path so they could sneak away from Mastery House to visit Fledge. Until today, it was the only rule she'd ever broken. Fledge's counsel and friendship was well worth the risk, as were the fruit and cakes he'd share with them during their visits.

"Lead on," Beau said.

They skirted the edges of the yard, hugging tight to the towering hedge. Luck was on their side—for even though it was midday, there was no one else around.

"Through here." Cressi pointed out the narrow passage in the thicket, then watched as Beau stepped through, his nerves clamping his jaw tight.

From the Manor side, the hedgerow encircling the grounds appeared lush, green, and thriving, the thorns obscured by the foliage. But on the far side of the thicket the colors bled out into dull shades of gray, brown, and black. Balding branches gazed upon a barren landscape and a molding heap of rotting wood and crumbling brick and stone. The ghastly pile stood two stories high, with a roof of hastily laid shingles. Small uneven paned windows squinted through thick metal bars, casting a curse over anything that dared step within its dark shadow.

Oblivious to the danger, Beau started to walk through straight into the yard when Cressi pulled him back. "This is as far as we can go."

"But where's Mastery House?"

"What do you mean, where?" Cressi whispered. "It's right here in front of us."

"This pile of rot?" Beau looked as if she'd slapped him. "It hardly looks habitable for pigeons."

Standing in the shadow of that horrid building again, Cressi tried to beat back the memories of all her years there. But how could she ever forget the bitter tang of urine clinging to cracked floors that threatened to swallow one up with every footfall? Cressi's sleep was still haunted by those unanswered cries echoing from the second floor, made all the louder by the hush of too many bodies holding their breath from fear. The powerful waft of orange oil, the scent Matron doused herself with from head to toe, would forever be associated with despair. If Cressi thought she was finally free of Matron's ability to inspire dread, returning now proved the stink of the place would never wash out.

Cressi was about to usher Beau back to the laundry yard when the side door swung open, sending a jolt through her hotter than a strike of lightning. She pulled Beau deeper into the protection of the hedge just as the ragged line of children emerged. All dressed in dull brown Mastery House uniforms, the children lined up in the dirt, silently arranging themselves in height order from the tallest twelve to the smallest two.

Matron had called for a surprise inspection.

Cressi scanned the line, carefully taking in each and every dear face. Even though she'd only been gone one season, they'd all grown so much. Sweet, funny Bea, who was only a two when Cressi left, stood next to Rory among the threes and fours now, her hands caked with dirt and mud from hole-digging duty. And Pervis, who stood at the top of the line, even looked to have some facial hair blooming.

But where was Nate?

"They're from the Badem?" Beau whispered. "They're so young and innocent looking."

"Of course they are. Did you think they'd be different just because they're poor and born in the Bottom?" Cressi hissed. "Your own mother was of the Badem. Or did you not know that either?"

"She rejected the Badem when she married my father," Beau replied. "It's different."

"Is it? So, you think—" Cressi bit back the rest of her thought as Matron stepped out of the house.

Dressed in her customary long black habit, her hair arranged into a high helmet held in place by a fortune of pins and netting, Matron strode up and down the line, slowly scanning each child from their matted heads down to their poorly shod feet.

Even safely hidden away in the hedge, Cressi felt as if she were back in the line, enduring Matron's scrutiny, waiting for her to level her judgment and deliver some unwarranted punishment.

"I'll ask again," Matron said, her pacing as slow and menacing as a panther on the prowl. "Who will tell me the truth?"

None of the children moved, except for Bea. She'd spotted Cressi and Beau in their hiding place in the hedge and was doing her best not to break out in a wide smile. Thankfully Rory gently squeezed her hand, forcing her attention back on Matron.

"You mean to tell me not one of you knows where he's gone? Surely he bragged about his latest scheme to one of you," Matron growled. "I told him, the next time he tried to run, instead of punishing him, I'd punish all of you."

Nate.

A wave of fury flowed over Cressi. Why couldn't he just obey the rules?

"Very well." Matron's toothy grin cracked her white powdered face in two. "You'll have reduced rations for three days. Let's see if hunger doesn't loosen your memories and your tongues."

Matron scanned the line, her head turning like a peacock

in the sun. She was always at her happiest when making a child cry. Yet none of the children had broken yet—not even Bea—so she fixed her upper lip and waved them off.

"Get to work," she sniped. "I don't want to see any of you again until nightfall unless you bring me news of Nate."

As the children went scurrying back to their work assignments, Cressi turned to leave, but Beau was just standing there, his mouth agape.

"My father can't possibly know about this. Can he?" His voice came hardly above a whisper now. "They're so young. That little one that smiled at me, she . . ."

"That's Bea. We should be grateful Rory was there to keep her from giving us away. Now, come on, we have to go. You ready?"

Beau nodded slowly, somehow looking more certain than she'd seen since they'd first met. Maybe this terrible gamble would be worth it after all.

After checking that the laundry yard was still empty, Cressi signaled Beau to follow her back to the tunnel. She knew the terrain well, zigging her way through the maze of laundry poles, easily jumping over several broken-off tree stumps littering the yard. But Cressi forgot the heir didn't know his way as well as she.

Until she heard it.

The unmistakable sound of a body hitting the ground.

Chapter Four
The Red-Throated Napper

It wasn't the dirt stuck between Beau's teeth, the metallic taste of copper pooling on his tongue, or even the excruciating pain in his nose that kept him facedown on the ground. It was the cold slap of utter humiliation.

Cressi made jumping over the stump look so easy, like a stag clearing a fence. It never occurred to Beau that he wouldn't make it over too. But arms pinwheeling and legs flailing, he hung suspended in midair for what seemed like an eternity before his own feet got in the way, sending him crashing to the ground.

Beau wanted so badly to jump up, brush off his knees, and make believe he'd never stumbled, but the pain was too intense.

"I've got you." With a steady grip, Cressi helped Beau across the yard to the back of a small outbuilding and sat him down on a wooden crate. Cupping his chin in her hand, she inspected his nose from all angles.

Her touch was gentle and careful, that is until her fingers brushed past the bridge of his nose. She might as well have punched him.

"Sorry." Cressi winced along with him. "I just want to check to see if it's . . ." She shook off the last word.

"Broken?" Beau struggled to keep the rising dread out of his voice. "How am I going to explain this? I wasn't even supposed to leave my apartments. Barger will kill me. What do I do?" Panic took hold and started squeezing.

"Just breathe." Cressi's voice was soothing, but her hands kept nervously hovering over her apron pocket—one moment about to dive in, the next retreating like it was a bad idea. Finally, she made her decision and pulled a small blue pot from her pocket.

"I could try this balm I made." Her uncertainty was clear.

"I'll take anything you can do."

Beau braced himself as she began applying a salve to his nose.

Any time Cratcher, the Manor's apothecary, had come to treat Beau, the ancient medic used the foulest salves and poultices, all of which burned Beau's skin and smelled of sulfur and misery.

But Cressi's ointment immediately began to soothe.

"No sting or stench." Beau sighed in relief. "I'd rather have you tend to my ailments than old Cratcher any day."

"Just rest for a few moments." Cressi quickly sealed the pot and tucked it back into her pocket. "I think you'll be more than fine soon."

A warm kind of stillness began washing away the shock of the fall, taking with it the throbbing pain. But along with a return to ease came visions of what true pain looked like.

Mastery House.

How could he have forgotten, even for one moment?

"I'm sorry for not knowing about Mastery House," Beau said. "I could never have imagined a place as horrid as that existed."

"Well, it does," Cressi said. "Still, I truly don't understand. You're the heir to the Land, next in line to rule. How can you not know what goes on?"

"I . . . I don't know. I guess if it's not written about in *The Histories*, if my father or my tutors don't tell me, then . . . You have to believe me, I had no way of knowing. Now that I've seen it, those faces, the horror of the place, I'm . . . What's worse than horrified?"

"Then you should see inside, the conditions are twelve times worse," Cressi said. "Those rations Matron threatened to withhold? A thin soup made from potato peelings and kitchen scraps. The entire building is riddled with holes. There's not a single fireplace, except for a ridiculously large one in Matron's quarters. The walls are covered in mold, the floors are rotting, and there's barely a blanket to be spared except for the very youngest ones. Until I was sent up to service, I'd sleep in the nursery so I could make sure the babies got some measure of warmth and comfort. Who knows what they're suffering from now." Cressi cut herself off and looked away.

But Beau couldn't look away.

"It's not right, it's not fair. I wish there was something I could do. Had some way I could help."

Cressi shifted her gaze back to him, the look on her face as if she'd been stuck with a pin. "You are probably the *only* person in the Land who can do something about it!"

"You're wrong. I wish I could. But I can't. I have no power."

"You have all the power of being the heir."

"But I don't. It's just rotten luck that I was born me."

"Oh. So, you don't like the fate you were born into?" Cressi mocked. "Neither do I. But how can you ignore that you have more power and privilege than anyone else?"

"That's what you don't understand. My father—"

"Exactly!" Cressi broke in. "*Your* father. *You're* the one who will inherit the Land."

"Maybe one day. Maybe."

"Well, we can't wait for one day," Cressi said. "The other children, the sick, the dying, none of us can wait for some day when you decide to claim what's yours. Begin now. Use what you've been given."

Beau had always thought of his title as a burden, a responsibility he wanted nothing to do with. He saw his father as someone to be appeased and avoided. He'd always been so careful to not anger Himself, it never occurred to him that he could have any influence over his father. But something about Cressi made him almost believe he could.

Almost.

"I'm not like you. My father would never listen to me. I can't make him do anything he doesn't want to."

"I believe you can." There was something about the way Cressi was looking at him—at, not through or past or above him—as if she saw something in him no one else did.

Beau laughed nervously. "I mean, it would be something if I could walk straight up to my father and tell him what I think, what needs to be done. That the cruelty has to stop. If I could do that, then I'd be able to do something, something real—" Beau stopped. Cressi was crumbling into a deep curtsy, her eyes glued to the ground.

"What are you doing? Why are you—" he began. Then he felt it, a hovering shadow.

"What is . . . this?" Barger waved his hand in disgust as he stepped in between Beau and Cressi.

Beau's insides melted into a swirling cesspool of dread. He wanted to run, to flee, but he couldn't do that now; he wouldn't do that now.

"I was coming back from the stables when I fell," he said,

pushing his voice to sound authoritative. "This girl saw what happened and she helped me."

Barger sniffed. "Is that so?"

"Yes?" Beau's bravado wavered.

"How helpful," Barger said. "In that case, she should run to the laundry as fast as those boney legs can carry her and not leave until every last linen in the Manor is washed clean. And if she's still standing here after I'm done speaking, she'll be doing the washing without her boney legs to prop her up."

Cressi began backing away when Beau stopped her with a hand on her shoulder. It was a risky move. Barger didn't make idle threats. He made promises. But now it was time for Beau to make some of his own.

"She doesn't work in the laundry," Beau challenged. "She's a nursemaid's assistant, a talented healer, and I want her to be my personal apothecary. Look at what she did for my nose. It feels so much better already."

Barger leaned in. "Your nose?"

"I know it looks terrible, but as soon as she put a salve on it began to feel better." Beau gently patted his nose.

No pain.

Then he gave a tentative squeeze. Still nothing.

Amazing! There was no swelling, no tenderness. All evidence of the fall vanished, gone as if by some kind of magic....

Beau's blood turned to pudding as he watched Barger's expression turn from ire to understanding, leaving him practically salivating at the realization.

"Wait." Beau wedged himself between Barger and Cressi. "It's not what you think. She's not a—" But Barger sprang before Beau could get another word out.

The chamberlain pushed Beau aside, drew his knife, and grabbed Cressi, pinning her against the wall with his blade to her throat. With his free hand, he pulled a whistle from his pocket and blew it loudly.

"No, stop! I demand you let her go," Beau yelled as three guards rushed in.

But his words were lost to the wind as one of the guards threw Beau over their shoulder—as easily as if he were a bag of rubbish—while two others took hold of Cressi.

"Escort our young master back to his apartments," Barger instructed. "See to it that he remains there, safe from fevers and other undesirable forces. We'd hate to see him suffer a similar fate as his mother."

"No! You can't do this!" Beau struggled to get away, but he was hardly strong enough to make the guard flinch. "She's not what you think. I command you to leave her alone!"

"You couldn't command a flea not to bite," Barger scoffed as he turned to the other two guards. "Bring the girl and follow me. I believe we've found our charmer."

Chapter Five

That Horrible Thing Called Hope

Time had never been a friend to Beau. When he was with his father, time dragged when Beau needed it to fly. Then when he was with Fledge and needed it to linger, time broke into a sprint. But the instant Beau opened his mouth and accidentally betrayed Cressi, time did something new; it froze in that single moment just before understanding set in. Then after the guard carried Beau back to his apartments, bolting every door and window in his wake, time revealed its greatest trick—it split clean in half.

From that moment on, time would forever be divided into the Once and the Now.

Once, Beau would've thought being locked in his apartments the worst thing that could happen to him. He'd have sulked that he couldn't go see Fledge or take a ride. He'd have sunk into a gloom, unable to escape how unfair his life was.

After a while, he'd begrudgingly surrender and try to find some small measure of happiness. He'd disappear into a game of Fist or weave stories in his head about a life lived traveling beyond the borders of the Land—a life where he hadn't been born into a fate he neither wanted nor could ever live up to.

But not Now.

Now, as he stood in the center of his sitting room, his bones aching with rage at the depth of his stupidity, Beau knew better. Being locked in his apartments wasn't the worst thing that could happen to him, it was the worst thing that could happen to Cressi.

And it was all his fault.

He'd been so eager to prove he could stand up to Barger, be the person Cressi thought he could be, he'd ended up walking her straight into the hangman's noose.

By the time day began its slow turn toward afternoon, Beau had already tried forcing open every door and window, but it was useless—they'd been bolted from the outside. He'd shouted himself hoarse, demanding to be released. He'd rung the bell so hard the pull cord ripped free. But no one cared, no one came.

Still, there had to be a way to save Cressi, to undo the terrible damage he'd done.

Beau was trying to pry out the hinges on the door to the balcony when he heard the chime, an announcement that a meal, clean linen, or an emptied chamber pot had arrived in the dumbwaiter.

The dumbwaiter.

Of course! How had he not thought of it?

Beau raced to open the sliding hatch in the dining room wall.

When he was younger, he'd been certain the hole in the wall had magical properties—how else could meals appear out of nowhere? Then as he'd gotten a bit older, he realized the dumbwaiter possessed another kind of magic, the power to drive his tutors mad. After discovering he was the perfect size to fit inside the lift, he'd ride up and down, teasing and taunting them until they figured out where he was hiding. It took one tutor half the day to find him. Himself ordered it sealed up after that, reopening it only after Beau had grown too big to fit inside.

But had he really?

Beau pulled out the chamber pot that had been sent up and squeezed inside, practically folding himself in half. Even with his knees pulled up tight to his chest and his head tucked down tight, he barely fit.

But barely was better than not at all.

Beau eased the hatch door closed and the dumbwaiter began its descent, plummeting him into a darkness so complete it had a weight all its own. With each revolution of the crankshaft, Beau's heart pounded harder, for there was every possibility he was descending right into danger. But it was also possible that luck might be on his side.

Might.

When the lift landed, Beau braced himself as he slowly eased the hatch door open and slid out into the empty alcove.

An excellent beginning.

But the door to the kitchen was open, and from where he stood, Beau could see at least two maids at work at the long wooden table occupying the center of the room. One of the maids, thin and rangy with a scar across her cheek, was standing at the head of the table peeling potatoes while the other, a small, squat woman with deep crevices creasing her face, stood directly across from the door kneading dough.

Seeing the kitchen again made Beau homesick for the days when he'd sit for hours reading by the large open hearth. Soothed by the whistle and hum of the cooking pots, it had been one of his favorite places in the Manor. He used to spend as much time as he could with Perta, the old, kind kitchener. She'd sing him songs and feed him a perpetual bounty of freshly baked biscuits, pudding pots, and delicate pastries.

Then one day, Perta died, Cook arrived, and Barger banned Beau from the kitchens. He said there were too many dangers—open cooking fires, large knives—to let the heir roam freely. He hadn't been allowed back since.

Beau waited until the maid facing the doorway left her station to get more flour before slipping past the kitchen. From there he crept down a narrow, winding corridor lined with an endless succession of doors. There was a room for nearly every purpose along these halls: cheese storage, meat storage, meat salting, meat brining, wine storage, wine decanting. There were also several other doors that led to stairwells offering discreet entry to rooms on the upper floors, such as Himself's library, the salon, the dining room. The chamberlain's office.

But even Beau knew Barger didn't use his office for his real business. A dank cavern leading to the dungeons served that more nefarious purpose.

Beau followed the corridor as it snaked around until he came to a dead end, or so it appeared to the unknowing eye. The first time he'd watched Barger disappear behind the wall, Beau thought it was some kind of magic. Then he'd seen the trick.

He'd never before dared to press the right side of the panel, easing open passage into a cavernous anteroom, but there was nothing he wouldn't dare now to save Cressi.

Lit only by a single torch, the room gave way to two gated doorways. One was locked with an enormous padlock. Beau pressed on through the other one. Halfway down the passageway, he heard Barger's voice ricocheting off the walls.

"Oh, she'll talk," he said. "I'll make her talk. I've no doubt that she knows. There's not a servant in the Manor who hasn't heard the rumors about Annina."

"She'd be lying if she said she hasn't," Cook replied, that croaking rasp unmistakably hers. "My maids tell me some even think Annina is alive and hiding out in the Bottom waiting for her boy to come of age."

Beau's knees buckled. They did not just say his mother was still alive, did they? He had to have misheard.

He eased a few steps closer.

"Oh, she's dead, believe me. I saw her buried myself," Barger bragged. "As for this maid, though, where did she come from? How did she slip through? Why didn't Matron see her charming ability early on?"

"Don't blame Matron. Those charmers are clever as snakes."

"That's one thing our heir isn't. The idiot didn't even realize he'd betrayed the girl until it was too late."

"But this is what I've been wanting to tell you." Cook lowered her voice. "Friedan told me she's been hearing stories about the girl. Rashes disappearing before the eye, coughs drying up under her care. Then this morning, that girl tended a guard after he cut his thumb. Friedan said the others told her as soon as the charmer girl put some salve on his wound, it closed up. No scar, nothing. But then he started weeping, couldn't stop. Kept asking for forgiveness, saying he was only following orders. They had to carry him away, confine him. And this was a captain of the elite guard, a man as tough as they come."

"That's perfect!" Barger cackled.

"Why's that?"

"There's our proof. I told Himself his suspicions were wrong, that his boy is no charmer," Barger said. "He has no spine, no spark. He could never have been responsible for the fever. But the girl is different. I knew the moment I saw her that she's the one behind everything that's been happening— including last summer's flood and the wheat blight. And look what I found. Finally. It was right there in his chambers, under his reading chair!"

The verdigris pawn.

Knowing it was in Barger's possession burned Beau like salt to a wound.

"It's beautiful. I've never seen such a vibrant color," Cook gasped. "You turned her apartments upside down three times over looking for it. How'd he get it?"

"I don't know," Barger replied. "All that matters is I have it now."

"You gonna try and use it? See if it works like it's supposed to?"

"No, there's time for that. First we deal with the charmer girl."

"Are you going to do it the same way as the last time?" Cook asked. "Oh! You should bring back the iron shoes. I'd pay good coin to see a charmer do that dance."

Beau's stomach lurched. He'd read about the iron

46

shoes—one of the countless unthinkable Badem forms of torture. After a victim was strapped into red-hot metal boots, their futile attempts to save themselves was referred to as a dance to the death.

Beau shook out his trembling hands, readying himself to march in and strike his bargain. His life for Cressi's. He would promise to name Barger High Chancellor once Beau became the next Himself, all but making him Beau's regent—granting him nearly equal power. All in exchange for Cressi's release.

"You're thinking too small!" Barger reprimanded Cook. "What's important is that Himself returns to find the Land in impeccable order, his heir dealt with, and the charmer who's been causing floods and fevers captured. It's for him to decide whether she dies or is put to good use. And how to reward me for my good work."

"That's easy," Cook cooed. "He'll name you High Chancellor, for sure. First one in three generations, most powerful man in the Land behind Himself. You deserve it."

"I do," Barger practically sang. "Now let's go see that charmer."

Beau slumped into a puddle on the floor as the sounds of Barger and Cook's retreat echoed through the dank hall.

His one bargaining chip was made useless. Barger had already won the game. He had a clear path to power under Himself. He had Cressi. And he had the verdigris pawn along with a plan to use it against Beau. Even if Beau raced after him right now demanding Cressi's release, Barger would only laugh. Then he'd see Beau locked into his apartments for as long as it served his purposes.

Beau had no moves left to play.

Just like all the games of Fist he'd lost, he'd failed to strategize. Except now he'd lost more than a game—he'd lost Cressi.

Chapter Six
Cressi In Deep

As Cressi sat huddled in the cold, dark cell, she realized she'd been right about one thing: this day was going to end with her neck on the chopping block. While she was used to her life being in peril every day she was in the Manor and wasn't surprised it had come to this—to be accused of being a charmer was absurd. And a death sentence.

But it was also a truth she'd been trying to run from for as long as she could remember.

She'd always had a healing touch. Back in Mastery House, she'd been able to remedy the other children's ills faster than anyone else. Then, when she was put into service and Friedan taught her about herbs and how to make remedies for everyday maladies, it was as if somewhere deep in her bones Cressi already knew so much. Even Fledge used to tell her there was something special in her.

"In time it will make sense," he'd say.

But all along she kept denying it, telling herself she was simply a gifted healer.

How stupid she'd been!

If only she'd gone to seen Fledge sooner, he might have been able to help her, tell her what to do. The stories circulating about her abilities would never have started, and she certainly never would have met the heir. She'd simply have gone on living the life of drudgery fate had handed to her.

Or would she?

Cressi was never one to allow anyone else to indulge in denial, to run from the life she knew they were meant to live. She constantly called Nate out on that very point, drove him crazy. She'd stepped way out of line to tell the heir who he had to be. What if this was her destiny? Who was she to try to dodge it?

Cressi gathered her thin skirt and ragged wrap closer around her. The damp had seeped into her bones, making her shiver and quake.

At some point she drifted off into a kind of cold-induced stupor. Thoughts of Nate, the heir, the guard whose hand she'd healed swirled around, hovered along the periphery of her dreams, tugging at her. It was as if all their voices were pushing in, begging to be heard, to be healed.

Then the sound of a key tumbling in the heavy lock punctured the dark, reminding her exactly where she was. Where she was headed.

A thin stream of light filtered into the dank pen as Barger entered, inevitable as the night.

"Get up," the chamberlain ordered as he hung a small lamp on a hook.

Cressi had always been able to read people, to see behind the masks they wore. A gift and a curse, it made it almost impossible for her to truly hate anyone. Even Matron, whose own pain and suffering roiled under the surface of her cruelty. But Barger was different. He wore no mask. The guile and greed he projected were his truest essence.

"You don't look like a charmer," he said, a combination of disgust and delight wetting his lips.

"I'm not a charmer, nor would I know what one looks like, sir," Cressi replied.

"I do. I've been deceived by one before. Saw the Manor nearly destroyed until we recognized her for what she was," Barger said. "How long has it been since you were sent up from Mastery House and put into service?"

"One season."

"Which is exactly how long the Manor has been plagued by one calamity after another beginning with the infestation that ruined half the wheat crop and the flood that followed."

Cressi clamped her jaw shut. Crop blights were sadly not uncommon. And whoever thought it wise to create a bridge across the river out of piled-up rocks rather than build a proper span was responsible for the flooding, not magic.

"Now we have a fever that's afflicting our guards," Barger continued. "If that's not the work of a charmer, I don't know what is."

"I don't either, sir."

"Don't think yourself clever. I know what you are and everything you've done. The maids with the hacking cough, the heir's nose. But reducing one of our bravest guards into a sniveling shadow of his former self was going too far. Who are you working for? The heir?"

At the mention of Beau, Cressi felt a kind of protective ferocity ignite in her bloodstream. She ought to hate him, but she didn't. Beau was willfully innocent and dangerously ignorant about the Land; still she saw something in him, something hiding under the surface. A tiny spark that needed to be protected, kindled, coaxed into a flame.

"I know nothing of the heir. I only found him lying on the ground then attended to his nose as I've been trained to do," Cressi insisted, fighting to keep her expression flat and clear.

"You expect me to believe that? He wanted you to replace the apothecary. Why? Because he knows what you are. Doesn't he?"

"If he does, he knows more than me. On my bond, I know nothing of the heir. I simply helped him as is my duty."

Barger rubbed his chin, his fingers making a shushing sound as they brushed against his afternoon stubble. Then he broke into a smile, a viper ready to strike.

"According to both Matron and Friedan, you have a clean record," Barger said. "No trouble, no punishments. Matron almost spoke well of you when she sent you into service. Said you were helpful in containing the unrulier children when you were in Mastery House."

"I do as I'm told, sir."

"It's too bad I'll have to kill you." Barger tutted. "Although there's always a place for servants who understand loyalty, particularly those with special talents."

"On my life, my loyalties are yours." Cressi bowed in deference.

Barger's nose twitched, a hare sniffing at a snare. "Yet you still refuse to admit to your powers."

"I know nothing about charming. Although, given the chance there's no knowing what I could do." Cressi locked on Barger's greedy gaze before adding, "For you."

"You know, I can end you any time I please." Barger sneered as he reached into his coat pocket.

Cressi went numb. She'd played this all wrong. He was going to kill her right here.

Yet the chamberlain did not pull a blade from his pocket.

"You might yet prove to be of use to me." Barger held a small object up to the lamp, turning it this way and that, allowing the light to play off the iridescent blue and green hues.

Fear for her life melted into a kind of deep yearning. Cressi had never seen an object like this before. She didn't even know what it was. But it wasn't the thing that she was drawn to exactly, but more the way it made her feel. Her hands itched to hold it, to protect it, shield it from harm.

"Do you know what this is?" Barger asked, holding it out just beyond her reach. "This is a verdigris pawn. Part of a Fist set that once belonged to an enemy of the Land. You do know how to play Fist, don't you?"

Cressi barely shook her head, consumed by a gnawing hunger to snatch the pawn from his hand.

"No? I thought all you servants yearned to play at overthrowing the Manor. No matter, you'd never understand the rules anyway; they're too complicated. Let's just say that whoever controls the pawn controls the board. And whoever controls the board *wins*."

Barger folded the pawn into Cressi's palm, releasing a wave of relief. It was as if she'd been missing a vital organ or just discovered she had an extra pair of eyes. With the pawn in her hand she'd been made whole, connected, part of something far larger than just herself.

Barger smiled. "I was right about Annina, and I'm right about you. Now the question remains if you're willing to be useful."

Being useful to Barger could only mean serving his interests, all of which were dark-hearted. But to Cressi, being useful meant defending what was right. And now it also seemed to somehow include protecting the pawn—whatever that meant.

"I am more than willing."

"You're smarter than you look," Barger said. "If you do well, you will live a long and comfortable life. If not, I will cut you down where you stand. Understood?"

Cressi slipped the pawn into her apron pocket next to the small blue pot of balm. Although there was no actual movement, it felt as if the two objects started vibrating together, like some kind of greeting or dance between friends.

"Agreed."

Barger reached one hand forward, the blade she'd been expecting earlier shining in the other hand.

Cressi stumbled back, although there was nowhere for her to go.

But Barger didn't come for her, instead he turned the blade against his own hand. "Heal me, charmer," he taunted, raking the sharp point across his palm, a thin red line rising in its wake.

Cressi fought to contain her rising panic. She truly had no idea how to control whatever powers she did have. If they even were powers. All she'd done was put a woodberry salve on the guard's cut and Beau's nose and fed phlegmatic maids a tincture of meadowspur and willow bark. There was nothing magical about those herbs at all.

Or was there?

Cressi pulled the blue pot out of her apron and quickly

slathered on a layer of salve.

Seconds, minutes slowly ticked past as she waited to see what would happen. Barger was watching, too, anticipation slowly morphing into impatience.

And then it began. The blood that had been slowly pooling around the gash stopped and began receding like the tide at midday. The gulf of flesh the knife had created started closing up until finally Barger's hand was as it had been before.

Cressi's insides uncoiled.

"Very good, charmer." Barger nodded in approval. "Now let's go. We've got work to do."

Chapter Seven
Torn Tethers

B eau found the stables deserted. There were no trainers, grooms, or stable hands anywhere. Even the chestnut filly was gone. And worst of all, Fledge was nowhere to be found.

How could that be? The stables were Fledge's workplace, his home, his center of gravity. He was never not there. He should have returned from delivering the blankets long ago.

Beau had been trying to keep his panic at bay, knowing that even when he got tangled up in the gnarliest of knots, Fledge would be there to unwind him. But without him, the knots tightened, leaving Beau immobilized.

Then the hard, flat notes of the bugles rang out with the call to assemble and Beau snapped to his senses. Himself's private guard hadn't left yet.

Fledge had to still be there, helping them ready for departure.

Buoyed by hope, Beau raced out of the stables.

As he approached the parade grounds Beau could see the first flank of the regiment slowly disappearing over the rise, Himself at the lead. With the danger of his father seeing him gone, Beau dashed over to the last of the guardsmen preparing to move out.

"Where's Fledge?" he called. "Have you seen the stable master?"

The guards all ignored him, likely taking him for a stable boy unworthy of reply. Then Beau spotted a solitary figure on the edges of the field slipping a chest plate over his head.

"Excuse me!" Beau ran over, his nerves close to unraveling. "Have you seen Fle—" But the rest of the name evaporated on Beau's tongue as the man lowered the armor to his chest.

"Fledge?" Beau sputtered. "Why are you wearing that? Why are you out here? I need you; you have to come with me!"

Fledge furtively scanned the area, then pulled Beau behind Striker, his dappled red gelding who was standing in wait nearby. "What's happened?"

"I lost her, Fledge!" Beau burst. "I had a plan, but it was all wrong. Stupid. And now I don't know what to do. You have to tell me what to do!"

"First things, slow down." Fledge gently took Beau's hands, calming the shaking. "Tell me everything."

"It's all my fault and now she's going to be—" Beau couldn't get himself to say the words, or even to draw a full breath.

"Beau, look at me." Fledge cradled Beau's face in his warm, reassuring hands. "Slowly, one breath at a time. One. Good. Now another. Two. Good. Now tell me."

"There's this girl. You know her. She knows you too. Cressi. She showed me Mastery House. It's an awful place. How did I not know it existed, Fledge? Why didn't you tell me?"

Fledge winced. "I know, I should have. I was going to, believe me, but first, what's happened to Cressi?"

"Barger . . . Cressi . . . he has her."

Fledge tightened his grip on Beau as if to hold himself steady. "Explain."

"I . . . I told him she was a charmer. I mean, I didn't say that exactly. That's what he heard though. And she might be one too. I don't know. My nose was . . . What do I do?"

Fledge raked his hands through the thick forest of curls clubbed messily at his neck. "I thought I'd have more time. I thought I could—"

Bugles blared, cutting him off.

"Hey, you!" a captain shouted, pointing at Fledge. "In line! We're moving out!"

Fledge delivered a salute, then waited for the captain to ride away before turning back to Beau. "Listen to me. I'm to leave with the guard to tend to the horses. There are too many of them. I can't refu—"

"What do you mean, 'leave'?" Beau couldn't make sense of what was happening. "What about Cressi? You have to help me!"

59

"I have no choice. You have to listen—"

"Master or not, you obey my orders while you ride with us!" the captain bellowed. "Move out!"

Fledge strapped his pack to his horse's back. "Think of the game, Beau. If your mage was trapped, how would you free her?"

"This isn't a game!" Beau nearly exploded. "This is real!"

"I know that. You have to trust me. You can do this, you above all others can do this."

"I will run you through where you stand!" The captain was red faced and fast approaching, his sword unsheathed.

"Just like in the game, use your ace to free your mage," Fledge said as he mounted his horse and took up the reins. "Find your ace, Beau. It's the only way we can win."

And with those few cryptic words, Fledge rode off, joining the ranks of the departing company.

Long after the regiment disappeared down the drive and away from the Manor, Fledge's words echoed in Beau's head: use your ace to free your mage.

What kind of advice was that? Life wasn't a game of Fist. And even if it were, Beau was a lousy player.

Still, Fledge would never lead him astray. There had to be some sense to this.

Well, obviously Cressi was the mage. That part wasn't cryptic. And *if* she was a charmer, then like the mage, she possessed powers. Under normal play, the mage functions much like the bishop in chess, but instead of guarding the king, it protects the verdigris pawn. Yet when the mage is played right, it can gain control over the king's guards, leaving him unprotected.

The mage does have a weakness though. If the king's guardsmen reach her first, they will claim her, and the king can use her powers to his advantage.

As for the ace, it too is unique to Fist. It operates like a field commander, organizing the guards, leading the charge into battle. When well played, the ace can shield the pawn and the mage from capture. It can lead a raid straight through the heart of the king's ranks, capturing two guards at a time and leaving a clear path for the pawn to unseat the king. It's also the only piece that can liberate captured pieces.

Yet while the ace's purpose in the game was clear, Fledge was the only person who could remotely fit the description. But then why would he have told Beau to find the ace?

"This makes no sense!" Beau picked up a rock and hurled it as hard as he could.

As he watched the rock land, he realized how far he'd walked. He'd crossed clear through the parade grounds into the barrier fields and all the way to the outer cow pasture, a place he'd never ventured before. This far from the Manor the air was sour and starchy, pungent and heavy, yet ineffably alive. Cows quietly lowed, birds sang, bees hummed. Their lives uncomplicated by malice, their only concerns were eating, building nests, collecting pollen.

Lucky them to simply be what they were.

Beau tried again to untangle Fledge's meaning, but he couldn't shut out the echo of Cressi's muffled cries as the guards carried her away. He was trying to shake it off, make room for ideas to blossom, when he realized the sound wasn't in his imagination. Something—or someone—was calling out from beyond a hedge of tall grass.

Beau raced toward the noise, part of him hoping it might be Cressi, only to find three calves tethered to poles outside a roughly hewn lean-to. Tied so tight, the sweet, young creatures could barely stand, let alone move.

"Poor things," Beau said, petting them each on the nose. "Who would do this to you?"

The calves strained at the end of their ropes, trying to nuzzle Beau.

"Let me untie you first, then you can thank me," Beau laughed.

After untangling the first of several tightly wound loops, Beau had just begun working on the second level of knots when something poked at his back.

"Stop that." Beau laughed. "How am I going to get you and your friends untied if you keep trying to get me to play?"

"I dunno, boy," came the sharp reply. "That depends on who told you to undo the beasts?"

Beau dropped the rope.

"Turn around," came the warning.

Beau raised his hands and slowly turned until he came face-to-face with two hulking guards, a pair of towering mountains.

"Looks to be a stable rat, Keb," one guard said to the other. "Why you out here touching them ropes, rat?"

"I . . . they were tied too tight" was the only reply Beau could manage.

"You hear that, Keb?" the guard asked his companion.

Keb eyed Beau as if trying to decide how he might taste. "I did, Boz."

"I meant no trouble. I'll be on my way." Beau nodded politely and moved to step away when Keb stopped him with a meaty hand on the chest.

"You're not going anywhere without our say-so," Boz growled. "You one of ours?"

Beau flushed. He couldn't afford Barger to find out he'd snuck out. "I . . . I'm allowed to be out here if that's what you're asking."

"We decide what you're allowed," Keb snarled, primed to pounce. "Answer him—you one of ours or not?"

There were only two choices here, and Beau was an awful liar. He'd have to try the riskier path.

"Fine. You found me out. Take me back to my apartments. I'm sure Barger will reward you handsomely for returning the heir, but I will see the sum doubled if you don't tell him."

"The heir?" Boz scoffed. "You?"

"Yes, I'm afraid so."

At that, both guards broke out into the ugliest laughs imaginable, something between a cackle and the sound of someone choking on their own spit.

"I seen the heir, plenty of times. Guarded him even. He ain't you," Boz boasted. "I took him out hunting. Big, tall kid, hair black as tar. He was training a falcon to hunt. Laughed when it snatched him a big rabbit."

"You never did saw him!" Keb snapped. "If you did, you'd know he's got gold hair and a big scar across his cheek from battling a mad boar that got into the Manor one night! He said he's gonna put me in his private reserves after he's made the next Himself."

"Fffffff," Boz sprayed as he poked Keb in the chest. "The only reserve guard you're fit to serve in are down by the pits."

"No, that's you!" Keb poked back, spraying Boz in a shower of spittle of his own.

As Boz and Keb argued, Beau slowly began backing away. He'd been intimidated countless times by his father's personal guards, but he'd never seen any as stupid as these two.

But Beau only got a few steps away when Boz spotted him. The guard's legs, thick as tree trunks and fit to bursting through the gray leggings of his uniform, carried him farther in one step than Beau could travel in three. Boz grabbed Beau up by the collar like a weed to be plucked and pressed his pock-riddled face inches from Beau's. "You try to untie them calves again and you'll leave as pig food. Now get back to work mucking them pens."

And with that, Boz threw Beau down, sending him skittering to the ground.

"Yeah, and you try and pass as the heir again and we'll come find you and see you gutted!" Keb added as the pair stalked away.

Beau sat stunned where he fell. His hands and knees were skinned, his clothes covered in dust and dung, and his head was spinning.

What just happened?

An obstacle as large as a team of oxen standing in his path had simply melted away.

What kind of magic was this?

Or was this what luck looked like?

Whatever it was, Beau wasn't about to question it. Where hesitation had resided, a new kind of determination took up residence. He'd find his ace, he knew it.

But first he had to get up, a feat that was proving to be a slow process of coaxing his head to stop spinning and his ankles to stop buckling under his weight.

Beau took a deep breath and tried to push himself up, but he was still too dizzy to see straight. He closed his eyes and was waiting for his vision to clear when someone grabbed him from behind.

Chapter Eight
Crafty

Jolted into action, Beau lashed out at his attacker, wildly swinging his fists. But rather than landing a blow, he only managed to lose his footing and went stumbling backward.

"Whoa! Steady. I've got you," came a voice from behind.

Willing his legs to hold, Beau turned to face his rescuer. While he had no idea who he'd find behind him, he never would've guessed it would be a boy. And although he stood taller and was closer to manhood than Beau—the beginnings of a fine fuzz having started to bloom above his upper lip— he looked to be around the same age.

"Oh. I thought you were Pervis." The boy's disappointment was palpable.

All Beau could offer in return was a quiet "Sorry."

The boy pushed back the fringe of hair hanging over his eyes—a gesture that proved futile for longer than a few seconds. "Pervis is the only one around here besides me with the guts to tangle with those two devils. I thought he finally decided to . . . Anyway, you did good."

Beau waved the compliment off. "Getting tossed to the ground like a bale of hay hardly takes guts."

"True, but even *I* never thought to tell them I was the heir. That brain-boiled pair are witless enough to fall for almost anything. But you should've considered your clothes when you came up with your plan." The boy thumbed Beau's filthy jacket. "Nice togs, but not nearly fine enough for the mighty heir. And I doubt he smells like cow dung."

"Don't be so certain," Beau muttered, brushing himself off.

"You're not from here," the boy said, his thick eyebrows disappearing under that fringe of hair. "Who do you belong to?"

"I . . ." Beau had no answer at hand, but thankfully the boy didn't leave him time to reply.

"Wait, let me guess." The boy circled Beau. "The tailor maybe? No, your buttons wouldn't be hanging like that. Not blacksmith, either, your hands are too clean. Probably not the cooper either. Okay, I give up. Who?"

Still quite uncertain how to reply, Beau asked, "What do you mean 'belong to'?"

"You're right." The boy nodded sagely. "They may think they own us. They don't. We're our own people, and the day is coming when they'll pay the price. You apprentices deserve your freedom, too, even if you do have it far better than us here on the Manor. So, who you training with?"

Understanding finally dawned on Beau. Like Cressi, the boy mistook him for an apprentice.

"Cordwainer." The lie slipped out with ease.

"There's worse places than a cordwainer's shop. At least you got those nice boots."

Beau looked down at his feet. Even covered in dust and splattered with dung, the fine craftsmanship of Beau's riding boots was glaringly obvious, especially when compared to the boy's own ragged and frayed boots.

"I should've been trained in one of the fine crafts," the boy continued. "I've got a good eye, clever hands. Matron almost said as much, too, but she also said I was a rancid minnow and she'd rather eat house sparrows for a month than see me move up."

The boy paused, a kind of faraway look clouding his eyes before he cleared it with a laugh. "I would have told her she was a nasty, old pillock if I'd been in the mood for eating grass that day."

Beau had no idea what a rancid minnow or a pillock might be, or why anyone should have to eat grass, but he did know enough not to ask.

"So when did the Manor remand you from the cordwainer's service?" the boy asked. "How'd he take that? I'd have thought they'd put a boy with skills like yours in the horse stable, not out here. That's just like them. Putting people down, never giving them a chance to show what they got. Why do they do that?"

"I honestly don't know," Beau replied.

"Me neither. But I'll tell you what it is—it's a waste." The boy picked something off the tip of his tongue, then flicked it away. "What do they call you, anyway? I'm Nate."

"Beau," Beau's mouth replied before his mind could stop him. Where was a lie when he needed one? Beau recoiled, ready for Nate to hit him.

But Nate simply shook his head in pity.

"Sorry to hear it. Lots of others over at Mastery House were named after him too." Nate turned and started walking toward the cow barn. "The heir be hung. You won't hear me saying that name, not 'til I've got him pinned to the ground begging for mercy."

Beau stopped. "Mercy?"

"You don't think that goat-livered heir deserves any, do you? Wait, you're not one of those apprentices who thinks you're better than us lowly orphans, are you?"

"No," Beau vowed. "And you're absolutely right, the heir deserves no mercy."

"Exactly!" Nate flung a rock the size of his fist across the field, watching as it flew off into the tree line. "All that's done in his name, leaving us to starve while he stuffs his face, ordering servants around to do his every bidding. It's not right, it's not fair. Why's he get so much, when we get so little?"

"I honestly don't know." The weight of that truth was almost too heavy for Beau to carry. "And now it's even worse over at Mastery House."

Nate halted in his tracks. "What do you mean?"

"Uh . . ." Beau hesitated. "I heard someone say Matron was making them do double duty and taking away half their rations."

"Why?" Nate pressed.

"Something about someone who'd run away and . . ." Beau let the words trail off as the pieces fell into place.

Nate.

This was the boy who'd run away.

"The pig-snouted snipe!" Nate kicked at the ground, sending dirt and grass flying. "She threatened to do it more times than I can count. I never thought she would."

"Maybe she'll change her mind when you go back?" Beau suggested.

Nate stopped kicking up the grass and looked at Beau as if he'd just suggested he cut off his own nose. "Would you willingly go back there?"

"Never."

"Exactly." Nate bobbed his head, a cocky kind of acknowledgment that of course he was right. "The only way for me to help them now is to go . . . Wait, how do I know you're not one of Barger's maggot peepers?"

"On my bond, I am the furthest thing from one of his spies," Beau vowed. "I'm the exact opposite."

Wholly unconvinced, Nate crossed his arms and planted himself inches from Beau. "Prove it."

Part of Beau wanted to run away, fleeing this boy's scrutiny. But there was something about him, his confidence, even his hatred for the Manor, that against all reason, Beau felt a kinship with.

"I'm not supposed to be out here. I should be back . . . at the stables, but I'm looking for someone. Someone who can . . . help."

A strange look overtook Nate, something between a glare and a dare as a new kind of interest in Beau ignited behind his eyes. "Help with what?"

"Free . . . people."

Nate narrowed his eyes, searching Beau's face for something. Then finally, after having reached some kind of a decision, he abruptly turned and walked away, the smallest nod of his head indicating Beau should follow him.

This was a boy who seemed to know things—things about the world that Beau wanted and needed to know. He trailed after Nate, propelled forward by the hope that maybe one of those things was where to find his ace.

Beau followed Nate into the cow barn and up a rickety

71

ladder to the hayloft. Only after they were safely ensconced in a far back corner did Nate look at Beau again. There was something at once both wide open and closed off about him now. "This isn't like me. Still . . . I've got a feeling. But just in case I've got you wrong, this someone you're looking for, describe them. What would they be like?"

That was easy; they'd be like the ace. But Beau couldn't very well say that.

"They'd be very brave, daring."

"What else?" Nate prompted.

"A clever strategist," Beau added. "You know, someone who's good at making plans. And, uh . . . they'd be good at rallying others. Strong, certain, a real leader. Loyal and clever."

Nate nodded sagely. "And what are you willing to do to find them?"

"Whatever it takes." Of that Beau was certain.

Nate sized Beau up, his head cocked to one side, a thinking face. Then he tossed his head—a decision made—and extracted a tightly folded parchment from up his sleeve. "Look at this. Found it stuck to the wheels of a wagon back from the Middlelands."

Beau unrolled the parchment. "Bounty for the capture of the Villain Doone! 42 coins!" was scrawled above a sketch of a man with straight, dark hair, piercing blue eyes, and a bloodthirsty grin.

Beau's stomach clutched at the familiar name and portrait. "Doone?"

Nate's eyes sparkled. "That's him. You described him perfectly, exactly how I've always heard it. They say he's the last of the Badem, and you know what means, don't you? It's in his blood to work for the good of all of us. I heard that when he was young, a charmer cast a spell to protect him from ever being found out or killed. He knows what we face, what we need. He's brave, he's clever as a fox, and he's our best hope. Imagine helping him right the wrongs done to all of us. Working with him to free Mastery House and liberate the Land."

Beau's head pounded, and his heart did too. The ace in Fist was sometimes called the liberator because it was the only piece that could free captured guards.

Still, this couldn't possibly be who Fledge meant. Doone was the enemy Beau had been warned about his entire life. Hiding out in the Bottom, a place riddled with traitors and thieves, Doone was actively plotting to overthrow the Manor, kill Himself and his heir. And with so many guards ill his chances of succeeding were greater now than ever. That Doone could be Beau's ace was unthinkable, and the very thought of going to the Bottom to look for him was terrifying.

And yet.

This day had already uncovered so many lies that Himself

had passed off as absolute truths. In some twisted-up way, it all made sense. It fit. Fledge had only said to go find his ace, he never said where.

"You really believe Doone can free the people of the Land?" Beau pressed.

"Every story I've ever heard about him tells how he's devoted his life to leading us to liberation. They say he even traveled across the seas seeking out allies, building up his strength before returning home again to lead us to freedom. He's the one."

Nate spoke with such conviction, such passion and knowledge. A boy raised in that awful Mastery House would have nothing to lose and no reason to lie. There was no question of who to believe, who to trust. While leaving with Nate to find Doone was scary and dangerous, and incredibly stupid, if it meant finding his ace, then it was necessary.

Judging from the last time Barger locked him into his apartment, Beau figured he'd have at least two, maybe three days before Barger came to check on him.

"How long will it take for us to find him?" Beau asked.

"Not long." Nate spoke with absolute surety, but there was also an air of caution. "You do understand what this means, right?"

"That we have to go to the Bottom."

"Yeah, but more than that. If we're going to try this, it means that you know too much about me and I know too much about you. We're bound to each other now and can never betray the other."

Beau felt lit up from inside. He'd never been bound to anyone or anything but duty.

"I guess we are." Beau offered his hand to shake, but Nate seemed unfamiliar with the gesture. Desperate to break the awkward silence that followed, Beau bolted for the ladder, adding, "All right then, let's go."

But Nate pulled him back. "Where are you going? It's not like we can just walk off Manor lands under the light of the sun."

"Oh . . . I know that," Beau said. "I mean, I just thought if we keep heading through the fields we'd eventually wind up—"

"Stuck in the tar."

"Tar?"

"Great wide moat of it circles the border of the Manor, except at the gatehouses where they got bridges over it. We'd never get past it. I know, I've tried. Got the burns to prove it." Nate pulled his pant leg up, exposing a patch of red and raw skin.

"That's awful." Beau tried not to wince.

"It's only ugly. Doesn't hurt much." Nate shrugged. "But see, I've tried to run enough times now that I've come up with a foolproof plan."

Beau liked the sound of that.

"If you can truly help me find my . . . Doone, I'll be forever in your debt."

"There's too much of that around already." Nate sank down into a pile of hay. "But you do need patience. You have any of that?"

The boy who'd spent his entire life waiting nodded. "Plenty."

"Good. I don't, but I do have a lot of good ideas. Only reason I'm alive now . . ." Nate paused and stroked the thin blush of hair above his upper lip. "I can't call you by that name though. Just thinking it makes me angry. I think I'm going to call you . . . Crafty."

"Crafty?"

"Sure, you've got a craft, and it was pretty crafty to try and pass yourself off as the heir to those goons. What do you think?"

Beau let the name roll around in his mind for a moment, then he smiled.

"I like it," he said, for it was more fitting than Nate could ever know.

Chapter Nine

Talent in the Bones

There were countless places Cressi imagined Barger might be taking her when he marched her out of the dungeon. Cook's pantry wasn't one of them.

There wasn't a servant in the Manor who hadn't heard about the finely furnished room located just off the kitchen, or about the glorious meals Cook prepared for a chosen few. Cressi understood immediately why the place inspired awe in so many. A large hearth dominated one entire wall, in front of which was situated a satin-covered settee and matching chairs—furniture far too lush for the servants' halls. But it was the shelves running the height and breadth of the opposite wall that enchanted Cressi. An array of brightly colored bottles, crocks, and lidded pots were arranged in size order on the shelves—a virtual treasure trove of herbs, elixirs, dried flowers, and extracts.

Were it not for Barger's ironclad hold on her arm, Cressi would've already been upon the shelves, opening every jar she could reach. And the pawn apparently felt the same way, for as soon as they'd stepped into the pantry it turned warm in her apron pocket, as if it recognized where it was.

"I was correct." Barger held up his nearly healed hand. "As I always am."

It was only then Cressi noticed Cook, standing proudly behind a large worktable laid out with neat piles of bowls, bottles, and jars.

"I never doubted you," Cook cooed, but her tone and temperature cooled as she pulled Cressi to the shelves. "I know all about you charmers. All your tricks and traps. You're not gonna pull anything over on us. Understand?"

Cressi nodded, though all her attention was focused on those glorious bins, bottles, and boxes lining the shelves.

"I got three combinations mixed up here." Cook set three small bowls out in front of Cressi. "From what I know, any one of them could work for our purposes. You're gonna give them each a sniff and tell me which one is gonna do what Barger wants."

"And what is that?" Cressi asked.

"You don't need to know that. Just sniff, we'll know the answer when we see it."

Cressi looked at the bowls. They each contained a combination of dried herbs, crushed flowers, pieces of bark, and other various fungi and flora. She recognized some of the components while many were unknown to her. Yet somehow, she felt as if she knew them all.

"Go on," Cook goaded. "Smell."

Cressi picked the bowls up one by one. The first two had pleasant aromas that evoked a sense of serenity and order. They were soothing and sweet. But the third was as rancid as week-old milk. Cressi recoiled, nearly dropping the bowl to the floor.

Cook grinned with pride as she plucked the offending mixture from Cressi's grip. "This is the one."

"That was easy enough," Barger said. "Brew it up, girl, and let's see if you've got the true touch of a charmer."

Cook ordered Cressi to empty the bowl into a small pot of water boiling over the hearth. Her nerves still on edge, Cressi took hold of the wooden spoon Cook thrust at her and mixed the concoction. As the brew began to boil and froth, the pantry filled with the vilest odor—a wretched combination of tar, rotting meat, and an overfull outhouse.

Overcome, Cressi covered her nose and mouth with her apron. Even the pawn reacted, turning hot as a coal plucked from the fire. But Cook and Barger hardly looked bothered at all.

"How can you bear it?" Cressi asked through her makeshift mask.

"We don't smell or hear the plants same as you," Cook drawled.

"What do you mean hear them?" Cressi pressed.

"Talking!" Cook snapped. "You can hear them telling you what they can do, can't you?"

"I . . ." Cressi hesitated. She'd never thought of it that way. It wasn't so much that she heard plants talking as she felt them, intuitively understood how they could be used to heal, or to harm. When she'd once told that to Fledge, he broke out into the widest smile, pride beaming like the noonday sun. At the time she thought he was just being kind, supportive. "Maybe, but not in words."

"Of course not words!" Cook spat. "A lifetime of practice and all I can do is poison and sicken, but you—"

"Cook!" Barger scolded.

Cook nodded dutifully to Barger and pulled a red-glazed canister off a high shelf. "Look here. Foxglove: useful to reduce swelling and heal new or green wounds. Can also be poisonous when mixed with complimentary herbs, such as that." Cook pointed to a glass bottle on another high shelf. "Wolfsbane: a poison with a strong taste and a nasty habit of making one bleed from the eyes."

A wave of nausea washed over Cressi.

"Now, this is what you really want." Cook stepped up on a stool and reached for a small black canister from the highest shelf. She climbed down, handed the canister to Cressi, and stepped back.

"Add a pinch to your brew."

Cressi pulled the cork and was nearly thrown back, over-whelmed by the smell of death and decay.

"Glorystem." Cook grinned. "See, when used by the likes of me, a person with no talent for charming, a few drops floods the blood with bile, turning it black and putrid. An awful way to die. But when handled by the likes of you, glorystem releases her secrets. Go on now, add it."

Daring not to disobey, Cressi added a small pinch to the boiling concoction. The odor that had been so vile turned sweeter, almost placid. "So now it will release its healing pow-ers?"

"If robbing someone of their will is healing," Cook snorted. "The body looks the same, they sound the same, but the mind isn't theirs anymore."

Cressi's mouth ran dry. "That's horrid. And you want me to do that to someone?"

"We simply want to teach you, help you understand what is possible," Barger said. "You do want to be useful, don't you?"

Cressi swallowed. She needed to keep herself in check long enough to take what they were giving. She'd figure out how best to use it all later.

"When you did what you did to the guard and the heir, what were you thinking?" Cook asked.

"To relieve their pain," Cressi replied.

"That's not what I mean!" Cook pursed her almost non-existent lips. "When you made one of our fiercest guards

81

break down like a wounded puppy, what were you thinking? Truly thinking about him. Was it that he's a cruel beast who deserved his wounds and you wanted to make him suffer? Or maybe you saw the scared boy he once was who deserved to be healed."

How did she know that?

"You charmers see people as they truly are, not as they want to be seen," Barger explained. "Everyone and every living thing is hiding something, a truth they don't want known. Pain, shame, lies. Only your kind can hear and see it, like you do with the plants. Then you get to decide if you want to use someone's pain to heal them or control them."

Barger retrieved a small, tightly sealed cask from the shelves along with a small crowbar. "Think of charming as a kind of hand spike, like this one, and this tightly sealed cask as someone with a truth to tell, information vital to the safety and well-being of the Land. I need what is inside. Now, I could smash the cask open, but in so doing I'd spill all the contents. Lose too much. It's easy to imprison, torture, and starve someone. Yet even then I can't force them to fully expose their secrets, to surrender their will. I can't ever truly know their mind, what they're thinking, what they're hiding. Who they're protecting. I can't ever make someone behave how I want. But a charmer can. A charmer is the most powerful weapon there is."

Cressi shuddered. Life in the Land was already beyond

horrible, but if the Manor came to possess this kind of power, present-day nightmares would look like fairytales in comparison.

She'd never do what he was asking of her, but he needn't know that.

"I am here to serve you, sir." Cressi dropped a curtsey. "And eager to learn all about the brews."

"You'll learn only what *we* need you to know," Barger snorted. "You just do the charming the way we tell you to."

"Of course." Cressi bobbed in submission.

"Pour your brew into this teapot," Cook ordered. "Then you keep your mind thinking only on being dutiful, loyal, subservient while you serve it to the heir. Understand?"

Cressi nodded and offered a sweet smile.

"Good. Now bring the tray and follow me." Barger headed for the door. "It's teatime."

Chapter Ten

Prodders at the Gate

Beau and Nate remained tucked away in the hayloft waiting for dark to fall. Nate slept, but Beau was hardly able to sit still as the remaining hours of daylight slowly ticked by. This was unlike any waiting he'd ever done before. Time was no longer marked by lessons, meals, or duties, but by the shifting of the sun, the cooling of the air, and the calls of birds. The expectation of a bold move.

When, at long last, the bells tolled eight, Nate rose and stretched. "I think this is our time, Crafty. You ready?"

Beau nodded and let Nate lead the way out of the barn into the cool of the evening. But just as they rounded the side, Beau stopped. There was something he had to do first.

"What are you doing? You can't back out now," Nate warned.

"No . . . it's silly. Don't laugh, but I want to untie those calves. They looked so miserable tied up."

The sounds of the calves' bellows echoed in the near distance.

"All right," Nate agreed. "If we're to be liberators, might as well begin with the beasts. Plus those two rump-faced dolts will get in deep for it too."

The boys raced through the hedge of tall grass to the calves and unwound the tethers. Yet once untied the calves only stood there staring at the boys, wholly uncertain what was expected of them.

"Go!" Nate shooed.

The calves didn't move.

"Run!" Beau said.

Still, they stood looking at the boys.

"Like this!" Beau started loping a wide circle around the calves.

"You look ridiculous!" Nate called from the sidelines.

"I know!" Beau crowed.

He ran until the calves finally understood and took off, their long uncertain legs gaining confidence with every step.

"Nice work, Crafty," Nate said. "But you know, I'm the one with the good ideas."

"Oh." Beau stepped back. "I'm sorry. I didn't mean to—"

"Relax." Nate gave Beau a playful shove as he led the way across the pasturelands under the cover of a darkening sky. "I'm just having a laugh."

"Right." Beau nodded. "I knew that."

He had so much to learn.

As they walked, Beau tried to keep track of the ever-increasing number of stars appearing above. He'd never been under the wide-open night sky like this. Himself always warned that the night was "home to revolutionists and would-be kidnappers, like the ones who killed your mother." And so Beau had always been locked inside his apartments when the sun went down, safe from those who'd wish to harm him.

More lies added to the ever-growing list.

The boys continued across the fields in expectant silence. But soon the lights from peddler's gate came into view. The guardhouse was lit up like a beacon of doom in the distance, making the reality of what they were about to do suddenly very real.

"It's much brighter than I thought it would be," Beau said. "It's nearly as big as the main . . . I mean merchant's gate."

"Don't worry. We're going to catch a ride in one of those outbound wagons, I can feel it."

"But won't they check the wagons?"

"They might, but I've got a way around that. See that out-building, there?" Nate pointed out a small shed tucked into the shadows on the Manor side of the gatehouse. "The one on this side of the road by the tree line? On my say-so, we slip down that embankment there. Watch yourself, it's made of slick rocks and riddled with glass shards and rusted spikes. If you fall you might never get up again. But once we're down, we tuck in behind the shed. That's where we're going to get our plank."

"Our what?" Beau asked.

"A wooden board. You know, because of the prodders."

It truly was as if the two boys spoke different languages. But Beau could only ask for so many explanations without giving himself away. So instead he simply nodded.

"Last time I tried this, I got all the way down to the wagons, but there were seven guards on duty. Three of them checking papers and the other four all prodding." Nate winced at the memory. "I had to turn back. That was before I got the idea for the plank. I bet if I had one then, I'd have made it out."

Beau counted three guards now, all of whom were busy inspecting the three inbound wagons.

"I think luck has decided to follow along," Nate said. "See that second outbound crate?"

Beau spotted a dray cart loaded with sheepskins parked behind a hay wagon emblazoned with the Manor's seal. By comparison, the dray cart was small and rickety. The wheels hung at a strange angle, and the driver, a haggard man with a tall shock of hair standing at all angles, looked to be ninety years old if he was a day.

"That's our ride." Nate looked at the run-down cart as if it were a golden carriage. "Driver looks old. Maybe even deaf, and prodders rarely bother with sheepskins—too heavy to move more than the top few. If I'm right, he's headed for the Upper Middlelands, probably delivering to a fuller or a weaver. It's not quite the Bottom, but it'll get us at least halfway there."

Nate spoke with such confidence; Beau couldn't help but trust his every word.

The boys remained tucked into the shadows at the edge of the field as the guards finished inspecting the first inbound cart. They'd been giving the driver a hard time, throwing the bolts of cloth he was carting to the ground and demanding he empty his pockets.

"The poor sap should just offer the bribe up now," Nate said. "They're never gonna let him get through 'til they get theirs, though that never stops some Middlelanders from trying."

No sooner had Nate said that when the driver, shaking his head in disgust, pulled out a small purse from deep inside his vest pocket. He began counting out a few coins when the tallest of the guards grabbed the purse. The driver's protests and the guards' ugly laughter echoed all the way up the hill.

With the stolen coins in hand, the guards soon got bored, leaving the driver to retrieve his fabric from the ground while they turned their attention to the first outbound Manor cart. The tallest guard started what looked to be a friendly chat with that driver while the other two guards picked up long poles and started ramming them deep into the hay piled on the back of the cart.

The prodders and the need for the plank made sense now.

With a large plank in hand, Beau and Nate would be able to make the prodders think they'd reached the end of the wagon. Nate was really the one who should be called Crafty.

"This is it," Nate said. "We've got to get behind the shed while the guards are on that cart. You ready?"

His heart pounding to burst, Beau readied himself for the sprint. After a silent countdown, Nate gave the signal. The boys dashed out of the field, zigzagging their way around the broken shards of glass and rusted barbs, down the slippery slope, and finally behind the outbuilding. The run was both terrifying and exhilarating, but they'd made it without the guards spotting them.

Now came the hard part.

Nate pulled a small knife out from his boot and began prying at one of the boards that lined the bottom edge of the shack.

While Nate worked, Beau kept an eye on the guards, but no one even glanced in their direction.

"Got it!" Nate soon whispered in triumph, holding up a plank of wood. "Now we wait until the guards move on to the other inbound wagon, then you're up."

"Me?" Beau balked. "What am I supposed to do?"

"You've got to hold that horse on the wool wagon steady without the driver seeing. Make sure he doesn't move or whinny while I climb in and set up our spot. You're a cordwainer's boy, you've got a way with horses, right?"

Beau knew exactly what a spooked horse could do to someone who was trying to control them, especially a workhorse. They might be slow, but they were strong and could break a man's back with one hoof. "I do," Beau said.

"Good. Wait for my signal before you come around to join me on the wagon. I'll make like a peeper frog. You know the sound, right?"

Beau nodded and Nate tucked the wooden board under one arm while they waited for their chance.

And then it happened. Like a flock of carrion birds, the three guards converged on a large inbound wagon covered by a tarp. They set to work tearing it apart, pulling every box and crate off the back, piling up what they favored and casting aside the rest, all while the driver stood by helpless.

At Nate's signal, the boys sprinted across the road. Heart pounding, eyes wide, Beau split off from Nate and slid into place just between the work horse's front legs. The horse flinched, but just as he was about to lift a hoof Beau grabbed hold of the bottom of the harness, stilling him.

From there he could see Nate's feet approach the back end of the wagon, then disappear up and out of sight. He was on!

Beau expected to hear Nate's signal at any moment, but it didn't come.

"Come on," Beau whispered to himself. "Where are you, Nate?"

Precious minutes passed and still no signal came from

Nate. It was just as Beau thought about releasing his hold on the horse and making a run for it that he heard it.

"By the Goodness of Himself, wake up, old man!" a guard shouted all too close by. "We got no guards to spare to ride with you. You get yourself robbed again like you did last time, you won't live to see another day. Now get on with you."

With the sound of a smack, the horse lunged forward. Quick as he could Beau let go his hold and rolled away, narrowly missing the fall of one of those heavy hooves on his neck. Once he was clear of the wheels, Beau jumped to his feet and made to climb into the back of the cart, but it was moving too fast!

He stumbled back, bewildered, the all-too-familiar twang of disappointment ringing in his chest, when Nate popped up from behind the sideboard. His arm extended down; Nate waved for Beau to run and grab hold. Beau sprinted forward, running faster then he'd ever moved before, finally managing to grasp onto Nate, who pulled him up into the cart. In the split second before the cart passed under the gateway, Nate pushed Beau into a hole he'd created in the front corner of the wagon and covered them over with sheepskins.

They'd made it! They'd actually made it!

As the cart slowly picked up speed, Beau sat stunned in disbelief. He was truly on his way to finding his ace, riding away from everything he'd ever known—hopelessness, inaction, lies—and onward toward possibility, help, and hope.

Chapter Eleven
Topend

After what felt like half a lifetime Nate pushed the sheep-skins back, exposing their hidey hole to fresh air and a view of the open road.

"We did it," Nate whispered, a smile blooming on his face. "We actually did it."

"I don't know how to properly thank you," Beau whispered back. "I could never have gotten this far without you."

"Don't go thanking me yet." Nate set the plank aside. "It's a long way to the Bottom, and we still have plenty of other gates to get through. We're found out along the way, our next stop will be the gallows. But for now, we feast."

Nate pulled two grayish lumps out of his pocket and held them out toward Beau. "A roll and a hunk of dried mackerel. Which one you want, or should we split even?"

"You have them," Beau said. He had no stomach for food.

He was still too wrapped up in disbelief.

When he awoke this morning, the day promised to be no different from any other. Yet dropping the pawn had set in motion a chain of events that landed him in a wagon running away from the Manor in search of a man he'd always been told was his greatest enemy, but who might just be his savior.

"You've got to eat." Nate broke one of the gray lumps in half.

"I don't want to take your food."

"There is no yours or mine."

Nate pushed the lump into Beau's hand, but one small bite of the roll was all Beau could manage. "What is this?" he asked, spitting it out.

"Awful, isn't it?" Nate chuckled. "I pretend it's one of those scones they give the upper servants. I've had one of those before. The memory helps the sawdust go down."

"Sawdust?"

"Sure, Mastery House bread is lousy with it. They mix it in with the flour; makes the provisions go further. It's not bad for you, but if you're not careful you wind up with some nasty splinters." Nate stuck out his tongue, revealing a painful-looking mess riddled with tiny white scars.

Beau tried not to cringe, but he couldn't imagine such a thing. His own food was so carefully prepared, the worst he'd ever suffered was a burned tongue on a bowl of soup.

"It doesn't hurt if you choose not to feel it."

It was clear, though, that it had hurt. Sadness lurked in the shadows behind Nate's eyes as he pulled a small knife from his boot and cut a slice from the second gray lump.

"Now, this you'll like." Nate pierced the piece of fish with the tip of his knife and offered it to Beau. "Nicked it from Matron's pantry. Go on, might be the best grub we get for a while."

Beau slid the piece of dried fish off Nate's knife, but he was more interested in the blade than the fish. A sharpened stone strapped to a wooden handle, the knife was nothing like the finely honed pieces of steel in Himself's collection. Yet it cut with a nice clean stroke.

"Not bad, huh?" Nate beamed with pride. "Go on, take a look."

Beau took the knife, playing with the weight, admiring the sharp edge. "The spine is nice and straight, and the swag point is perfectly rendered."

"Took me nearly three seasons to hone that edge." Nate took another bite of fish. "Almost got caught with it once or twice too. There's a price I'd never want to pay."

Nate slowly ran his thumb over the sharp edge. "You have to break rules if you want to survive, Crafty. Everyone does it."

"They do?"

"Sure. At least the rules they know they can get away with. Well, everyone except Cressi. She never stepped over a line in her life."

"Cressi?" Beau fought not to wince at the mention of her name. "Who's that?"

"Someone I came up with," Nate said between bites of fish. "She'd like you."

"I doubt it."

"No, she would. She's got this thing where it's like she's seeing right through you. It's creepy. Still, she knows a good sort when she sees one." Nate flicked a fish bone off the side of the cart. "But if she doesn't watch herself, they'll have her tending to that dog-hearted heir."

"Maybe he's nothing like Himself though." Beau tried to throw the idea out as almost an afterthought. Odd how he felt the need to defend himself—a self he never wanted to be.

"Only someone with eggs for brains would think he's not exactly like his father. The only thing that spoiled rat-swallow cares about is becoming the next Himself. That's how they work, to stay in power at any cost. Keep people cold, hungry, and stupid and they'll believe anything you tell them. No, we need a leader who can bring us real change."

As Nate spoke, a heat rose in Beau's throat. He was right. Even if Beau believed he could, he'd never liberate the Land, let alone free Cressi or the Mastery House children on his own. That's what an ace was for. An ace that just might be Doone.

"You look like you saw the skunk in the flesh," Nate laughed. "Don't worry, Crafty, we'll find Doone soon enough. All we got to do is look out for the runner's code."

"What's that?"

"They say runners leave messages behind for each other, symbols that tell them where it's safe to go, when to turn back. And where to find Doone." Nate flicked his knife into the sideboard of the cart, but when he pulled it back out, he moved too fast and cut his finger.

As a fine ribbon of blood trickled onto the white sheepskin, Beau started to rip a piece of his shirt off the way Cressi had earlier.

"Leave your togs intact." Nate wiped the blood off on his own jerkin. "It'll be fine. I've had worse. But then again, I used to have Cressi to tend to me. She could heal anything."

Beau tried to mask his surprise—did Nate know about her? "You mean, like she's a charmer?" he tested.

"No!" Nate laughed. "Cressi just knows what to do for cuts and maybe a fever. Charmers were more than healers. They were listened to, respected, and relied on by great leaders. They were special."

"You don't think she's special?"

"Well, I guess to me and the others at Mastery House she is. But there are no charmers left, Crafty. The Manor killed them all. Even Himself's own wife. They say he killed her himself when he found out she was one. Don't you know that?"

"That's not tr—" Beau began to protest, but what did he know about the truth anymore.

"No," he corrected himself, "I'd never heard that before."

"Well, they say that's what happened."

Beau turned away, for if Nate saw his face right now, he'd know Beau was lying. But Nate had taken a sudden interest in the view as they passed the first of Topend's enormous houses.

"Whoa, look at that!" Nate exclaimed.

Lit up with enough candles to turn night into day, the fifteen-room manse belonged to the Parvenues, one of Topend's wealthiest, most powerful, and nastiest families. Beau had been there several times when he was younger. Himself and Mr. Parvenue, a bore who never passed up the chance to try and impress Himself on subjects as fascinating as the oat tax and why Himself should award him a title, had tried to force a friendship between their sons. But the meetings thankfully ended after Kender locked Beau in the servants' outhouse.

"That one's even bigger!" Nate pointed to the next house down the road. "And look, they've all got private guards stationed at their doors. Unbelievable! Give me a two-room cabin and I'd feel like the richest man in the Land. And look at that one! It's bigger than the last two put together. Wait, are those statues of Himself planted in front of them all?"

Topenders designed their homes with only two things in mind—outspending their neighbors and trying to impress Himself with ever larger, grander, and more costly monuments in his honor.

As Nate continued commenting on every house they passed, Beau lay back in the sheepskins. He'd be happy to never see Topend again. But no sooner had he begun to slowly unwind when the bells began tolling nine.

Nine bells was when Beau was expected to go to bed. What if Barger had decided to check on him? Just because he ignored Beau for three days last time didn't mean he'd do it again. And if he did, having found the heir gone, he'd raise the alarm, waking the entire Manor to begin an exhaustive search. Riders would take off in every direction, tearing the Land apart. They wouldn't stop until they found Beau.

What had he done?

"What if they send riders after us?" Beau pressed. "What do we do then?"

"They wouldn't waste the metal to shoe the horses on the likes of us," Nate laughed. "Worst case, they'll post notices. But by the time they do that, we'll be safely with Doone. Don't worry, Crafty, we're not worth the effort to them."

If only that were true.

Or maybe it was.

Beau tried to picture Barger admitting to Himself that he'd lost the heir.

He couldn't see it. Barger would never admit to having failed in his duties, for to do so would condemn him to the same fate he'd walked countless others to—pain, shame, and a cruel and merciless death.

No, the chamberlain was too ambitious to ever expose himself that way. He'd handle Beau's disappearance the same way he handled everything—with coercion, bribery, and deceit.

That meant they probably had a bit of time before Barger sent someone after them. At least enough time to find the ace and get back to free Cressi and the others.

"Lay back and enjoy the ride," Nate yawned. "Try to sleep. I'm thinking we won't hit the border with the Upper Middlelands until well after sunrise. I'll wake you if anything happens."

"But if you're asleep, how will you know?"

"I don't know what it was like sleeping at the cordwainer's," Nate yawned again, "but in Mastery House if you don't sleep with your ears wide open, you might never wake up."

Tucked in between the sheepskins, Beau slowly allowed himself to unwind. The world outside the cart was dark and quiet, no sign of guards or trouble of any kind. For the first time ever he could simply be. He'd always been expected to be busy studying, answering, groveling. Never just being. And so, even as he knew he should try to stay awake and vigilant, the rocking of the wagon soon lulled him into a deep sleep.

Chapter Twelve
He's Gone

Tray in hand, Cressi dutifully followed Barger out of Cook's pantry on a silent march past the kitchen, through a succession of triple-locked doors, and up three flights of stairs. It seemed the heir was confined behind nearly as many barriers and bars as the Mastery House children.

When they'd arrived at yet another triple-locked door at the top of the stairs Barger stopped.

"This will be the first test of your abilities and loyalty. The heir will be preparing for bed," Barger explained. "I'll tell him I was wrong about you, and that as a gesture of goodwill, I've placed you in his service. He'll be suspicious of me, and that's where you come in."

"You want me to use the brew to . . . rob him of his will?" Cressi had prepared herself for this moment, but that didn't stop the very thought from turning her spine to ice.

"No!" Barger said. "You and your brew will simply make him want to become the heir his father deserves. To come to see me as his mentor and role model. And on the day he is named the new Himself, he will name me as his regent, requesting I rule in his stead."

In other words, turn Beau into a mindless and submissive puppet for Barger to control. The chamberlain had found a way to both increase his personal power and serve his master.

As Barger said, control the pawn, control the board. It all made sense now.

"I understand perfectly." Cressi readied herself as best she could. The game was about to begin.

The sheer opulence of the heir's apartments was overwhelming. Smooth marble floors as shiny and cold as a sheet of ice reflected the light of large chandeliers dripping with candles. Overstuffed upholstery looked ready to swallow one up, and everything was either dipped or edged in gold.

Prisons apparently came in all shapes and sizes.

"Set the tray over there." Barger gestured to a small table in the center of the sitting room. "I'll retrieve the heir, then you'll pour the tea for him. You're clear on what to do?"

Cressi nodded, but no sooner had she agreed than the pawn began quaking in her pocket. Although this time it was a different kind of dance—nervous and tense with a hint of excitement.

Cressi waited until Barger disappeared into the next room before pulling the pawn out of her pocket. Clutching it tightly, she marveled at how the blue-green hues shimmered and glistened, exposing a swirling depth of color such as she'd never seen before. But the light also exposed something else. The game piece wasn't moving at all. There was no shaking, no jumping. The pawn sat in her hand still as a stone.

And yet the quaking still reverberated through her bones, producing a perfect mixture of excitement and dread as if she was about to take a big leap.

Clearly her imagination had taken over every part of her, for it was almost as if she was feeling someone else's emotions.

But this was no time to worry about feelings, hers or anyone else's. She had to find a way to make it look as if she were somehow charming Beau without actually doing so. She opened the teapot to re-stir the brew, thoughts of trickery fixed in her mind, when a string of curses splintered the silence.

"That mouse-hearted, bloodsucking viper!" The chamberlain stormed back in, upending two chairs and a side table.

"Where is he?!" Barger backed Cressi up against the hearth.

"I-I don't know," Cressi stuttered as the heat of the fire played at the hem of her uniform. "On my bond, sir. The last time I saw him was with you."

"LIAR!" Barger shouted. He reached to grab for her, but

then his gaze landed on the pawn in her hand. Suddenly calmed, he stepped back, smoothing his hair and clearing his throat as if trying to erase the rage he'd just unleashed.

"You already knew he was gone, didn't you?" Barger's upper lip was curled so tightly it might as well have been up his nose. "The pawn told you, didn't it?"

"I . . ." Cressi stumbled to understand.

"Don't pretend with me. I knew Annina's pawn was charmed when I gave it to you. She'd admitted as much before she died. But how does it work? What does it tell you about the heir?"

So the emotions Cressi had felt whenever the pawn began dancing weren't her imaginings. They were messages from Beau of some sort.

"Truly, sir," Cressi said, her eyes wide and clear. "I don't know."

"Curse me for thinking someone like you was smart enough to understand!" Barger roared, and before Cressi could resist, he dragged her out of the apartment.

Cook, who was sitting at her worktable opposite a pair of guards, jumped up as soon as Barger and Cressi barreled into the pantry.

"Leave," Barger snarled at the guards.

"My boys are as trustworthy as me, you know that," Cook said. "Besides, they've got some news you're gonna wanna hear. Go on, tell him."

The guards were a nasty pair of matching brutes. The only discernible difference between them was their hair color; one had a mop of straight, straw-colored strands while the other sported an oily, mousey-brown mane.

The mousey-headed one stood up and cleared his throat nervously. "Well, Mr. Barger, it's this way. We was on patrol, like we was ordered, you know, right where we should be, nowhere else, following orders. Right, Keb?"

The other guard jumped to his feet, his head dutifully bobbing up and down.

"As we was patrolling past Mastery House, the doorkeep calls us over. 'Bring word to the Manor,' he says. 'We got a runner.'"

Cressi shifted nervously. Nate. It had to be.

"Why are you wasting my time with this." Barger shook his head in disgust. "You should know what to do."

Boz, the mousey-headed one, looked to Cook for reassurance before continuing. "Well, that's the thing. We thought we seen him out by the calf enclosure."

"Then why are you here?" Barger snapped. "Go find him!"

"Well, then the doorkeep described the runner, and we realize he ain't the one we seen. See this boy, the keep said, was skinny, tall, had dark hair that's always falling in his face. That ain't the boy we seen, even though we seen him too."

Barger calmly—too calmly—turned to Cook. "Translate this gibberish before I have their tongues removed."

Cook smoothed the front of her apron and explained. "There were two boys out by the calves. They passed the one with hair in his face after Keb and Boz had told the other one to get back to work. They figured he was assigned out there too. But the one I said you'd be interested in was about this tall." Cook held a hand below her own shoulders. "Clean hair. Cut like them Topend boys. Nice teeth all sitting straight in his mouth. And it sounds like he was wearing riding boots, like the ones Be—"

Barger threw up a palm. "Don't. Say. It."

As he began to pace, his anger seething like a pot about to boil over, Cressi went pale as milk. Nate and Beau—together? The thought of it made her stomach churn.

Nate was like her very own blood. They were as close as any two people could be, even though they were exact opposites. Where Cressi was methodical and patient, Nate was hotheaded and impulsive. And he hated the heir with everything he had.

"It's not my boys' fault," Cook cooed. "They didn't think anything of it until they heard about the runner, then they realized the description of one didn't match the other. That's when they came to me. Besides, it's Miss Charmer's fault. She's the one that shoulda known."

As four pairs of eyes shifted in Cressi's direction, she slipped her hand into her pocket and held the pawn tight. Even though it was lying still, as she thought of Beau she was filled with the most wonderful, expansive feeling. Freedom—the exact opposite of what she was experiencing.

It was Beau who'd taken a great leap. There was no question about it, Cressi was certain he was gone. And while what he was doing was dangerous, he wasn't in danger. Not now.

Nor he was alone. Beau was out traveling somewhere beyond the Manor walls with someone she knew all too well.

"I don't fully understand it, but I know now the heir's gone," Cressi said. "And . . . he is with that Mastery House runner, the one they call Nate. I have no doubt. He's been trying to run since he could walk."

"Blast them!" Barger slammed his fist on the table, sending plates and cups rattling. "Where'd they go?"

The pawn wasn't telling her where they were headed, but Cressi had long known if Nate ever left the Manor there was only one place he'd go—to find Doone.

"They're not there yet, though their destination is clear." Cressi shivered as if frightened to the bone before adding, "The Bottom."

"That mewling heir! Gone to the Bottom?" Barger began turning several shades of red. "Don't you dare lie to me!"

"Never would I." Cressi raised her hands in innocent surrender.

"Why would the heir go to the Bottom?" Barger pressed.

"I don't know. Maybe the runner took him captive in hopes of getting paid for him. What I do know is I can find them.

Send me. I'll bring the heir back to you. And the runner too."

"What makes you think I'd let you out of my sight?" Barger snapped.

"Because I'm the only one who can find them without attracting attention. Unlike guards or an official search party, I can travel without raising any suspicion, gossip, or fear."

Barger scoffed. "I'm meant to believe a girl who's never stepped foot off the Manor could navigate her way through the Land?"

"The pawn will lead me to him."

Barger's nose twitched. She was clearly making him second-guess his own cunning. "Be careful. I can see you dead in less time than it takes to butter my bread."

"I know. Send me to find him. He trusts me."

Barger's pointer finger traced a line back and forth across his lower lip before summoning the guards to stand. "You two will take her. Go fetch a wagon. We'll dress you as couriers, give you papers so you can cross the borders of the Land without questions."

"You mean we get to leave the Manor?" Boz asked.

"You get to find the heir," Barger corrected. "And make certain no one knows he's gone missing."

A mixture of elation and fear ran up Cressi's spine as Keb and Boz made for the door. Her gamble had worked. She'd won this round.

She got up to follow the guards out when she was yanked back.

"You have four days," Barger said, waving four impeccably manicured fingers in her face. "You're not back with him by then, I'll come after you to finish the job myself."

"Four days? That's barely enough time to—" Cressi began.

"Make it to the Bottom and back," Barger snarled. "Not so certain of your powers anymore?"

It was all Cressi could do to keep her lips from curling into a snarl of her own, but she managed to tame them into a soft smile. "Four days it is."

Chapter Thirteen
On the Town

Beau awoke with a start, Nate's face inches from his own.
"Don't move." Nate's words were barely audible, although with one hand slapped over Beau's mouth and the other gripping his knife, his gaze fixed outside the wagon, his meaning was clear.

"All the coin!" a voice like rolling gravel demanded from outside the wagon, while a trio of others echoed the call. A thin, reedy voice rose up, begging for mercy as Beau felt the wagon rocking from the push and pull of a struggle up in the driver's seat.

Thieves.

Grunts and moans filtered in beneath the sheepskins along with the stray bits of intelligible chatter. "We gonna take the skins?" someone asked.

The reply that came was inaudible.

Beau's skin prickled with cold, waiting for the moment the skins were thrown back, exposing him and Nate. While Nate might be fast enough to get away, Beau would be easily caught, a rabbit in a snare.

But then the most astounding thing happened: Beau heard the sound of horses riding off, carrying away riders cackling in triumph.

They'd survived undetected.

But what of the driver?

Nate slowly eased off Beau. He was wondering the same thing.

But before they could peek out there came the creak and whine of the wheels as someone slowly—possibly painfully—climbed into the driver's seat and started the wagon down the road.

Both boys collapsed with relief. They were safe, at least for now.

Sometime later the wagon passed through a thinly guarded gate without a search. Sounds of life and the smell of fresh baked bread infiltrated their hiding place, leaving both boys drooling. They waited silently as the wagon came to a full stop, the sound of the brake engaging and the driver groaning as he climbed out of his seat. Shuffling footsteps were enough to tell them he'd walked away. The time had come.

On Nate's signal, the boys threw the skins off and went

scrambling out of the wagon across the cobblestoned street to the safety of an alleyway. From there they peeked out at the marketplace, surveying the scene.

There were people everywhere in the town square; ambling amidst the stalls, talking, and hawking their wares. Dogs barked, people argued, and everywhere were the sounds of commerce. Everyone had somewhere to go, something to do, and not one of them was taking note of the two boys with their heads peeking out of an alley. If Beau's tutors were right in their descriptions of the Land, this had to be the Upper Middlelands Marketplace.

But wherever it was, Nate looked as if he were staring into the face of heaven.

"You see the cordwainer anywhere? Anyone else you know? What's that over there? And what's that amazing smell?"

"I don't see him," Beau replied, choosing the easiest lie to tell.

"Good!" Nate started for the square then doubled back to the alley. "First thing, I need to pee or else I might drown."

"Me too." Beau scanned the area, looking for an outhouse, when he realized that Nate had simply turned his back and began relieving himself. Right there, out in the open!

"Come on, what are you waiting for?" Nate said. "I want to get out there."

Beau laughed nervously as he took up a position by the wall. While Nate rambled on about what he wanted to do and see out in the market, Beau fought to relax. He'd never done his business anywhere but in a chamber pot. Then again, he'd never climbed into the back of a wagon and run away from the Manor before either. Rebellion took some practice to get used to.

"So—what do we do now?" Beau asked once they'd both finished.

"First we get some food. Then we look for signs of the runner's code, then find another ride headed south." Nate made to step out of the alley when he stopped. "Wait, what if someone recognizes you in the market?"

"No one ever pays attention to the apprentice, only the master." Beau spoke with authority, for he'd experienced this countless times. No one ever noticed him or anyone else while in Himself's presence unless ordered to do so.

"Makes sense," Nate said. "All they see is the one who holds the coins. So, which way?"

Beau looked out on the maze of stalls and parked wagons trying to decide how to proceed. Everything was so new to him. Unlike the High Street in Topend with its tidy row of shops, here there were vendors selling their wares out in the open air, offering everything from bulk cloth to copper pots to salted meat. A kind of controlled chaos pulsing with life and vitality filled the square.

"We head straight into the heart of the market," Beau decided. "Better chance to melt into the crowd."

"Good thinking. Let's—" Nate stopped and raised his

nose high in the air. "Hold up. You smell that? What is it? I've never smelled anything like it."

Beau had. That thick, syrupy nectar wafting on the breeze was the unmistakable aroma of sweet, melty sugar. "It's candy."

"Wrong. It's heaven," Nate declared as he took off into the marketplace, a hound on the scent.

In and out of stalls, around wagons, Nate led the way to a far corner of the square where a confectioner was cooking sugar-coated almonds over hot coals.

Busy at her work, she didn't notice the boys at first, but when she did her expression turned to stone.

"No money, no looking!" The woman waved her wooden paddle in Nate's face, narrowly missing his nose.

"That's not right," Beau snapped, his voice sounding hard and sure. "We can look even if we're not going to buy."

The confectioner nailed Beau with a sneer. "Until a dirty little rat like you runs the Land, I decide who gets to look at my sugared almonds. Now get before I raise the alarm on you."

"You're the one who should be taken in—" Beau began when Nate elbowed him in the ribs.

"We're going." Nate threw his hands up in mock surrender, grabbed Beau by the arm, and dragged him away down the lane. "Wow, Crafty, I didn't know you had it in you to stand up to someone like that."

Beau tried to shrug it off, but in truth, he hadn't known

until now that he had it in him either. Yet the impulse had come easily.

"One day, we'll have all the sweets we want. But for now, we'll have to settle for some apples from that cart." Nate wiggled his fingers and mimed plucking an apple from the neatly stacked rows.

"No." Beau planted his feet. "We're not stealing."

"Unless you've got some coin hidden or something of worth to trade, we'll not have any food then."

"These people work hard. They deserve to be paid."

"And we deserve to eat."

"We'll find a way," Beau said, determined to make certain they did.

But as the boys continued winding their way past carts piled high with hand-pies, breads, and fruits, Beau's resolve began chipping away. Was it really so wrong to snag a pear or two off the back of a cart? How much could one loaf of bread really mean to a baker?

Beau was about to give in when he spotted a bustle of activity up ahead. People were leaving the market stalls and gathering around an enormous statue planted in the center of the square. Carved from gleaming white marble, the statue depicted Himself as a powerful ancient warrior standing guard over the marketplace, the very picture of the protective commander.

Beau's stomach twisted. His father's image was everywhere.

"I think we should avoid that crowd."

"We should hear what's got them rattled," Nate countered. "Just keep your head down and your ears open."

Beau tried to push away the churning sensation in his belly as he tucked his chin and followed Nate into the crowd. Once there, he could see two men standing at the base of the statue. One, a robust, bearded man dressed in the signature fur-trimmed red cloak of a wool merchant overshadowed his companion, an old man who, like his clothing, was worn thin and ragged. Beau had never seen the man in the red robes, but the old man's shock of scraggly white hair was all too familiar.

The cart driver.

"Isn't that—" Beau began when the wool merchant's voice boomed out over the crowd.

"Quiet down!"

A hush descended and the merchant turned to the cart driver. "Tell them again, exactly what you told me."

"I was jumped, robbed, right below Topend." The driver's voice was shaky, and Beau had to strain to hear him over the crowd's low grumbling chatter. "Thieves, not sure if they were from the Bottom or Lower Middlelands. They got my purse, gave me a fat lip and this lump on my head. At least they left me the skins."

The crowd erupted in a buzz of whispers, while someone shouted out, "Soon they'll be robbing us all in bright daylight! Right here in the square!"

"Let him finish!" the man in red shouted to the crowd.

"Himself rode out yesterday, surrounded by his elite guard headed to the North Hills and Torin's territory."

At the mention of Torin's name, worried grumblings began echoing through the square.

"Calm yourselves!" the wool merchant warned. "A deal with Torin is a great boon for us. They're coming to protect us, guard us."

"How do you know?" someone shouted.

"Because the Manor tells us so!" the wool merchant scolded. "Himself values us, our goods, our coin. We've already seen what can happen as the fever takes ever more guards. There are bandits roaming the roads. We've had two shops broken into at night! We should be grateful to have Torin guarding us. He will protect us, keep things from getting any worse. By the Goodness of Himself, we will be safe from the thieves, pilferers, and villains who want to take what's ours. As for all of you, rest your gossiping tongues and get back to work knowing the Manor is looking out for our safety."

"Those Lower Middlelanders are just waiting to take what's ours!" a woman clutching an infant tightly to her chest cried out. "Not even Torin could keep us safe if they spread the fever to us here!"

"The fever hasn't moved beyond the guards' barracks," the wool merchant scolded. "The only thing you need to worry about, Mary Bellwright, is making sure you can pay your taxes."

The woman withdrew, but the crowd was no closer to calm.

"It's the work of a charmer!" another woman shouted. "There's one among us."

Nate leaned in and whispered, "If only there were still charmers. This lot deserves to suffer as much as the rest of us. Another flood or maybe a drought might teach them."

It was a terrible thing to say, but there was some truth there. From what Beau could see, the people of the Upper Middlelands showed little interest in the common good, unless it benefited them.

"That's enough now!" the wool merchant shouted the crowd down. "There are no more charmers! The Manor has it all under control. Now go back to your work, and put your trust in Himself. He will see that we and those in Topend are safe."

"We should get out of here," Nate whispered as the crowd begrudgingly began to disperse. "This lot doesn't sound like they'd take to new faces. Which way do we go?"

Beau tried to muster some semblance of confidence as he led Nate down a narrow lane, then down another, and yet another. He'd hoped they'd eventually wind up in the out-skirts of town, but in truth they were only going in circles.

"Do you even know where you're heading?" Nate's bitter tang cut deep. "I need to eat. Now. And I don't care how we get it."

He was right. Everywhere they went the smell of food

cooking followed, turning pangs of hunger into a stifling ache. Why had Beau promised to find them food? What did he know about it? The most work he'd ever had to do to fill his belly was open the dumbwaiter.

Beau was ready to admit defeat, when he landed on the answer. He turned and marched into the center of the marketplace, his head on a swivel looking for just the right thing.

"Glad you changed your mind," Nate said, his fingers twitching and ready to pick some rolls off a nearby stall. "My stomach says it's worth the risk."

"Not like that. There's where we get our next meal." Beau pointed out a cartman slowly loading barrels onto a wagon.

Nate squinted at the cart. "Why would he give us food?"

"Not give, pay in exchange for our labor."

"He doesn't look like he's got two coins to rub together. We need to hit on someone who looks prosperous."

"I don't agree. Look at him struggling. His arm is bandaged, he needs help. And if he can't pay us, we'll try someone else."

"You better be right," Nate grumbled. "I've done enough work in this life for no pay."

Chapter Fourteen
Half a Coin

"Wait! Let us help you!" Beau called as he and Nate rushed in to help the carter lift his cask onto the wagon.

"Kind of you," the carter said, yielding the barrel to the boys. "Had a little accident yesterday, it's slowing me down."

The man tugged at the bandage on his arm, a small pool of dried blood staining the wrappings.

"We can load the rest of your barrels, if you like," Beau offered.

"For half . . . a full coin," Nate emphatically added.

The carter looked the boys over. "All right. Half a coin each if you load the entire wagon."

Nate brightened. "For half a coin each we'll drive it too!"

"Might take you up on that." The cart man winked. "Go on, get to work. I got places to be."

Beau was nearly bursting with pride as he and Nate got to it. His idea had actually worked. With every barrel they moved, they were that much closer to finding Doone, to freeing Cressi. And, if everything Nate said about Doone was true, liberating Mastery House.

By the time they'd finished loading the last barrel onto the wagon, Beau's arms were aching from the labor, his stomach howling with hunger. At least their meal would be an honest one.

"Fairly done." The carter counted out two half coins from his purse. "Too bad I won't have help this good down the way."

"Down the way?" Nate asked, his palm out and ready to receive payment. "Where down the way?"

"Lower Middlelands. I'm hoping to do some trading there." The carter poured the coins from one palm to the other as he leaned in to whisper, "There's a gathering."

Beau had never even heard of such a thing, but Nate was practically salivating. "You mean like they used to before they were made illegal? With music and games? That kind of gathering?"

"And all the food you could ever want. Too bad you can't come along. I imagine your mothers will be missing you for supper."

Beau and Nate exchanged a look.

"Actually, we're heading south too," Nate ventured. "We have an aunt down there. She's not well, and we're being sent to tend her pigs."

"Imagine the chances." The carter's smile exposed a mouthful of crooked, yellowed teeth. "I'll tell you what, you come with me to the gathering, unload my wagon, and I'll pay you double. A full coin each. Unless your dear aunt can't wait."

"She can wait!" Beau and Nate replied in unison.

"We've a deal then." The carter dropped the coins back in his purse and tucked it into his pocket. "There's room for you in the back. You can watch the barrels, make sure they don't move."

"Oh . . ." Nate hesitated, as he watched the coins disappear out of sight. "We thought to get some food first."

"You got nothing packed for your journey?"

"We forgot." Nate shrugged. "Too worried about our aunt."

"Right." The carter nodded. "Well, I've got bread, a cheese rind, and a couple of pears. If that'll do you, it's yours."

"That's perfect," Beau said. "Thank you."

And with that the two boys climbed aboard the wagon, ready to ride out of the Upper Middlelands, with full bellies no less.

"I'm thinking I should change your name again." Nate wiped away the beads of pear juice dripping down his chin.

"Why?" Beau asked between bites of bread.

"Seems like Lucky might be the better name for you. Every time I tried to run, I always got caught before I could find my way onto a wagon. Then you come along. We get a free meal and a ride on a southbound wagon that just fairly pranced right through the gate on our way to a gathering! You're not a charmer, are you, Crafty? You the one causing the fever? If so, watch out, I might just turn you in for the reward." Nate laughed, then in a swift shift of mood added, "You gonna eat that pear?"

Grateful to not have to answer, Beau surrendered the fruit. Nate was right again. It wasn't only Himself and Barger who suspected a charmer was behind the fever. As the sickness spread, people were getting anxious and hungry for answers, or in the absence of truth, a scapegoat. Beau needed to find Doone and fast.

"I could eat these all day," Nate crowed, finishing the pear. "Only fruit we got in Mastery House were half-rotten gostberries. Nasty, seedy things. But I did once have a peach hand-pie. It nearly ruined me. Made going back and facing a bowl of watery gruel too hard. After that, I told Fledge to spare me the knowing."

"Fledge?" His friend's name yanked Beau out of his thoughts. "The master of the stables?"

Since Cressi knew Fledge, it made sense Nate did as well. But somehow it stung that Fledge had kept them hidden from Beau.

"Me and Cressi used to sneak out to go see him. He'd feed us, then send us back with food and sometimes warm clothes for the others. He'd teach us things, too, like how to read. But after Cressi got sent up to service, I stopped going. Couldn't trust anyone else with Fledge's secret."

"His secret?" Beau asked as blithely as he could muster.

Nate leaned back against the barrels. "I shouldn't say it, but since you and I are bound to each other now, I guess I can tell you. Fledge came from the Badem. Himself's charmer wife brought him to the Manor. She told Himself she wouldn't give him a child until he vowed to protect Fledge, always. So Himself made Fledge apprentice to the old master of the stables when he was a ten, and that's why he is where he is now."

The story hit Beau like a blow to the head. "That's not true."

"You're calling me a liar?" Nate leaned in, a hint of smoke smoldering under the surface.

"No," Beau backed down. "But I can't believe that's true."

If Fledge had known Beau's mother, he would have told him.

He should have told him.

Why hadn't he told him?

Beau pitched forward over the edge of the wagon until all he could see was the ground racing past in a blur. Road became indistinguishable from rocks, truth from lies. Friends from enemies.

"Well, there are stranger things than that," Nate laughed, brightening. "You wanna know my secret?"

Beau hesitated. He couldn't handle knowing Nate to be anything other than brave, smart, and his friend.

"Well, I have two, actually," Nate said. "The first is stupid, probably every kid in Mastery House has the same one. See, up until I was a five or a six, I used to think I was there by mistake. That I'd been stolen from my parents, sold to the Manor by their enemies, and any day they'd figure it out and come for me."

"Every child sold to Mastery House has been stolen from their parents by their enemy." Beau shook his head in disgust since that enemy was his father. "That's why we have to see them all freed."

"True enough," Nate agreed. "But I used to think my parents were rich and lived in one of those fine Topend houses I'd heard so much about, so when they came for me, I'd be rich too. But know what? Even if they were the richest people in the Land, I wouldn't want that now. To live like that when so many others don't, means you only see what you want to see. That's not me. I see it all. You know?"

Yes, Beau knew all too well.

"I'm a lot like Doone in that way," Nate continued. "I tell you, Crafty, we're so close to finding him, I can taste it."

But no sooner had Nate spoken than the scent of roasting meats wafted past on the breeze.

"Or is that a roast? You smell that?" Nate asked. "Where's that coming fro—"

And then they saw it. Just off the right side of the wagon, down below in a wide bowl-shaped field lay a glorious assemblage of tents, wagons, and people. The gathering.

The sight of all those people freely laughing, dancing, playing set Beau's blood bubbling. With so much to do, to see—games, hammer throws, dancing—it was like some kind of dream of freedom.

"Once we get paid, I'm going to watch that lot over there playing Hazard." Nate pointed out a tight huddle of people gathered around a game of dice. "Study the game. Afterwards, I've a mind to try turning our two coins into a whole lot more."

"No, we can't chance losing what we have."

"If you want more, Crafty, you've got to be willing to risk what you've got."

"I know, but we need to keep going. Find Do—" Beau began when the cart man appeared at the end of the wagon.

"You not gonna find anything until you empty my cart," he snarled.

"We'll get it done." Nate jumped off the wagon. "You only need worry about having those coins warmed up and waiting for us."

"You mean these?" The cart man plucked two coins from his purse and waved them in Nate's face.

"That's them." Nate tried to snatch the coins away, but Beau stepped in between them.

"Don't worry, sir," Beau said. "We'll get it done."

The cart man pulled a long-bladed dagger from his boot and outlined a large rectangle on the ground. "Line them barrels up in rows of five right here. Not one over the line."

"Easy coin." Nate winked at Beau. "You roll the barrels to the edge, I'll grab them off the wagon and line them up, neat as a pin. You'll see, Crafty, we'll be on our way in no time at all."

Chapter Fifteen
The Power of Power

The thrill of leaving the Manor for the first time carried Cressi far into the night. Watching the Manor recede into the distance filled her with a joy she had to fight to contain. She sat primed and ready, wedged into a wagon between the two Manor guards, pawn in hand, waiting for it to tell her where to find Beau and Nate.

But several leagues past Topend and the pawn still remained silent.

There were no movements, no feelings welling up to overpower her own. The only thoughts occupying her mind were hers alone.

All she could do now was trust that something was pushing her forward.

Eventually the journey grew tedious, the rumbling over rutted roads wearying. She slept on and off through the night and into the next day, waking to the sounds of the guards eating, arguing, and snoring. It was only after the late afternoon sun began its lazy journey to the west that they entered a large town.

Unlike the Manor with its one magnificent building surrounded by workshops and outbuildings on the outskirts, here there were buildings of all sizes, shapes, and ranges of magnificence. Some were as tall as three stories, others low and squat, and most hosted shops on the ground floor.

"Where are we?" Cressi asked.

"What, don't your pawn tell you?" Keb laughed.

"That's not how it works," Boz snorted.

"What do you know about how it works?" Keb shot back.

"Forget about the pawn," Cressi said. "Where are we and why have we stopped?"

"Upper Middlelands." Boz climbed out of the wagon and tied the horses to a hitching post. "You and that pawn ain't getting us nowhere, so we figured we'd ask around if anyone's seen the heir."

"Are you serious?" Cressi pressed. "No one is meant to know he's gone from the Manor."

"You ain't too smart, Miss Pawn," Boz clucked in pity. "We're not gonna mention his name. Just gonna ask who's seen a boy with nice teeth and clean hair."

"As if they won't figure out who two Manor couriers are talking about from that description!"

"No, they won't," Boz countered. "You don't know nothing about being a spy. We been trained. Don't go telling us what to do."

"Yeah," Keb added.

As the two guards proceeded to launch into a series of one tall tale after another about their supposed spy craft, Cressi caught wind of a scent on the breeze.

Flowers? Trees?

No. Something else, something far more powerful . . .

Cressi looked up and down the street searching for the source. But the fishmonger's, the baker's, nor the cordwainer's shop could be home to what she was smelling. Then she spotted it. A tidy little apothecary shop tucked in at the end of the lane.

"You know," she said, interrupting Boz, who was busy bragging about how he single-handedly discovered who was stealing cabbages from the kitchen gardens, "I think you're right.

"We should ask if anyone's seen a boy of that description. As long as we don't mention it's the heir, they won't suspect a thing. Although . . ." Cressi shook her head as if terribly disappointed. "We should split up; all go in separate directions. It'll go faster that way."

"No way, missy," Boz said. "Barger said to keep you in our sights at all times and that's what we're gonna do."

"You're right." Cressi threw her hands up in surrender. "It'll be fine. So what if it take us three times as long? We'll still have two and a half days before Barger expects us back. All right then, let's go."

Cressi made to set off, but she could see Boz was considering the idea, his face twisting and contorting as he tried to look for the trap. Finally, after a quick huddle with Keb, he grumbled, "Fine. You go asking, and we'll go asking. But don't go pulling anything funny."

"I want to find the heir as much as you do," Cressi said. "I'm going to go ask at that row of shops. You can follow me, spy on me, do what you like, but I intend to find him."

If Cressi had been mesmerized by Cook's pantry, the effect was tripled the moment she stepped inside the apothecary shop. Three entire walls were lined with shelves and drawers, all filled with plants, flowers, and barks of every variety. Cressi stood there, her eyes wide and her mouth agape until the proprietress stepped out from behind the counter.

A tiny woman with a face like a rotting pumpkin, the proprietress donned a pair of spectacles and stepped up to take a closer look at Cressi. "Never thought I'd see one of you in my shop ever again."

Cressi cringed as she dropped a quick curtsy to hide the guilt in her eyes. Was it really that obvious?

"I think I've made a mistake." Cressi backed up to the door. "I'll be going."

"Not without what you came for first." The shopkeeper

stepped in front of Cressi and closed the door.

Cressi froze. This was the worst idea she'd ever had. She shouldn't have allowed her instincts to take over and drown out reason. Everyone had heard the stories of what the Upper Middlelanders had done to suspected charmers after Himself's final decree. Drownings, hangings. Far too many people with a talent for herbs were killed simply because they had no friends in high places to protect them—friends like this woman obviously had.

"You're a young one, aren't you?" It was hard to tell if the shopkeeper was disgusted or impressed. "Makes sense though. Why waste someone with more experience? Better let your sort be exposed than us, especially the way they say the guards in the Lower Middlelands barracks are dropping from the fever."

Relief flooded in. She hadn't seen Cressi as a charmer but as a lowly nursemaid come to treat the guards down with the fever.

"Yes," Cressi replied a bit too brightly. "I'm here to help with the fever."

"They expect me to give you supplies, no doubt." The proprietress clucked her tongue. "By the Goodness of Himself, I'll do it, it's my duty to the Land, but I want it taken out of my tax for the season. Understand? You tell them, nothing for free."

"Yes," Cressi said, mustering a tone of authority. "I believe that will be fine."

The proprietress wiped her hands and turned to scan her well-stocked shelves. "You'll be wanting some willowbank and this green nettler, I assume?"

She offered the jar of nettler to Cressi to smell.

Green nettler was conventionally used to clear congestion, but as Cressi inhaled, a thousand tiny pinpricks broke out over her skin. It felt like in her hands the nettler could be used to raise a rash.

"Yes, we need that," Cressi said. "But the fever victims are having a hard time sleeping. They're very restless. Something to help them sleep, deeply, for a long time would be best. What do you recommend for that?"

"Linden flower will do, or valerian root. Or . . . these." The proprietress set a jar of large red berries down next to the linden and valerian. "Ferrita."

Cressi breathed deep of all three. The linden and valerian evoked only a slight sleepiness in her, but the ferrita berries smelled of a long, deep sleep.

Combined with the nettlers, she'd have the makings of the perfect brew to sidetrack the guards when the time came.

"I'll take all three."

While the proprietress weighed and packed up the herbs, Cressi found herself drawn to a large glass jar sitting on a corner shelf behind the counter. It contained a thick, gelatinous substance, the color of which was almost an exact match for the verdigris pawn. It didn't speak to her the same way herbs and plants did. Rather than evoking a kind of physical or emotional state in her, whatever this was, it enchanted Cressi into an almost empty-minded kind of trance. She could have stayed there gazing at the swirl of color all day, all year, for the rest of her life had the proprietress not stepped in between her and the jar.

While the woman's disposition had not been exactly sunny up to this point, it turned decidedly stormy. "Anything else?"

Cressi shook off her fascination and deposited the five packets of herbs in her apron pocket. "You've done enough, thank you. This will help immensely."

"That's four and one-half coins' worth you have there," the proprietress scolded as she followed Cressi to the door. "You make sure they reduce my tax by that much. You hear me?"

"Yes, ma'am," Cressi replied as she exited the shop.

Cressi tucked her head and hurried back to the wagon. Keb and Boz were nowhere in sight, leaving her ample time to stow away the packets from the apothecary alongside that vile brew Cook had prepared.

Her plan was beginning to take shape.

Chapter Sixteen
The Vexing Man

By the time Beau and Nate finished moving the final cask, the day was growing long.

"That's the last of them." Nate approached the carter, his hand outstretched. "We'll take our coin now."

"You get paid after I sell them. All of them," the carter grumbled.

"That wasn't our deal!" Nate shot back. "You can't change the terms after we did the work."

"I can do what I want as long as the coin is sitting in my pocket and not yours. Now get on the wagon and out of my way. I've got customers approaching." The carter pushed past Nate and greeted three men pulling a wheelbarrow behind them.

Knowing Nate wasn't likely to drop it that easily, Beau wrapped a friendly arm around his shoulder. "He's only got fifteen more casks to sell. We'll be rid of him soon enough."

Nate shrugged Beau's embrace off and flexed his fists. "I know how to be rid of him even faster."

"Fighting will only call attention to us. We just need to get our coin then be on our way to finding Doone."

Nate reluctantly shook out his fists. "You don't have be so sensible all the time. Sometimes the only way out is to act. Dare to risk it all."

"You mean like when we climbed into the back of a wagon to escape the Manor?" The implication that he was too compliant stung. Shades of his father's disapproval hovered overhead. "Being daring doesn't have to mean being stupid."

That glint of lightning flashed in Nate's eyes. "Are you calling me stupid?"

"Never. But I am saying we can be smarter than him and get our way."

Nate weighed Beau's words before easing back. "A frog is smarter than him."

"So is a rock," Beau added with a chuckle. "That's why we should *help* him sell off the last of these casks. Here, watch."

Beau cleared his throat and took a few steps closer to where the carter was negotiating with his buyers.

"Of course, we have to be patient." Beau raised his volume a little too loud and turned his tone up a little too bright. "Goods this rare don't come around all that often, and gents smart enough to see their worth are rarer still."

"That last one saw the worth, though, didn't he?" Nate replied, picking up on the game.

"He sure did," Beau announced. "Three casks' worth."

The carter shot Beau through with a nasty glare, but Beau saw his customers' body language had softened. Gone were their hunched, protective stances, replaced now with the open posture of three people eagerly waiting to spend their coin. In less time than it took for the carter to return his full attention to the transaction, the customers were demanding to buy two casks each.

After the men left, six casks in tow, the carter moved on the boys, pinning them against the wagon. "What game you playing?"

"Just helping you move your goods, sir," Beau said, summoning a smile.

"Who told you to do that?"

"Common sense," Nate said. "We want our coin, the sooner you sell your . . . whatever you're selling, the faster we get paid."

"Oh!" The carter's yellow teeth flashed in the fading light of day. "So you wanna get paid, do you?"

"You know we do," Nate shot back.

"Well, boys," the carter clucked. "Afraid it won't be up to me much longer if you get paid or not."

"What does that mean?" Nate's fingers were twitching, itching to grab his blade.

"You two know what the reward is for returning runaways to the Manor? Enough to buy me a proper house."

"We're not runaways!" Nate snarled, but his voice cracked, leaving room for the truth to leak out.

"It don't matter if you are or aren't. Mastery House will take you all the same."

Beau felt the air contract around him, squeezing his chest tight. "You . . . you'd sell us to the Manor? How could you do that?"

"You maggot scum!" Quick as a flash, Nate pushed the carter as he pulled his knife and lunged forward. But the cart man moved fast too. He swung his bandaged arm out, knocking Beau down to the ground as he went after Nate.

As Beau scrambled to get up he saw the carter hit Nate, sending him flying backward in one direction, his knife in another. Before Nate could rebound or Beau could find his own feet, the carter planted his heel on Nate's chest.

"Who you calling scum?" he spat.

"Did I say scum?" Nate snarled, his voice strangled by the foot on his throat. "I meant vermin."

As the carter twisted his heel deeper into Nate's chest, Beau charged forward. He was no match for the man, but he didn't care. But just as he was within striking distance, he felt himself being dragged back, the collar of his shirt pulled tight around his neck.

"That's enough of that," came a smooth, silvery kind of

voice from behind Beau. "Leave him be, Grater."

All Beau could see then was the expression on the carter's face turning from smug satisfaction to a kind of cowardly terror as he scrambled back and away from Nate.

"I didn't see you there," Grater sniveled. "Didn't know you was here."

"Apparently not," came the voice.

The hand holding Beau's collar released him then, leaving him to stumble forward. And that's when Beau got his first view of the stranger. Tall, powerful, and almost too handsome by half, he exuded a kind of cool control as he stepped to Grater.

"Now perhaps you'll explain to me what's going on here."

"Just getting the boys to do the work they said they'd do." Grater shrank back even farther.

"That's a lie!" Nate said retrieving his knife. "He wouldn't pay us what he owes us. He was trying to sell us ba . . . to the Manor."

"That's not very nice, Grater," the stranger said.

"You gonna believe these two over me?" The cart man tried to laugh it off.

"I'll believe anyone over you. And get that bandage off your arm," the stranger said. "I warned you not to try that nonsense just to catch pity and unwitting children."

"I got cut!" Grater mewled.

"You did not. I see you trying to siphon mercy off from

those that deserve it again, you'll have cause for more than one bandage." The stranger turned to Beau and Nate. "How much does he owe you?"

"Four coins. Two each." Nate flipped the fringe of hair back from his eyes.

All it took then was one look from the stranger for Grater to open his purse and count out four coins.

"Good," the stranger said once the boys had their coin in hand. "Now back on your wagon, Grater. I don't expect to see you, that fake wound, or your shoddy goods around here again. Understand?"

"There are them that can't afford what you—" Grater began but quickly withered under the stranger's glare. "Fine, I'll sell elsewhere."

"You do that." The stranger waved Grater off, then wrapped an arm around each of the boy's shoulders. "How about we go and get you some of that good roasted meat or maybe some sweets?"

"Why not both?" Beau replied.

"Now there's a fine idea," the stranger laughed as he led the way toward the festivities.

The stranger bought two large plates for the boys; one brimming with roasted meats and the other piled high with strawberry hand-pies.

Beau happily pulled one of the pies off the plate and was

about to take a giant bite into the sweet, syrupy treat when Nate ripped it out of his hand.

"Hold on. The last person who gave us free food just tried to sell us to the Manor. What are you looking for in return?"

"Not a thing. You're free to enjoy as much as you like or throw it away. I've got a game to get back to. You two would be wise to watch who you get involved with out here." And with that the stranger gingerly plucked the berry tart from Nate and handed it back to Beau before walking off.

As he receded into the crowd, Beau couldn't help but feel there was something oddly familiar about him. It wasn't so much that Beau thought he'd seen the man before, as he recognized his confidence. He walked with a kind of swagger and surety that left Beau expecting to catch a whiff of cloves, for the only other person he'd ever seen carry themselves with such authority was Himself. Although the stranger, with his clear, bright eyes and that confident tilt of his chin, exuded a gentler kind of authority. Like someone you could trust.

"That was . . . odd," Beau said. "I feel like we should thank him properly."

"He didn't seem to care." Nate took a bite of food and rolled his eyes skyward in bliss. "All I know is now we've more coin to do with as we please. Come on, I wanna see the hammer-throwing contest up close and proper."

"What about finding Doone? It's still so far to the Bottom."

"We can spare some time for fun, Crafty," Nate said.

"Can we really?" Cressi had already been in Barger's custody for more than a day. Who knew how long he'd wait to level his punishment?

"Besides," Nate continued, "we need to find a ride out first. In the meantime maybe we'll hear something about where exactly to find Doone."

Nate was right—they couldn't exactly walk to the Bottom. And maybe they'd get lucky again. "Fine, but we focus on finding a ride, all right?"

Nate agreed and led the way through the gathering. After they'd stuffed themselves full of food, they wandered every corner of the festivities. From the archery and wrestling matches to a rousing match of stoolball, the boys got swept up in the excitement of the games. At one point Beau heard someone mention Doone's name, but a fire-eater happened to swallow a flaming sword nearby at that same exact moment, and the explosion of delighted *oohs* and *aahs* drowned out their words.

As daylight dimmed, the games came to a sudden end, and the crowd began assembling in the center of the field. Though no less festive, the mood of the crowd had shifted into something more restive and expectant. The air crackled with heat as right before a storm.

"What's happening?" Beau asked.

"I heard someone say something about the vexing man."

Nate replied. "I've no idea what that is, but I sure want to know. Come on."

Beau resisted; they'd already spent too much time. "No. We need to find a way to get out of here now."

"You kidding me? It's just starting to get good."

Nate grabbed Beau by the wrist and dragged him into the center of the crowd. For the first time now Beau could see what everyone was assembled around—a larger-than-life straw effigy. Adults and children alike were taking turns stuffing things into the straw before stepping back to rejoin the crowd. Though the face of the effigy was roughly hewn and comical in expression, the likeness made Beau's bones tremble.

"Is that meant to be . . . Himself?"

"Yes, and look there, perched on his shoulder." Nate laughed. "None other than that snake heir of his."

Beau followed Nate's gaze to where a large snake sat coiled atop the straw man's shoulder. While the body was serpentine, the face was made to look like a younger version of Himself.

Beau's mouth ran dry. "Why are they doing this?"

"It's an old tradition that's long since been outlawed to get rid of worries and vexations," a woman who was standing next to Beau explained. "Those who can write put it in words, the rest tuck rotten fruit or moldy bread to stand in for their troubles and woes."

"What kind of troubles?" Beau asked.

"The usual." Though her face, hands, and back had been ravaged by time, the woman held her chin high. "Fear, hunger, sickness. Not enough coin. The Manor's never-ending cruelty. All of them go in the vexing man."

"Then what?" Beau asked even though he wasn't sure he wanted the answer.

"We burn it," the woman said. "Send all our problems up in smoke."

"We should do that too, Crafty," Nate crowed. "Wait, we need a scrap of parchment."

While Nate ran off to find something to write on, Beau remained stuck to his spot. The gathering, which had looked to him like the epitome of freedom and joy, wasn't just a brief reprieve from the difficulty of people's lives. It was an act of rebellion.

"Does it work?" he asked the woman.

"You tell me," she said. "Season in and season out, we still got to pay our taxes to the Manor or risk losing our farms, our families. The best pickings of every harvest get sent up north to feed them that have so much more than us. Himself and his heir don't care for our misery, only their comfort."

Beau wanted to tell the woman she was wrong about the heir. He wasn't anything like his father. If he had any power at all, he'd never let greed or injustice prevail or let people suffer. But he couldn't say that without raising the crowd's anger, putting his chances of freeing Cressi at risk.

Instead he simply said, "I hope it does work one day."

"The Manor will fall." The woman spoke with certainty. "All things eventually do. Until then, thanks to the fever, we get this chance to once again burn the vexing man and get a taste of what freedom will be like. Look, they're lighting it up."

The crowd roared with delight as three men bearing torches set the vexing man aflame. Cries of "Liberty!" and "For All!" bounced through the assembly like soap bubbles from a wand. Here was one thing Himself had not lied about—the people of the Land were ripe for a revolt. Yet if this was a revolutionary act, it was nothing like the menacing and destructive mayhem Beau had been warned about all his life. People trying to unburden themselves of their woes, envisioning a better future was nothing if not hopeful and creative.

As the shouts and whoops of joy filled the air, Beau too felt his spirit soaring, getting carried away with the promise of freedom. A better life for all was possible. But then the flames reached the heir-faced snake, and the cheers turned to jeers. People shouted obscenities and threw rotten fruit, hastening the snake's destruction. Their hatred of the heir burned with a passion as bright as the flames.

Beau shrank away from the bonfire, certain every pair of eyes in the crowd could see straight through to the truth of who he was. Those all too familiar feelings of shame and worthlessness began to rear their heads, but Beau beat them back. He had no time, no use for them.

Already determined to find his ace to free Cressi, to put an end to Mastery House no matter what it took, Beau's search took on ever more urgency. He needed an ace, but so did the Land, and neither of them had much time.

Chapter Seventeen
Welcomed

Beau wove in and out of the food vendors and mead stands, searching for Nate. He checked by the parked caravans, peered into every cluster of people. Nate was nowhere to be found. His hunt was further frustrated as the crowds began to flow away from the vexing man and toward the back corner of the gathering where the high-stakes games of Hazard, Chess, and Fist were being played out.

Pulled along like a log on the waves, Beau thought he caught mentions of Doone's name, and of Torin's, but it was too hard to hear anything specific. Only when he reached the games corner did the crowd grow quieter in respect for the players. Under any other circumstances Beau would have been the first in line to watch a real Fist match, but not now.

Beau was about to take another run through the gathering when he heard his name called out.

"Crafty!" Nate raced toward him, wild with excitement. "There you are!"

"I've been looking all over for you too! We have to go, Nate. Now—"

"We can't leave now!" Nate panted. "Just follow me."

Nate pulled Beau through to the front row of spectators until they had a view of two players hunched over a Fist board. Carved from a glistening slab of wood, the game board was inlaid with copper to delineate the squares. And the keep— the square at the very center of the board where the king sat—was encrusted with tiny verdigris-colored stones.

It had to be the most beautiful Fist board ever made. Beau loved his mother's and Fledge's sets, but they paled in comparison—with the exception of his mother's verdigris pawn, which glistened with a light all its own. Nothing could ever match it.

"Look." Nate nodded toward one of the Fist players. "It's him!"

Beau tore his gaze from the game and looked up at the player. It was him, the stranger who'd saved them from Grater. From the looks of the board, he was only a few moves away from victory.

"Good for him, but we need to find—" Beau began but was summarily hushed by people on every side as the stranger's opponent made his next move.

Like a fool the opponent shifted his king back one square.

He'd left the stranger the perfect setup. In one fell swoop, Beau and Nate's rescuer captured a total of three guards then scooped up the verdigris pawn, ceremonially replacing his rival's king on the keep.

The spectators erupted in a rousing round of applause for the victor and jeers for his bested opponent.

"Now, now," the stranger playfully scolded as he pocketed his winnings. "We should always be gracious in victory. No gloating."

"Ready for a better challenger?" someone in the crowd shouted.

"Another time, perhaps." The stranger tipped his head at a man who'd been busy packing up the board to follow him as he strode away, cleaving the crowd in two.

"Come on. This is our chance!" Nate shouted as he sprinted off to follow in the stranger's wake.

"What do we care about him?" Beau asked.

But Nate was gone. Beau had no choice but to race to keep pace with Nate as he ducked and dodged, beating a line through the crowd until finally he caught up to the stranger, planting himself in his path.

"You're Doone, aren't you?" Nate blurted out.

The stranger laughed. "Am I?"

Beau had been certain he'd recognize Doone the instant he saw him. That the meeting would be momentous, that it would hit him like a strike of lightning.

Had he really mistaken his ace for a kind stranger?

"I've been trying to run from Mastery House for the last four seasons to come and join you!" Nate was nearly breathless with excitement as he pulled the WANTED poster from his sleeve and thrust it at the stranger. "I can't believe I didn't realize it was you."

The stranger looked the poster over.

"I can't blame you—it's a terrible resemblance," he said. "But I'm not sure I understand why you'd be looking to join me."

Nate checked over his shoulder before leaning in close. "To be part of the rising."

"Is that so? You hear that, Trout?" Doone turned to his companion, who gave an indifferent shrug.

Trout cut a stark contrast to Doone. His misshapen nose collided with narrow-set eyes and sunken cheekbones that looked like they might slip off if not for the great wedge of a jaw holding it all together.

"Everyone says you're the only one who can make it happen." Nate was trying to remain calm, but his enthusiasm was seeping out the edges. "I . . . I mean, we want to be part of it."

"Sorry, boys, not sure what you're meaning. Trout and I travel light, but I wish you the best. Stay safe out here." Doone patted them both on the head and walked off.

Beau's stomach twisted in on itself as he watched hope walk away, but Nate wouldn't be deterred. He sprinted after Doone.

"We've got valuable things to offer you!" Nate panted as he trotted alongside Doone. "Crafty here has skills, he can make you things. And me, well I'm clever and as slippery as you need. I know ways in and out of the Manor no one else does."

That was enough to stop Doone's progression. "You say you ran from the Manor?"

"Yes, slipped out in the back of a wagon," Nate boasted.

"These are fine togs for children of Mastery House." Doone was clearly dubious.

"I stole them from the laundry." Nate tossed his head with pride. "Kept them hidden in a barn. Only put them on days I tried to run."

"And you?" Beau's heart threatened to stop dead as Doone felt the quality of the cloth of his sleeves.

"Crafty's not from Mastery House. He's the cordwainer's boy. See the shoes?" All of Nate's coolheaded composure had evaporated in Doone's presence. "Who else but a cordwainer's apprentice would have such a fine pair?"

"Yes, who?" Doone studied Beau, taking his measure. "Healthy, aren't you? You've got fat on your bones, teeth in your head, and a craft to support you. Why run?"

"He was remanded by the Manor," Nate said. "Sent to tend to the calves. Terrible waste of talent."

"They would've given you back to the cordwainer. Eventually. Yet you gave up the promise of a comfortable life to run."

"A life of comfort isn't always worth the price you have to

pay," Beau replied, a truth he knew all too well.

"Wise words from a boy who spends his days cobbling shoes."

"Not just shoes!" Nate volunteered. "He can do anything you need. Repair saddles, fashion sheaths. He can make one for you. You'd do that, Crafty, right?"

"Sure . . . I could do that." Beau fought to make the lie sound easy.

Doone looked impressed. After a quick glance around he gathered the boys into a huddle. "This talk of a rising is dangerous business," he warned. "Trout here and I are dedicated to helping the people of the Land, to right the wrongs so that one day, instead of burning their woes in a straw effigy, everyone will be free. We've seen it's possible, out there across the sea. Life is different in other lands, freer. But what we do is not the stuff of stories. It's real, hard work. Is that what you two are looking to join?"

Beau felt a burst of energy rise from the bottom of his feet and rush up to the top of his head. He might not have recognized him for who he was at first, but only the ace would think like this, dare like this! Doone was the one to save Cressi, liberate the children of Mastery House, and free the Land.

Beau and Nate both nodded fervently.

"Good." Doone smiled. "Then we welcome you."

˄˅˄

Beau thought he knew what it was to walk in the wake of power. To feel its effects on a crowd of people. Power was palpable. And so was the fear it incited. He'd seen it compel otherwise pompous men to bend and arrogant women to demure in Himself's presence.

Power was cruel, absolute, and unbending.

Or was it?

For even as the crowds parted for Doone and people stopped to watch him pass, there was no fear or trembling. Only admiration and hope. Lots and lots of hope. But as they walked through the crowd, basking in Doone's shadow, Beau realized something else. He'd been so focused on finding his ace, he hadn't yet considered how to actually get Doone to free Cressi or the children of Mastery House.

"So how do we do this?" Beau whispered to Nate. "Do we just come out and ask him to help us free Mastery House?"

"No!" Nate snipped. "We have to prove ourselves first. Let him see we're worthy of his trust."

"But how long will that take?" Beau pressed. He'd already been gone for over a day. He only had another couple of days at best before Himself returned to the Manor.

"Knowing me and knowing you, no time at all." Nate tossed the hair out of his eyes, exposing that all-too-self-assured grin of his. "Don't worry, Crafty. The hard part is over."

"I hope you're right," Beau sighed. He'd better be right.

By the time they reached Doone's horses, Doone had flipped countless coins into waiting children's hands, helped a mother find her lost son, and broken up a fight. With each act of generosity Beau felt himself calming. Doone was worth a short delay, he knew it.

"Nate, you'll ride with Trout. Crafty, you're with me." Doone adjusted the saddle on his dappled gray stallion, then lifted Beau up as if he were no more than a sack of flour and placed him atop the horse.

Without thinking Beau hooked his feet into the stirrups, fixed his back and shoulders, then took hold of the reins, thumbs tucked, and hands crisply creased at the wrist—exactly as Fledge had taught him.

"You look like one of Himself's guards up there. All you're missing is the helmet and armor!" Doone laughed.

Beau chuckled weakly, collapsing his back into a half-bent curve. "I used to see them ride by the cordwainer's. Bunch of pillocks."

"That they are," Doone agreed. "Now make room for me up there. You've not earned your own horse yet. Nate, up with Trout."

While Nate figured out how to climb up onto Trout's horse, Beau kept his head down to hide the red streaks of horror burning into his cheeks. He'd nearly given himself away! If he was going to enlist Doone's help, he'd truly have to be Crafty.

Chapter Eighteen
Anka

By the time Keb and Boz returned to the wagon the sun was beginning to fade, and so were they. They looked exhausted, and their courier uniforms were smeared with sticky fingerprints, crumbs, and stains.

"What happened to you?" Cressi asked as they stumbled into the driver's seats.

"We ate," Keb grumbled. "Lots."

There went her plan. In their absence, she'd added large quantities of sleeping herbs to their food thinking she'd suggest they stop to eat once they were nearing the Bottom. But from the looks of them, neither guard was likely to want to think about food again until morning.

Time for a new plan.

Feigning a sore neck, Cressi asked if she could sit in the back of the wagon. Fortunately the guards were so overfull they were glad to have the driver's bench to themselves.

Cressi had just settled into the back of the wagon when she spotted a throng of townspeople led by the apothecary proprietress heading across the square. Some were on foot, several others were on horseback, and they were all heading straight for the wagon.

Cressi's blood turned cold. Had the proprietress found her out?

"Let's go! Drive now!" Cressi urged, but the guards were too busy arguing about who would drive and who would sleep.

"We don't take orders from you." Boz turned back to snarl at Cressi when his eyes grew wide. "What's this? Hang you, Keb! I told you not to take that coin!"

"It was your idea," Keb shot back.

"You stole coin?" Cressi pressed. "From who?"

"We didn't steal," Keb protested. "We took back what was ours after the sweets lady wouldn't sell us any more."

"Stop yattering and drive, Keb." Boz shoved Keb into the driver's seat, but it was too late. The riders surrounded the wagon on all sides, while the rest of the horde, led by a man dressed in bright red robes, closed in.

The proprietress, marching in step with the man in red, pointed up at Cressi. "That's her! Gave her four and one-half coins' worth of remedies to use on the guards at the barracks."

The crowd rumbled.

Cressi girded herself, preparing to be ripped away from the

wagon, when the man in red threw his arms open wide. "By the Goodness of Himself, I bid you welcome!"

Welcome?

"I'm Master Woolever, wool merchant and mayor of this humble corner of the Land. I told the good people of the Upper Middlelands not to worry, that the Manor would send help. And no sooner had I said it than you arrived."

"What?" Boz was, as always, completely confused.

"You mean you ain't mad about the coi—" Keb began, but Cressi stopped him with a sharp elbow.

"Please allow us to escort you to the barracks," Woolever continued. "We want to ensure your safe arrival."

"The barracks?" Boz repeated. "We ain—"

"That's very kind of you," Cressi called out over Boz. "Do you mind if we have a moment?"

"Not at all!" Woolever beamed benevolence and patience.

Cressi leaned in toward Keb and Boz. "They think we're on our way to the Lower Middlelands barracks to tend to the sick guards."

"Why they think that?" Boz gawped.

"'Cause that's what you told the lady with the sweets," Keb said. "She asked if we was here cause of the fever, you said, yeah—"

"I ain't going nowhere near no fever." Boz hunkered down in his seat, trying to make himself immovable.

"Too bad, we have no choice," Cressi shot back. "You

heard him, they're desperate for the Manor to do something to help their guards. Unless you want to admit you stole back your coin. Best case it'll land you in jail, worst case you hang."

"What about finding the heir?" Keb asked.

"We'll find him after we've gone to the barracks. I'll do what I can for the guards. You can stay in the wagon and sleep, far from the fever. We still have two days to find him. All will be well."

This couldn't have fallen more perfectly if Cressi had planned it. The Lower Middlelands were close enough to the Bottom for her to make her way there on her own.

Cressi turned back to Woolever. "Thank you for the offer! We appreciate it."

"Is there anything else you need before we go?" Woolever asked. "Name it, it's yours!"

"Got any more of them sweety almonds?" Keb asked.

"Perhaps just some food or cider if you have it," Cressi interjected.

"You heard her. Go!" Woolever clapped his hands and several members of the crowd ran to their respective shops. "I will be writing to Himself to commend you. He should hear all about your dutiful service."

"No! Don't do that!" Cressi exclaimed. "There's no need."

"Don't forget to mention me and Keb," Boz shouted. "Boz and Keb, you got that?"

"Yes, of course!" Cressi could practically smell the relief emanating from the mayor's pores. "And you, miss? Your name?"

"It's not necessary, I assure you." Cressi collapsed back into the wagon, hoping to put an end to the conversation. But no sooner had she begun to collect her thoughts when the proprietress appeared around the side of the wagon.

"Shhh! Make no fuss," she warned as she reached into her apron pocket and thrust several small pouches at Cressi. "Take these. I would've given them to you at the shop, but you can never know who's listening or looking."

Cressi looked at the pouches filled with herbs, confused. "I don't understand."

"I hate delaying you by sending you to the barracks," the woman whispered. "But it's the safest way, trust me. When you get there, you tell Anka I sent you. Understand?"

"Um . . . no, I don't."

"You will. Now put those with the rest of your herbs. But keep this separate." The proprietress pulled a small bottle from up her sleeve. A familiar flash of green and blue blinded Cressi for a hair of a moment before the woman pressed it into her palm. "Tuck it away safely on your person."

Cressi started to open her palm when the proprietress covered it over with her own hand. "Don't touch it, and do not smell it. Try not to even look at it or think about it, unless you need it. It's the only brew that can be used against a charmer. But it's also how I knew who you were for certain."

"Why would I need it?" Cressi feigned innocence. "There are no more cha—"

"Just keep it." The woman's hand was soft and warm resting on Cressi's. There was a kindness there, a reassuring calm.

"I truly don't understa—" Cressi began when two merchants loaded down with a supply of cider and food approached the wagon.

"May luck follow you, and don't forget to send my regards to Anka." The proprietress snuck off and soon emerged around the front of the wagon, shouting orders to the others. "Hurry up and get those things loaded. The ill can't be kept waiting!"

And with that, the wagon, surrounded by the mayor and several other riders, headed out of the Upper Middlelands, carrying Cressi ever closer to the Bottom.

As they traveled south, Woolever showered Keb and Boz with a seemingly endless string of compliments and the promise of rewards for their service. Keb and Boz blossomed under the attention, but Cressi understood their escorts were only trying to ensure they reached their intended destination. At least it gave Cressi time away from prying eyes to examine her newly increased store of herbs. Some she could name, others she couldn't, but she quickly came to recognize them for what they were. As for the bottle of blue-green liquid, she didn't try to open it or even look at it. She could feel its power, a strength she knew enough to avoid.

When they finally approached the barracks' gates the mayor and other riders insisted the wagon drive in ahead of them. Keb and Boz preened as if they were nobles getting their due. But as soon as they'd cleared the gates, two riders raced up and locked the wagon inside the compound.

Cressi had been expecting this, but Keb and Boz were stunned.

"You goat-faced rotters!" Boz shouted. "You tricked us!"

"Heal the guards, stop the fever, then you'll go free!" the mayor called back as he and the other riders set off.

"Why they do that?" Keb whined.

"Because they trust you as much as I do," Cressi muttered before adding in a full voice, "Well, let's see where we are."

Lit up by large torches, the forbidding fortress of stone and iron loomed up ahead, like a wolf about to pounce. But more than that, there was a pall hanging over the entire landscape— the kind of stony silence that accompanies illness and death.

"I ain't going no closer!" Boz declared from the safety of the driver's seat.

"I don't expect you to," Cressi said. "But I do hope you'll leave some food and cider for my return. We'll need the supplies as we travel on."

Cressi pulled a bottle of cider out of the back of the wagon and reluctantly handed it to Boz.

"We eat and drink what we want." Boz pulled the cork and took a long draw.

"As you say." Cressi dropped a quick curtsy and headed for the barracks confident they'd be asleep within minutes. She'd dosed the cider with enough ferrita berries to ensure a nice long sleep. "All right, pawn, let's search out this Anka so we can get on to finding Beau."

She hadn't gotten very far down the drive when someone carrying a torch came racing toward her.

"How many sick you got?" a woman called out, her wrung-out urgency echoing through the dark. "I've barely room for even one more!"

"None," Cressi replied. "I've come with supplies. I'm looking for An—"

"By the Goodness of Himself!" The woman's relief was clear even in the dark. "Woolever finally heard my pleas. I wrote to him countless times, and each time the messenger returned with the same answer: 'No one can be spared.' Yet here you are!"

"Yes," Cressi replied. "I've brought herbs. The apothecary sends her regards. I'm looking for Anka. Are you—"

"I'll take any help I can get," The woman turned and led the way inside through a cold and cavernous gallery. In better times the great hall probably would have been the place for taking meals. But now it reeked of illness and the suffering of the guards laid out on straw mattresses, many listless, too ill to move, while others tossed fitfully, moaning restlessly.

"How many nursemaids do you have helping you?" Cressi asked.

The woman adjusted the white cap covering her hair as she led Cressi down a series of narrow corridors. "None. It's just me."

They made their way down empty halls ringing with the silence of the sick, through a small dining room, then finally into a warm, well-lit kitchen. Once inside, the woman locked the door behind them, pocketed the key, then exhaled deeply.

"Now we can speak freely, and no one will hear us. Sit." She gestured to the small table in the center of the room. "I'm sorry for being so short. This is the only safe place for us to speak. So the Upper Middlelands apothecary sent you?"

"Yes. I've brought some herbs to help with the fever."

"I'm sure you have. Now tell me what you are really doing here."

"I—I don't know what you mean."

"I told you, there are no eyes or ears in here that don't belong. This kitchen was charmed a long time ago. It's a safe haven. A place to keep secrets. But time is running low. At least fifteen of those guards out there are close to waking up. If they do, they'll realize they don't have the fever unless I get more of my soup in them and fast. If you'd tell me why you are out here, alone—"

"They don't have the fever?" Cressi pressed.

"Most of them do." The woman began filling a large soup tureen with broth she had bubbling over the hearth. "I've been trying to keep them comfortable and quiet. I haven't lost any of them yet. But that left me with a few others who were so agitated by fear of the fever I was afraid of what they might do to innocent people in the name of keeping the peace. So I've quieted them with some black fern powder. It raises similar symptoms without the risks of dying. Only I know who is really ill and who has been sidelined."

"Are you a . . . a . . ." Cressi couldn't dare say the word, for to do so would be to fully expose herself. "You are Anka, aren't you?"

"I am, but I am not a charmer, like you. Perhaps while you're here you could make me a brew or two. I've always found truth to be one of the most effective weapons out here."

"I'm not a . . . Why would you say that?" Cressi balked.

"Because it's true." Anka dropped the ladle back into the soup pot and turned to Cressi. "If you won't tell me what you know, I'll tell you what I know. Two boys ran from the Manor and were seen on a cart heading south. I know without a doubt one of those boys was Beau and the other was Nate. What I don't know is why they're out here now, unprepared for what lies ahead, and why you are not with them."

"I . . ." Cressi could hardly feel her hands, although the warmth the pawn began emitting at the mention of Beau's name was hard to ignore. Was this for real? Or a trap?

"Had I more time now, I'd explain how I know what I know. But I'll say this: Scattered throughout the Land, there are those of us who have a way of remaining connected. Like roots, we spread out far below the surface. We're here to help you. And Beau." Anka placed the soup tureen on a tray along with several small bowls. "Redosing the guards can take some time; I'll be back as soon as I can. In the meantime, consider this kitchen yours."

"I'm sorry." Cressi rose and slowly began to back up to the door. "I don't think you understand. I need to be going."

"I understand everything, and I know exactly where you have to go, which is why you must wait for my return." Anka unlocked the door then handed the key to Cressi. "Lock yourself in. Should there be any trouble at all, that other door there will lead you to safety. But I'd hate for you to go without instructions. It would be a gross dereliction of my duties to let you go without you understanding into what you are headed."

"Your duties?" Cressi repeated, for she could hardly find her own words. "What am I headed int—" But Anka, tray in hand, was gone, the door slamming shut in her wake.

Chapter Nineteen
The Bottom

They rode through the night without stopping.

Even though Nate had told him to wait, Beau tried several times to find a way to ask Doone to turn north, to devise some way to get him to free Cressi and the children of Mastery House. But Doone wasn't interested in conversation, insisting instead that Beau sleep and rest up for the day ahead. And so Beau did sleep, if only fitfully. Every time he awoke, they'd traveled farther and farther south—the terrain turning ever harder, harsher, the fields and orchards of the Lower Middlelands slowly thinning into nothing more than brushwood.

By the time the sun rose, the horses were picking their way through a tangled and thorny landscape bristling with balding trees and scrub. The only colors were a wash of brown, black, and gray. Such a sad and gloomy place could only be the Bottom.

Doone brought his horse to a stop in the middle of the rutted and narrow road. From this point on it cut through a forest filled with young, skinny trees and bare scrub competing for what spotty bits of sunshine could fight through the gloom. Thick with damp, the air had a strong tang, a kind of acrid burning odor, both unpleasant yet somehow familiar. There were no fields, no houses, no animals skittering past. It was almost as if Beau could hear them tucking into the bushes, whispering, tittering tales that couldn't be shared. This was a place of secrets, and it was also a place that somehow felt like home.

"We'll walk from here." Doone dismounted. "The horses deserve a break. You boys lead them for us."

Trout pushed the half-sleeping Nate from his saddle and lumbered over to join Doone as he walked off ahead of the boys.

Nate landed on his feet, stretching and yawning as if waking from the most restful of sleeps. "I haven't felt this good in the morning, well, ever."

"Really?" Beau moaned, slowly slipping off of Doone's horse. "I'm not entirely sure I can feel my legs."

"There's the rebel spirit," Nate teased.

Beau rolled his neck, trying to work out the cricks. "We're hardly rebels."

"Yes, we are." Nate turned deadly serious. "That's exactly what we are now."

Beau hadn't thought of himself that way, not even as he stood watching the vexing man burn. Yet everything from going to Mastery House to escaping his apartments then running away to find his ace all been outstanding acts of rebellion. If that didn't make him a rebel, what did?

"But we won't be outlaws for long," Nate said. "One day soon, we'll be part of the leadership bringing a new beginning to the people of the Land. Once Doone topples the Manor, ridding us once and for all of the scourge of Himself and his vile heir, everything will change."

Beau stopped. Fighting for freedom was one thing, but he didn't sign up for killing. Himself was many things, but he was also Beau's father. There had to be another way to bring about change to the Land.

"The burning of Himself and the heir was only symbolic," Beau insisted. "That can't be what Doone actually means to do."

"So you think the Manor would just give power over to Doone? Let him rule over the Bottom? That Himself will simply roll over and say, 'Of course we'll let the children of Mastery House go and here's the Land.' That the heir won't fight for his title?"

"Maybe the heir doesn't want to rule. Maybe he'd be sympathetic, want to help, try to convince Himself to change."

"Why would you think that?"

"I don't know." Beau tried to shrug it off. "He just doesn't seem like a bad person."

"You've seen him?" Nate drilled Beau with a look of utter confusion. "Why didn't you say so before? Where? When?"

"I . . ." Beau grasped for the quickest lie. "I saw him in the stables one day. He was there for a lesson while I was working. He looked like . . . well, you. Or me."

"Well, he's not. He's nothing like me or you. Nothing."

True. The heir was nothing like Nate. He wasn't even like Crafty. Since meeting Cressi and leaving the Manor, Beau had done things he'd never imagined possible. The heir—the boy who was blind to everything but his own woes and knew nothing about the Land or its people—was gone.

But if Doone truly was Beau's ace, he'd never resort to murder. The ace relied on strategy to win, not mayhem.

They walked on in silence, Doone and Trout leading the way far up ahead. Aside from the sound of their footsteps, everything was quiet and still. No birdsong, no rustling leaves, only silence. Yet the deeper into the Bottom they walked, the more Beau began to feel that this wasn't the silence of nature at rest, it was something much louder. Somehow more sinister.

And then he saw it.

Or so he thought.

Just off to his right he caught sight of an old dead tree that seemed to move, the bark twisting and turning like a dance or a twitch.

Beau blinked and looked again.

All was still.

"Did you see that?" he asked.

"See what?" Nate stopped to scan the area.

"That tree over there," Beau replied. "I thought I saw it m—"

A loud whistle broke the air followed by Doone calling out, "Hurry up, boys. Trout will take the horses from here."

Nate went barreling ahead, Trout's weary horse tagging along behind him. Beau looked back at the tree before following with Doone's stallion, but there was no more movement, nothing. His imagination was working tricks on him.

Doone stood waiting near a fallen tree, his boot resting on it as if he'd pushed it over himself. While Trout took the horses, Doone turned to the boys, a glint shining in his bright blue eyes.

"Do you know what this is?" he asked.

"Firewood?" Nate laughed.

"No," Doone corrected. "It's a sign."

"Of wha—"

"The runner's code!" Nate nearly exploded with recognition. "It's real?"

"As real as you and me," Doone replied. "See how one end has been shaved to a fine tip, and how it's pointing into the woods there? It's directing the way to the next sign. Let's follow it and see what it says."

Doone stepped off the pathway and through some new growth trees beyond which lay a sunken patch of ground surrounded by burned grass and blackened moss. The earth turned boggy under their feet, almost pliable, and the tang of sulfur and peat hung heavy in the air.

Beau recognized the odor as something dark and ugly but couldn't place where he'd smelled it before.

"Always skirt the edges." Doone cocked his head at the pit. "You want to test the ground ahead, make sure it's solid. Don't ever get sucked into a sand pit, you'll never get back out."

A sand pit, of course. Beau should have recognized the stink. The Manor's apothecary touted the hot, molten sand as a cure for anything and everything. But Beau found all it did was nauseate the stomach and burn the skin.

"Matron used to threaten to drop me into a pit almost every day," Nate said. "I thought it would be more like an endless hole you'd never stop falling through."

"You get stuck in one of these above your ankle and soon that will be true." Doone continued past the sand pit and stopped in front of the ragged remains of a hollowed-out tree stump.

"Here we are." He presented the stump as if it were a precious relic. "Look closely. Tell me what you see. Take your time."

The boys circled the stump. At first all Beau saw was

rotting wood, but as he inspected the stump more closely, he began to see there were symbols etched into the cracked and peeling bark—one on each of the four sides.

"You mean like this?" Beau pointed to a line crossed by five hash marks carved into the side of the tree pointing back to the road.

"Exactly!" Doone beamed.

"And these too!" Nate added, pointing out the other three symbols arranged on all sides of the stump.

"What do they mean?" Beau asked.

But before Doone could reply a high-pitched scream pierced the air, sending Beau jumping and knocking straight into Nate.

"Calm down, Crafty," Nate sneered. "Haven't you ever heard a pig scream?"

"No!" Beau confessed before catching himself. "I mean, yes, but not like that."

"I'd think you'd be used to hearing pigs being carried off to the slaughter," Doone said. "Being a cordwainer's apprentice and all."

"I am," Beau bluffed. "I just, I guess I didn't expect it out here is al—" But before Beau could finish, another cry echoed through the woods. This one most certainly human, a wail of despair, heartbreak.

"Some people just get too attached to the animals they raise." Doone shook his head in pity. "Can't say I blame them, but everyone's got to eat."

Doone turned back to the tree stump. "Anyway, this mark that Crafty spotted means there's a safe road in that direction." Doone pointed south. "A crosshatched square is a warning. Maybe someone was attacked by bandits over that way. And this cockeyed *T* on the north side means you'll surely receive a beating if you continue down that path."

"Because that's the way back to the Manor!" Nate volunteered.

"Clever boy." Doone winked at Nate. "You learn to follow these signs, and you'll never get lost. Now, let's keep moving."

Doone led the way back to the path.

A short while later, the forest began to thin out, revealing the burned-out remains of a cluster of buildings, the remnants of a village. Beau stopped and stared at the charred skeletons of the abandoned homes. Though the air was clear, he could almost smell the smoke of fires long extinguished.

"That's Torin's work," Doone explained. "His weapon of choice, what they called northern fire, a flammable liquid they used to lay waste to entire villages. Burned down most of the Bottom."

Beau was about to correct Doone and tell him that *The Histories* made no mention of any such weapon. But gazing out over the destruction brought back a ghost of a memory, a footnote he'd once discovered buried deep within the text. The Manor's power, it said, had been bolstered by Torin's mastery of incendiarism. When he asked his tutor what it meant, he referred Beau to his father. But Himself refused to answer and instead made Beau repeat the Oath of Himself, the vow his father and seven generations before had all taken. The very vow Beau was supposed to one day take.

"By right and by might, by virtue of the blood by which I have been born, I am the Land. My word is its credo, my actions its fate. Anointed by birth, I am the law, the truth, the past, and the future."

Beau hadn't asked anything more about it for fear of incurring his father's wrath, but now it all made perfect, horrible sense.

Incendiarism, to maliciously set fires. To incinerate.

Of course Himself had cut off any questions on the matter, for how could anyone be at peace with causing such devastation?

"It's horrible," Beau said, the destruction catching his breath like a sail toppled in a gale wind.

"Yes, but we survived and one day will be revived. We're made of tough stock down here. See?" Doone pointed out a small cabin tucked into the corner of the burned-out village. Untouched by char, it was a tiny oasis amidst the rubble. And there, out front in the garden was a woman, stooped over, trying to rake down the torn-up and ragged soil.

"Mistress." Doone tipped his hat and nodded at the woman, shining a bright smile at her.

The woman looked up from her work. Though her hair had not yet turned gray with age, she held herself like an old woman, hunched and hurt. She was clearly startled at first, but after recognizing Doone she offered a smile, even as it sat stiff and tired on her squared-off jaw.

"It's a hard life we live here," Doone sighed. "All right, boys, on we go. We're almost there."

"Where is there exactly?" Beau whispered to Nate.

"I don't know." Nate shrugged. "But if Doone's there, that's where we want to be."

Chapter Twenty
Cordwainer Cordwain

There was a surprisingly well-built house situated at the bottom of a hill. Much like the homes they'd passed in the Middlelands, the homestead stood in a clearing large enough to support several fields, a cookhouse, barn, and several other outbuildings.

"Look at this place!" Nate exclaimed, throwing his arms wide open. "Now, that's what freedom looks like. I heard the house once belonged to Palus Whynde, the vanquished leader of the Badem."

"That's not possible," Beau said. "His house was burned with his family still inside."

"Maybe it wasn't." Nate shrugged. "Besides, if the Badem could charm people, why not a house? It sure looks charmed to me."

Beau surveyed the landscape, a shiver of possibility tickling at the base of his neck. It was so peaceful. Open. Plenty of room and good land to build on—homes, work, maybe even a proper school for the children of Mastery House. He could practically see Bea running through the fields, Rory at her heels, laughing. Playing.

Nate was right, it did look a lot like freedom.

Judging by the exterior of the house, Beau assumed they'd be met by a cozy and humble dwelling. Something like Fledge's quarters in the stables. Yet the interior of the house was surprisingly well furnished, especially Doone's sitting room. Between the richly upholstered furniture, heavy woven tapestries, and a jewel-studded candle clock, the room might have been located in one of the lesser homes in Topend.

Far from humble.

But if Beau was surprised to find such finery in the Bottom, Nate was nearly knocked sideways. A quiet yet powerful "Whoa" escaped his gaping jaw as he stood frozen in the doorway.

"Come, sit!" Doone motioned the boys to join him around a table set in front of the hearth.

Eager to please, Beau took his place at the table, his mind at work on how best to enlist Doone's help. Nate, however, took longer to settle in at the table, his eyes apparently hungrier for the riches arrayed around the room than his stomach was for food.

"This is . . . this is all so . . ." Nate stumbled, truly at a loss for words.

"Just some things I collected on my travels beyond the Islands," Doone said. "They help make this place feel more like a home. One I hope you'll come to think of as yours too. Please, eat."

Following Doone's lead, Beau and Nate ripped freshly baked bread apart with their hands and slathered it with jam and honey. No linens, no forks, just pure enjoyment of food; the meal a feast for the soul.

After they'd eaten well past their fill, Doone poured himself a draft of cider and leaned back in his chair. "Now, tell me about your escape from the Manor. No easy feat. I know grown men and women who were crushed trying."

"It was a lot easier than it should have been, thanks to the fever," Nate said licking jam from his fingers. "I spotted the perfect wagon waiting at the gate and told Crafty, 'that's our ride out of here.' And it was."

"Luck lives with you!" Doone beamed. "I hope you'll share some of it with us."

"We'll share everything we have with you," Nate declared. "All we've got are a couple of coins, but they're yours for the taking."

"Keep your coin. You two possess a far more valuable commodity."

"Comoddity?" Nate repeated.

"It's another word for goods, something to be traded," Beau offered before realizing he'd do better not to show off his vocabulary. "I mean, I think, I'm not sure."

"That's exactly what it means." Doone tipped his chair back to rest on the two back legs. "It's the single most important instrument of engagement in any battle. You know what I'm talking about, don't you, Crafty?"

Beau fully understood what Doone was referring to; it had been drilled into him for as long as he could remember. "Information."

"Precisely!" Doone beamed, bathing Beau in the light of his regard. "History isn't made with swords and arrows, but by the transfer of knowledge. The right information can change everything."

"You can't win a battle without weapons," Nate said. "I mean, look at what Torin's northern fire did."

"I think what he means is that force without good intelligence about your enemy is easily wasted," Beau explained. "Think of Cressida the Bold. The Manor would never have won the second battle for the Bottom if she hadn't sold out Palus's position."

"Perfectly stated," Doone said, his beam still trained directly on Beau. "Now, tell me about the mood on the Manor. How much has the fever loosened Himself's hold? How ripe for rebellion are the servants?"

"The conditions are awful," Beau began. "Servants falsely

accused of horrible crimes are being held in the dungeons, sentenced to dea—"

"Nothing they go through could be worse than what we face in Mastery House!" Nate tipped his chair back, a shadow of Doone's posture. "No food, not a proper bed in sight, ragged clothes, and Matron working us to the bone. There's not a child in Mastery House who wouldn't sign on to do whatever you asked of them. If I'd known I was going to get away for sure this time, I would've brought as many of the others with me as I could. That's what you would have done, Doone, isn't it?"

"I would do whatever saves my life first." Doone got up and laid another log on the fire. He had an effortless way of moving that made him look like he was almost floating. "You had a chance to escape and you took it. We're no use to anyone dead. But . . . now you're in a position of strength to go back for them."

Beau couldn't believe it. It was happening! He didn't even have to push or convince Doone.

"You mean it?" Nate jumped to his feet. "When can we go? Today? Probably better tomorrow . . . or today. Whatever you think."

"Soon, very soon. But first, we have to prepare. Make a plan." Doone retrieved a long, thin leather rectangle off the mantel and tossed it to Beau. "Do you think you can make a sling worthy of Himself's own guards out of that?"

Beau caught the roughly tanned piece of hide, the oily skin a foreign sensation in his hand.

"I . . ." Beau began, "I have no . . ." What could he possibly say? That he had no idea how to fashion a sling? That he'd never even seen a piece of raw leather before?

No. He was too close to securing his ace's help. A lie would have to do.

"Tools. I have no tools."

"I'm sure you'll find everything you need out in the forge. And there's a room upstairs there for you boys to sleep. You'll make yourselves at home."

"A whole room, just for us?" Nate crowed.

"With a bed each." Doone opened the door, gesturing for the boys to leave. "Go on, take a look, then work up a sling for me."

Beau tried to come up with something to say, a rationale to get out of making a sling, a plea for them to leave for the Manor now, but Doone was already guiding him to the door.

"What do you want me to do, Doone?" Nate asked.

"Go with him. Maybe you can learn something from our young shoemaker."

"Oh." Disappointment deflated Nate's thin frame. Head hung and eyes downcast, he made for the door. "If you need me, you know where I am."

"Yes, I do."

As the boys slowly marched out of the house, each doleful

for their own reasons, Beau realized two fundamental truths. First, Doone was right: luck had been accompanying him and Nate. But that created the second truth: at some point, luck could just as easily decide to up and leave them.

As the boys passed the cookhouse, Nate called out to Trout, who was busy building up a fire in the cooking pit. "Where's the forge?" His voice was still heavy with disappointment.

Without looking up Trout threw a thumb over his shoulder in the direction of a well-built stone building.

"I can't see why Doone keeps that sullen oaf around," Nate whispered. "I'd be a better second for him. Wouldn't I?"

Beau nodded but he had no words to spare. The lies he'd told were piling up, and now Cressi's life depended on him crafting a sling worthy of Himself's own collection. What was he thinking? Lost in his own worries, Beau barely looked up as they entered the workshop, but Nate's gasps of delight brought him back into the room.

"This is incredible! I feel like I could learn to do anything in here!"

One look at the well-provisioned workshop, complete with a large workbench and countless tools, and Beau almost felt the same way. Well-lit and bright, it was the kind of place even Beau could feel empowered to craft a sling.

At least that's what he hoped.

Beau dropped the doe-colored piece of leather onto the

workbench, trying to will the scrap of hide to reveal an answer. Meanwhile Nate roamed the workshop oohing and aahing as he opened every cabinet and touched every tool in the place. But his loudest declaration of joy came as he threw open a set of double barn doors revealing a large covered shed.

"Crafty! You have to come out here!" Nate shouted.

Grateful for a break, Beau dropped the leather and followed him outside.

"Look at this!" Nate gazed at the large stone forge as if it were the most miraculous thing he'd ever seen. "I used to tell Matron she should apprentice me to the blacksmith. She'd laugh and say I wasn't worthy of learning a trade, especially not something as important as smithing."

Nate grabbed hold of the giant bellows and pumped them up and down with glee until he'd created a gust of wind that sent ash flying. But not even a face full of soot could dampen his spirits as he moved on to inspect a rack stacked high with round metal balls.

"Look at these." His voice turned serious as he admired the orbs, which were perfectly sized to fit in the palm of one's hand. "What are they? And how'd they get these holes in the metal?"

"With a mold I suspect," Beau replied.

"What are they for, do you think?" Nate pulled a ball off the top of the pile. "They're heavy. Feel that."

Nate tossed the ball to Beau, who, to his own surprise,

caught it without stumbling. It was quite heavy. It was also somehow familiar. And while Beau couldn't exactly recall ever seeing anything like them, the balls called up a ghost of a memory.

"Look at this." Nate had moved on to admire a large metal cone that had been left leaning against the rack of balls. "I have no idea what it is, but it's amazing. I'm going to ask Doone if I can learn to make these . . . whatever they are. You've got to finish that sling first. If he likes it, we'll have it made, so make it good."

"Right, of course," Beau replied, trying to summon every ounce of confidence to make himself sound convincing.

"All right then, it's time to cobble!" Nate rubbed his palms together and led the way back inside "What's the finest piece you ever got to work on?"

"Finest?" Beau ran through the Manor's weapon collection in his mind, searching his memory for something simple, yet impressive.

"There's this sling I once saw," Beau began. "It was an oval of leather with a cup at the bottom, and the whole thing was held together by only a few stitches. It was a favorite among generals and commanders."

"Too modest." Nate's lip curled. "It should be fancy, you know, to match Doone's status."

"But that would take more time," Beau countered. "We want to get back to Mastery House fast, right? So we need to make something quick."

Nate shook his head, his teeth working at the inside of his cheek. It was hard to tell what he was thinking sometimes. Was he annoyed or impressed?

But finally the shake turned to a nod of approval.

"I'm glad I met you, Crafty." Nate sat down at the workbench, his eyes eager and wide. "Now teach me all you know."

Beau swallowed hard. He'd teach Nate something, but exactly what he wasn't sure.

Chapter Twenty-One
Charming Cressi

The kitchen came alive overnight. Or maybe it was Cressi who did, as if waking from some thirteen-year dream. She hadn't even realized the entire night and most of the morning had passed until she pulled the cauldron off the fire and set it down to cool next to the other stewpots.

There were four brews in all now, far more than she'd intended to make when she began working. One brew led to another, to another, and before she knew it, she'd passed the entire night mixing and matching plants, fungi, and roots.

When Anka first left the kitchen, Cressi was quite uncertain what to do. She thought about leaving, but to go where? The pawn was silent and without its guidance she had no idea which direction to go. But there was something else keeping her there; the kitchen seemed to have the same effect on her as the apothecary shop. Without even thinking she started to sift through the packets of herbs in her sack, taking time to feel, taste, and listen to what they each had to offer.

Some were familiar enough—chamomile, tarragon, chervil, and comfrey. They were all upfront and honest about what they could do, the healing they offered available to any- and everyone.

Others, like fox-spur, bitter althea leaves, and rue, were more hesitant to reveal their secrets. Cressi spent more time with these, gently sifting through them until slowly they too began talking.

Then there were those she didn't know, even though their scents were somehow familiar, as if they were part of a past she'd long forgotten. Some revealed their names, others only their powers. A select few refused to divulge anything at all. Cressi felt the greatest affinity and respect for these, for gaining their trust seemed to be the highest calling she could imagine.

Soon she was overcome by an idea—or maybe it was a feeling—and she began adding herbs and plants to a large pot of water. Mixing and matching, stirring and sniffing, she continued until the air in the kitchen was filled with hints of green coated in honey and morning dew. The aroma was cooling with just enough of a brackish twang to add bite.

That pungency told Cressi she'd hit it right.

Truth.

This was exactly what it smelled like, wasn't it?

Energized by her success, Cressi began another brew, this one intended to heal fever. It came to her so easily, as if the answer had always been there and all she needed do was turn her head to see it.

With each success she grew more invigorated and emboldened, until finally she was ready for a true challenge—shifting the guards' allegiance away from the Manor and to the cause of liberty.

She could wipe their memories, leaving them to believe they were Lower Middlelands peasants subjected to the Manor's cruelties. Or she could make them too frightened to confront their own shadows, let alone pick up a sword. But inflicting harm and engaging in cruelty were things Barger might consider, not Cressi.

No, it was a matter of enhancing and strengthening rather than deleting. But what?

Unsatisfied with her assortment of herbs, Cressi spotted a rack in the corner of the kitchen heavy with plants hanging upside down to dry. Guided by nothing more than the idea, she carefully gleaned a handful of lovage leaves, several stems of spikenard, and some goldburr roots.

Sniffing, stirring, blending, adding, she didn't even think about what she was making until the brew came together and presented itself to her.

Loyalty.

But this wasn't the blind, servile, painful obedience elicited by the brew Barger had compelled Cressi to cook up. There was a softness, a kind of guiding hand to turn one's intentions away from selfish wants and toward a more common good.

Satisfied with her work, Cressi moved on to compose another brew.

She was just completing it when Anka called from the other side of the door.

"You still here?"

Cressi let Anka back into the kitchen. She looked terrible, wrung out.

"Lock the door," Anka wearily warned, unloading her tray. "Always lock this door."

"What happened?" Cressi reengaged the lock, then returned the key to its proper owner. "I should've thought to come help you."

"I had it all in hand. I always do." Anka sniffed at each of the brews Cressi had made. "Tell me what you've made. What's this one?"

"I've just finished. It's for the fever. I believe it will work."

"Good. It's a dreadful blight that no one deserves to suffer. But I will need more of my black fern powder brew in the meantime. I'll be relieved to see all the guards healed one day soon, but I don't want them back to health yet. Not while you and Beau and Nate have your work to do." Anka moved on to the second brew. "This is perfect. Smells exactly like the truth brew Annina made all those years ago."

"She made a brew for you? So the stories aren't lies. She was a charmer."

"The very best."

"And you knew her?" Cressi pressed.

"She's why I'm here and not serving in the pits, or worse, and why I have the benefit of this charmed kitchen. She did everything she could to see we were protected."

"We?"

"The young ones. Me, Fledge, a few others." Anka pulled her hair back and splashed her face with cold water from the wash basin. "

Cressi balked. This information was coming a bit too fast for her to digest. "You know Fledge?"

"Of course I do. We were all hidden together during the war until Annina married Himself. Only reason any of us lived was because she made him promise to see we were protected. Always. He agreed as long as we were kept separate from each other. Fledge was apprenticed to the master of the stables, the others were scattered around the Land. And I . . . Well, they didn't know what to do with me, so they sent me here. Even so, we've found our ways to keep in touch." Anka dried her face and tidied her hair. "Fledge has been telling me about you for seasons and seasons now. He saw it in you when you were very young, younger than it should have been noticeable. He said that spoke to the depth of your talents."

"Fledge knew about me, about this . . ." Cressi bit back the words she really wanted to say. He knew about her abilities, yet he did nothing! "Why didn't he tell me? Help me?"

"He was waiting for your talents to bloom." Anka pulled out a loaf of bread and began slicing off thick slabs. "Besides, he's no more a charmer than I am. The best any of us can do is fill in a few gaps in your knowledge. But I see you're well on your way."

"I don't know about that. This could all be soup or weak tea for all I know. I just listened to the plants is all."

"Oh, is that all?" Anka set a plate of bread and cheese in front of Cressi. "That's everything. Listen, you're no longer at the Manor. You're free to rely on your own good judgment. Now, what's this one you're working on for?"

"It's meant to evoke memories long buried or lost to time and pain," Cressi explained. "The plants guided me there. It felt like a wise thing to bring out."

"I agree. And this one? What is it?"

"I was trying to rework a brew Barger intended me to use on Beau."

"You made a brew for Barger?"

"Not exactly. Cook made the combination, but I was made to tell them if it would work or not, then cook it up. I didn't mean to, but they clearly read it on my face. I never intended to use it, certainly not on Beau. It wasn't so much a loyalty brew as a soul-crushing killer."

"Loyalty." Anka let the word roll around in her mouth

before asking, "That's what Barger wanted you to use on Beau? Loyalty to who?"

"Well, to Himself, but also to Barger. He wants to rule as Beau's regent one day."

"I see." Anka began stirring and sniffing at the loyalty brew. "But why remake it? For what use? Far too many people in the Land have been raised with the single purpose of serving the Manor. Why enhance that in anyone? I should think you'd work on something less nuanced, something to crush the souls of those who've crushed us."

"I could never do that!" The very suggestion made Cressi feel oddly protective over her brew. She took a clean spoon and began stirring as if to remove Anka's negativity. "Blind allegiance isn't the only kind of loyalty there is. There's also knowing what's right. What could be simpler than that?"

"What if the truest beliefs of the person you charm are that Himself and the Manor are the rightful rulers of the Land. That they deserve dominion over everyone else? There are those who think like that."

"They might have convinced themselves of that to survive," Cressi replied, "but everyone knows no one's life is less worthy than another. Especially when that other is so very cruel."

"I wish that were true. And I appreciate, even after all you've been through, that you believe that," Anka said. "But there are plenty of people, not only those of means, who willingly exchange their freedom for safety. And they're more than happy to let someone else bear the brunt of that exchange."

Cressi stopped stirring the pot. "Someone like the children of Mastery House?"

"Exactly. I think this is too personal. You've bitten off more than you know how to chew."

Of course she had. This entire endeavor was more than Cressi knew how to manage. But that wasn't reason enough to stop. Especially not as she was just beginning to understand what these powers could do.

"You told me to rely on my own best judgment, to listen to the plants. That's what I've done," Cressi said. "Yes, loyalty can be self-serving, but reading people is the one part of charming I understand down to my bones. Even Keb and Boz, who are the picture of loyalty to Barger and Cook, truly only want to be safe."

"That may be. Still, you're young. You don't know what you can do."

"That's true, I don't," Cressi said. She had no idea what she was doing, but for the first time ever, rather than that being a problem, it was the source of her strength.

It all fell into place then.

Cressi pulled a small bottle down off of the shelves and filled it with her loyalty brew.

"What are you doing?" Anka pressed.

"If I can turn Keb and Boz's loyalty away from the Manor, I can do anything. Please, let me out."

"I don't think this wise." Anka planted herself between Cressi and the door. "What if it doesn't work? What if they figure out what you're trying to do?"

"They already know I'm a charmer, and they've made it quite clear they'll drop me where I stand if I even look like I'm betraying Barger. I'm well past being worried about what they'll do to me."

Anka remained immovable. "I don't like it."

"You don't have to," Cressi countered. "But you can't keep me here. I'll find my way out even if I have to charm you."

"You'd do that?" Anka challenged.

"Without a second's thought."

They stood there, silently facing off, each daring the other to blink, until finally Anka's grimace slowly began to melt into a bemused smile. "I'd hoped that's what you'd say."

Cressi had to stop herself from snapping. "So all this was some kind of a test?"

"More a test of Fledge." Anka extracted the kitchen key from her pocket. "He was absolutely right about you. You are as powerful as he hoped you'd be."

Chapter Twenty-Two
Magic of a Kind

There was only so long that Beau could stall. He'd already gathered every tool that looked remotely appropriate for the task. He'd even soaked the leather in hot water for a good long time—he had Nate to thank for that idea. But every moment of delay meant it would be that much longer before they could get to Cressi and the children of Mastery House.

There was no more time to waste. "Well then," he said tentatively. "I guess we're ready to begin."

"Do you think I could do the cutting?" Nate asked. There was a new kind of uncertainty in his voice, a shy almost tentative questioning.

"Sure, I guess that would be all right." With relief cascading off his brow, Beau handed Nate a razor-sharp tool with a short handle. There was no way he'd have been able to cut the leather without butchering it or his own hands. And so, after sketching the outline of a sling from the Manor's collection, Beau watched as Nate cut out the pieces for the cup, then the strap.

Even Beau's unpracticed eye could see Nate had a gift, an almost innate familiarity with the tools. Thankfully, he was also stubborn and insisted on doing everything himself. After a while he'd even stopped asking for Beau's council, instead charging ahead with his own ideas on how to perfect the design.

While Nate worked on stitching the cup to the strap, Beau stepped outside to get some water from the rain barrel. If their luck held out, they'd be riding back to the Manor with Doone before nightfall. Beau closed his eyes against the sun and breathed deep of the air, relishing the smell of meat roasting over an open fire. For the first time since Doone assigned him this task, Beau's shoulders began to unwind.

He remained outside, enjoying the quiet until Nate shouted for him. "Crafty! You've got to see this!"

Beau stretched and went back inside, but Nate wasn't at the workbench, and neither was the sling.

"Out here!" Nate called. "Hurry!"

Beau stepped out into the forge to find Nate cradling one of the small metal balls in his hands while Doone stood close by, examining the nearly completed sling.

"You're never going to believe what these are!" Nate's cheeks were flushed with excitement. "Tell him, Doone!"

"How about I show you instead and give your sling a test in the doing. Crafty, you see that barrel?" Doone gestured to a barrel in the corner of the workshop. "Take the scoop hanging on the side, fill it halfway, and bring it here. And Nate, go back into the workshop and fetch me one of those waxed cotton braids on the shelves and the brown jug next to them."

While Nate went back inside, Beau fetched the powder.

"Good. Now hold this." Doone handed Beau the metal ball and took possession of the scoop and poured the contents into the ball. "Stand still. Try not to move. Nate! You coming?"

Nate ran back in with a coil of waxed cotton about the length of his forearm and a small brown jug. "I wasn't sure how much you needed."

"This is fine." Doone worked one end of the braid deep inside the metal ball, leaving a few inches hanging down the side, then poured in a measure of the liquid. "Now, it's important you move slowly, Crafty, or it could get fiery around here."

"Fiery?" Beau repeated, the word sticking in his throat. "What exactly *are* these?"

"Magic!" Nate crowed.

"Of a kind," Doone corrected. "I discovered them in my travels out beyond the seas. Just one of these marvels has the potential to change the Land forever."

Beau's stomach quivered. How could something so small have so much power?

"Come, I'll show you." Doone turned to lead the way to a large field out back. "Nate, go fetch a torch and meet us out there."

"I'll be right back!" Nate exploded into action.

"Enthusiastic, isn't he?" Doone asked as he led Beau away from the workshop.

"He's . . . we're devoted to you and to freeing the Land," Beau replied, trying to keep every footfall slow and careful.

"It's impressive that a child of Mastery House was able to hold on to his spirit, his fight. Gives me hope for our future. Don't you agree?"

"Yes, sir."

"But for an apprentice like you to risk everything? It makes little sense for you to run. Unless there's something you're not telling me. Some secret you're hiding?"

Beau desperately tried to will his mouth to remain untwisted, his brow unwrinkled, and his hands steady.

It didn't work.

"I knew it." Doone clapped, looking as pleased as if he'd won a bet. "You've been lying to your friend."

Beau's marrow curdled as Doone threw an arm around his shoulder.

"You weren't really remanded to the Manor, were you? You chose to run, didn't you?"

Relief flooded over Beau, bringing back with it his beating heart. Doone might have spotted some cracks in Beau's facade, but they weren't wide enough to let the light out.

"Don't worry, I won't tell him," Doone soothed. "He doesn't seem the forgiving type. But why would a boy guaranteed a position care about anything other than protecting his future, one with a home, a trade, coin. Yet you seem determined to . . . well . . . blow up the entire system."

"Because it's not fair," Beau said. "It's not right for some to have so much, while others have nothing at all."

"High ideals." Doone ruffled Beau's hair just as Nate arrived, waving a small torch.

"I got it!"

"Perfect," Doone said. "We'll go out just a bit farther. I don't think Crafty can cradle that grenade much longer."

"Grenade," Nate repeated. "It's such a good word. I'd never heard it before."

But Beau had.

Volume III, Chapter 18, Section 3 of *The Histories: Defeating the Terror*, in which an account was made of everything confiscated from the Badem after the last Battle of the Bottom. Among the artifacts of the demolished culture was a detailed drawing of a pile of small metal balls with thick rope wicks sticking out the top. They were labeled grenades, with no explanation beyond that. Beau remembered thinking at the time they must have belonged to some kind of game.

"This is far enough." Doone halted the procession in the middle of the large, overgrown field. "Crafty, set the grenade in the sling. We'll see if this design of yours works or not."

A surge of anticipation filled Beau's veins as he placed the metal ball inside the leather cup. It held, at least it actually held.

"Now light it up, Nate," Doone ordered. "Then both of you run back to the tree line. You should probably cover your ears too."

The fuse lit with a crackle and hiss, sparking and sputtering as a tiny flame moved up the cotton cording.

"Go!" Doone pulled the sling over his shoulder then flung it, launching the grenade in a high arc out into the field. A high-pitched whistle sang out triumphantly as the metal ball hurtled through the air.

The boys raced back to the trees, arriving just as a clap of thunder shook the ground. A flash of light—or was it darkness?—exploded overhead, sending them reeling back. Stones, dirt, and debris soared high into the air hovering for the briefest moment before raining back down.

A shower of destruction.

As the air slowly began to clear, Beau swiped away the mist of dirt from his eyes and nose. But nothing could clear the confusion and awe of what he'd just witnessed.

"What was that?" he asked, but his own words were swallowed by the hum and thrum of white noise.

Beau looked around for Nate. He should have been right next to him. Where was he? But just as a wave of panic began wrapping itself around Beau's shoulders, Nate emerged from the dust with Doone. Jumping wildly, his arms flung wide, joy and excitement unbound, Nate looked like he'd just seen the future.

Maybe he had, for Doone had harnessed a plain black powder and transformed it into pure power.

Back in Doone's sitting room, the hum slowly faded and Beau could once again hear ambient noises—the creak of floorboards, squealing door hinges, Doone's satisfied sigh as he sank into his chair by the hearth.

"What did you think?" Doone prompted.

"I know you said it isn't magic, but that was magic to me!" Nate bellowed.

"No need to shout. I can hear you." Doone tapped at his own ear. "Pour yourselves some cider. It'll calm you."

While Nate poured two goblets of cider, Doone turned to Beau. "What about you, Crafty? You like what you saw?"

"I don't even understand what it was," Beau said, all pretense of being a rebel gone. "Why would we need that?"

"Why wouldn't we?" Doone said. "If rumors are true and the Manor plans to once again ally with Torin, we can meet their northern fire with some heat of our own. It's the means of our liberation, beginning with the children of Mastery House."

The buzzing in Beau's head returned, but this time it wasn't the explosion rendering him hard of hearing, but rather deep foreboding. "But if you use them at the Manor, people . . . the children . . . could get hurt, or worse."

"Do you think I'd let that happen?" Doone winced as if hit by a barb. "The grenades are simply diversions. They'll deflect attention in one direction while we do our work in another. No harm done."

Like a true ace, Doone had a complete tactical scheme for the mission—accounting for every possibility in order to liberate the children of Mastery House. Maybe it was as Nate said—sometimes you have to risk it all to win.

But Doone's plan didn't include saving Cressi. At least not yet. Beau would to have to find a way to change that.

"I think that's—"

"Brilliant, Doone!" Nate crowed. "So when do we go? Today? The sling worked, so we can go now, right?"

"We're going to need more than one sling," Doone replied. "How soon can you boys make ten more?"

"A day, maybe less. Two tops," Nate said. "Come on, Crafty, let's get back to work."

For once Beau was grateful for Nate's impatience—the sooner they could go the better, even if Beau had no plan in place yet. But as the boys made for the door, Doone caught Beau by the shoulders and pulled him back to the table.

"First, you take a break."

"That's all right," Beau replied. "We'll just get going on the—"

"You deserve a little enjoyment." Doone retrieved a box from the mantel above the hearth and planted it on the table.

Though the box was made of simple, unadorned wood, there was nothing ordinary or unfamiliar about it. Beau might as well have been standing in the center of the blast zone, for it was all he could do to not fall back as if he'd been hit between the eyes.

The box was an exact replica of the one that housed his mother's Fist set. How was that possible?

"Pull your chair up, Crafty," Doone said. "We're going to play a little game."

"Oh," Beau faltered. "It's all right, I'll watch. Let Nate play."

"He will. After you." Doone's usual beaming glow burned a bit cooler now.

"Sure, I'll go second." Nate smiled at Doone, but shot Beau a look of warning. "I'll learn from your mistakes."

"I'll play king side, you'll attack," Doone explained as he set up the board. "Your goal, with the aid of your ace and your mage, is to capture my king. Mine is to destroy all your blue guards. Yet neither side can win without winning control of the pawn."

"Is that this one?" Nate pointed to the verdigris pawn. "With the ruined color?"

"Far from ruined," Doone tutted. "It's verdigris."

"Verdi*what*?"

"A color achievable only by an act of alchemy," Doone said. "Our cordwainer can explain, I'm sure."

"Oh, yes. Alchemy is, well, it's a kind of magic, but not magical," Beau said. "It's a process that transforms one thing into another. Verdigris is only achieved through an alchemical reaction."

"So the pawn becomes the king?" Nate asked.

"Not quite." Doone placed the verdigris pawn on its starting position, the black square in the far-right corner. "The pawn is far more powerful than the king because it's the only piece that can threaten his rule. Neither side can win without taking the pawn."

"Oh, I see!" Nate was clearly working through the idea, untangling knots as he went until it all fell into place. "So whoever controls the pawn controls the king."

"And whoever controls the king controls the game." Doone sat back and took a deep draft of his cider. "Don't just stand there, Crafty. It's time to play."

Chapter Twenty-Three
A Game of Fist II

For the first time ever, Beau sat down at a Fist board trying not to play his best, but his worst. He asked a lot of questions and blundered even the easiest of moves. But as the match progressed, everything Fledge had taught him—the tricks and tactics—began to take over. He was playing instinctually. Guided as if by second nature, he positioned two yellow guards to block the rear flank of Doone's king.

Doone looked impressed. "I've only known one other player to use their yellow guards so effectively."

"You . . . you played the same move in the match we watched at the gathering," Beau said. "It worked for you, so I thought I'd give it a go."

"Clever. You see how he's playing?" Doone asked Nate, who'd been hovering over his shoulder the whole match. "Crafty indeed."

"Nice." Nate sounded impressed, but the look he shot Beau said something altogether different.

"Too bad you didn't think it all the way through." Doone took one of his rear flank guards and, in an exceptionally bold move, used it to take out another of his own players. It left his king exposed to the north, but it also completely blocked Beau's advance from the south.

"Guess I'm not that clever after all," Beau said.

"No, you're not," Nate scoffed. But his scorn melted away as he turned to Doone. "Too bad you can't use one of those grenades. Now, that would be something. If you had one of those mage pieces that really had powers, and an ace with grenades, you'd be invincible. The game would be over before it began."

"That's not how the game works." Beau couldn't resist taking a small swipe back.

"I'm not talking about the game, Crafty. I mean in life." Nate pulled his chair up closer to Doone's. "Think about it. You already have grenades. You could demolish the Manor if you wanted to. But what happens if Himself has them too? The field is leveled."

Talk of blowing up the Manor was braiding Beau's stomach into knots.

"It's a good point," Doone said. "The smart warrior always assumes your opponent knows as much, if not more than you. But even if the Manor has grenades, the best powder they could ever hope to get would be that soggy dust Grater was peddling at the gathering."

"That was powder?" Nate exclaimed. "The black-hearted viper didn't even warn us. We could have been blown up three times over."

"Never. It's so wet it wouldn't light in a bonfire. Even if they hit us with a thousand grenades, they'd be throwing torches into the wind."

"That's good. But still, it's too bad there are no charmers left." Nate shook his head dolefully. "Imagine all you could do for the people of the Land if you had a charmer's help. Crops could grow in the Bottom again; people could feed themselves and keep their children. Even rule themselves. Guided by your wisdom, of course, Doone."

"That's true!" Beau brightened. Here came his chance.

"It's a fine dream, but there are none left." Doone's voice took on a wistful tone.

"But what if there was one?" Beau asked, testing the waters.

"He just said there are no charmers left," Nate scowled. "Are you deaf?"

"I heard him loud and clear. But your friend . . . Crossi. She could be one."

"Her name is Cressi, and that's the stupidest thing I ever heard," Nate sneered.

"It's not stupid," Beau hit back. "Think about it. You told

me yourself that she had a way with healing, right? Something about cuts knitting back together faster than anything. That sounds like the work of a charmer to me."

"If she were a charmer, I'd have known." Nate glared at Beau. "No one was closer to Cressi than me. Now drop it."

"No, I want to hear more." Doone leaned forward in his seat. "What else was she able to do?"

Nate's ire vanished under the spotlight of Doone's attention.

"Well, she could clear up your cough faster than anyone," he began. "And not one of the babies died under her watch that I can remember. She had a way with cuts and bruises. No one ever wanted Matron or her nursemaids to tend to them when they were sick, knowing they might never recover. But Cressi could get you back to health before you knew it. I . . . I never thought of it, but . . . could she really, maybe be a charmer?"

Doone cocked his head as if he'd caught the scent of something delicious. "She's still in Mastery House?"

"No, she got sent into service for the Manor more than a season ago. Right before the fever broke out."

"As a nursemaid?"

"Posted in the back barns, last I knew." Nate was sitting up straighter now, as if suddenly imbued with some kind of authority. "That's where they've got the sick Manor guards."

"I'd like to meet her."

Beau could hardly contain himself; his plan was working!

"You should!" Nate crowed, giving voice to Beau's own elation. "We can find her when we go free Mastery House. She can help with the little ones too."

"No." Doone looked like he'd bitten into an unripe cherry. "We're not ready yet. That operation requires proper planning and preparation. Those slings to begin with. Trout and I will go and find her. You'll stay here and keep working."

"But how will you know her?" Nate pressed. "You'll need help."

"That's true. She could be anywhere," Beau chimed in. "Even in Barger's custody."

"Cressi?" Nate scoffed. "She's never been in trouble, ever. If you knew her, you'd know how stupid that was."

"The details are mine to sort out. Oh, look." Doone held the pitcher of cider upside down. "Drained. Nate, would you fetch us more from the cookhouse, and bring more wood for the fire while you're out."

"Of course." Nate stepped away from his post behind Doone's chair and left the room, but not without first glaring at Beau, a warning not to get too close to Doone in his absence.

Beau tried to offer a smile in return, a peace offering, but Nate looked away.

He hadn't meant to compete against Nate for Doone's attention. As soon as Cressi was safe and the children of Mastery House freed, he'd step away, leaving Nate to bask in the sunshine of Doone's admiration and trust.

First, he had to play his hand out.

"Your move, Crafty," Doone said.

Beau fought to keep his face relaxed and his mind focused. This was likely to be his only chance alone with Doone. He had to make it count. He searched for the most benign move he could find, advancing a blue guard one square forward then asked, "So you're convinced that Cressi is a charmer?"

"I never said I was convinced," Doone scoffed. "I said I was curious."

"Right, of course." Beau regrouped. "But don't you think that anyone else who's heard similar things about her might be curious too?"

"Why do you care so much?" Doone asked. "I thought she was Nate's friend, not yours."

"She is." Beau tried to shrug it off. "But, like he said, having a charmer on your side could mean nothing short of victory."

"It could also mean treachery. Charmers can be slippery, their allegiances easily bought and traded. The Badem lost control of a charmer once, and it cost us everything."

"Yes, but just because Cres . . . Nate's friend is named for Cressida the Bold doesn't mean she's anything like her."

"Cressida the Bold?" Doone scoffed. "More like Cressida the Deceitful. She wasn't a charmer, just passed herself off as one to the Manor. No, I meant that traitor Annina. May she rot evermore."

Beau flinched. He couldn't help it; it was too hard to mask his feelings at hearing his mother vilified.

"Sure, she was gifted, but not nearly as talented as my own mother. She was one of the best to ever live." Doone almost sounded wistful. "They were close once. Like sisters. But unlike my mother—a pragmatist, a realist, a true loyalist—when Annina spouted all those high ideals about peace and unity, they were nothing more than cover. She was a traitor of the highest degree and got everything she deserved. Still, it's not every charmer that could've turned the heir to the Manor."

Beau fought to keep his voice from betraying him. "What do you mean?"

"Himself was cut from the same cloth as all those who came before him—rough, colorless burlap woven through with nettles and greed. Then he met Annina and renounced it all to marry her."

This was exactly the story Beau had always hoped to hear—that his father once had a loving and compassionate heart. That there once was hope in the Land. "So he married her for love?"

"That's what he thought." Doone plucked up one of his guards and planted it next to the verdigris pawn, putting himself within one move of ending the match. "But right after Annina had their son, Himself's father, who'd raged against their marriage, turned blue and died. Clearly charmed. The next day Annina's husband, newly named Himself, also began to turn blue. If not for their apothecary, he'd have followed his father to the grave, leaving the new baby the title. It didn't take Himself long to realize who Annina truly was. *What* she was. That the only love she had was for power—power for her son and herself. The way I heard it, Himself's ragged heart truly broke then. But like everyone else in his bloodline, he mended himself by breaking other people's bones, lives, and spirits. Your move."

Black spots clouded Beau's vision as he grabbed the first game piece he could.

This tale about his mother couldn't be true. Not in a million lifetimes.

"Maybe she was set up," Beau said. "Someone else concocted a poison and made it look like a charming. Or maybe she was trying to unite the Land, put an end to war and pain by giving the Land an heir to both sides."

"An heir to both sides?" Doone mused. "Interesting idea."

Beau had thrown the idea out in desperation, but hearing it echoed back, it hit him like a revelation. Maybe that's exactly what his mother had wanted him to be—a bridge reconnecting the Bottom and the Manor.

If only Beau were capable of fulfilling her dream.

"Maybe," he sighed. "But an idea is all it will ever be."

"Not necessarily," Doone said. "Not if the girl is a charmer."

"What does she have to do with it?" Beau asked, his voice pinched and strained.

"Everything. Think it through," Doone instructed. "What could a charmer do for me?"

"Like Nate said, make the crops grow, the rivers flow, the—"

"I asked what you thought, not to regurgitate feeble-minded ideas," Doone hissed.

"Nate's not feeble-minded," Beau hit back. "He's brilliant and he's devoted to you."

"And he will serve his purpose carrying cider and wood and whatever else I have him do. You, on the other hand, have the mind of a strategist and belong at my right hand." The clean, handsome lines of Doone's face hardened, making him resemble more closely the villain on the WANTED poster. "You've already said it. You know exactly what the charmer could do for me."

Beau didn't want to say it, for it would mean everything he'd come to believe about Doone—his ace—was wrong. That instead of saving Cressi, Beau had exposed her to even greater danger. That the children of Mastery House were no closer to freedom. That he'd been wrong about everything.

"Say it," Doone pressed.

Beau swallowed back his revulsion, his regrets, his rising rage. "She could charm the heir?"

"Exactly." Doone blazed with admiration. "Compel him to kill his own father, then once he's the new Himself, she'll charm him to appoint me regent. He'd be known, for a while at least, as the great uniter, leaving me as his heir apparent upon his untimely death. And if the people suspect a charmer at work, as they did with Annina, we'll offer the girl up on a platter."

"You'd use her like that?" It was getting harder for Beau to keep his anger from seeping out around the edges.

"We'd be fools not to," Doone said. "You going to play that guard or not?"

Beau looked down at the yellow guard in his fist, knuckles wrapped so tight they were turning white. Unable to think about a move, he placed the guard on the first empty square he saw, realizing only after he'd lifted his hand that the move had exposed his mage.

"You're going to need your rest tonight, Crafty," Doone said. "Leave the making of the slings to Nate. You're coming with me in the morning. We've got a few friends to collect from the Manor."

Up to this point, Doone's play had been careful and methodical. Nothing hasty, each move executed like some kind of a slow dance. But now he swooped in like a hawk on a mouse. His last remaining blue guard clutched in his talons, Doone knocked out three of Beau's yellow guards.

The game was over.

The pawn was his.

Chapter Twenty-Four
Into the Woods

With a vial of her loyalty brew safely tucked next to the pawn in her apron pocket, Cressi headed out to the wagon.

Boz and Keb were already awake, perched on the driver's seat exactly where she'd left them. Though she knew they both had slept—how could they not have with all the ferrita she'd fed them—they sat there stiffly coiled, a pair of springs ready to be sprung.

"Took you long enough!" Boz shouted. "We need to get out of here before the fever catches us."

"That's not how it work—" Cressi stopped herself. "It doesn't catch *you*; you catch *it*."

"I ain't caught nothing!" Keb held his hands up to prove they were empty.

Cressi looked the guards over, shaking her head as if they

were painted blue, then muttered a fretful "Oh, goodness."

"Why you say that?" Keb turned white. "What do you see?"

"Nothing." Cressi made a big show of trying to laugh off her concern before turning dead serious again. "You do feel all right, don't you?"

"We feel fine," Boz growled. "Long as we get outta here."

"Good." Cressi clutched her heart in relief. "Then you have no aches, no pains, no stiffness?"

Keb and Boz exchanged a sideway glance, neither wanting to be the first to admit to anything.

"I see." Cressi paused as if to think before tentatively adding, "Those are some of the first symptoms."

"I told you it wasn't cause we slept funny!" Keb punched Boz in the arm.

"Touch me again and I'll break you," Boz barked.

But for all his bravado, he looked just as scared as Keb.

"Don't fret," Cressi counseled. "I have something that might help."

Cressi reached for her pocket but Boz batted her away. "You ain't giving us none of your charms. Cook warned us good to take nothing you give us."

Cressi threw her hands up in surrender and sighed deeply. "I told her that's what you'd say."

"Told who?" Boz asked.

"The nursemaid here. She makes this, uses it herself, every day, and she's healthy as can be. I told her you'd never take it."

Keb leaned in, loudly whispering to Boz, "I think we should take it."

"She's lying," Boz warned. "Probably about to turn us into frogs."

"That's not how charming works. This isn't a fairy story," Cressi said. "And I already told you, I didn't make it. Go inside and ask her yourself if you don't believe me."

"We ain't going no closer than here."

"I understand," Cressi said. "I do. But when you break out in a rash, don't say I didn't warn you."

"A rash?" Keb pulled his sleeves back to inspect his arms.

"Or worse. You might lose all control of yourself, piss your pants, or—" Cressi stopped as she spotted Anka running up from the barracks, waving and calling to get their attention.

"Who's that?" Boz asked.

"That," Cressi said, "is the nursemaid."

"By the Goodness of Himself, there you are!" Anka's cheeks were flushed pink from her run, brightening her face with a sunny glow. "I came to check on you, make sure all is well."

"That's kind of you." Cressi dropped a small curtsy. "But I'm not sure it is. These men are complaining of some aches and pains. I suggested they take your tonic to keep the fever from taking hold of them, but they refuse."

"Oh, but you must. You have to stay healthy. The Manor relies on you," Anka replied without missing a beat. "May I?"

Anka stepped to Keb and took his palm in her hand, gently examining it from every available angle. "Does this itch at all?"

"Why? You see a rash? Is there a rash?" Keb paled and went to work itching his palms madly. "I knew it."

Anka then turned on Boz. "Are your eyes always that bloodshot?"

Boz shrank back. "I . . . I don't know."

Anka shook her head as if terribly aggrieved. "It's not my place to tell you what to do, you're both far wiser than I. But I won't lie, I'm worried about you."

Boz hadn't taken his eyes off Anka once, and that's when Cressi realized Anka very well might be the first woman, aside from Cook, to pay them any attention. "You made it, not her?"

"It's how I've survived this long out here with all these sick guards."

"Well . . . if you says to . . . maybe we should. All right, girlie, give it to us."

Cressi handed the brew over to Boz and watched as he drained half the vial before passing it off to Keb.

"I never had medicine like this. Tastes like bamberries," Boz said.

"No, it don't," Keb said, wiping his mouth. "Tastes like Cook's apple cake."

"Apple cake?" Anka clasped her hands in surprise. "I have

some in the kitchen. You wouldn't want to come have a slice before you leave, would you?"

Boz and Keb exchanged another of their looks. It was clear they both were desperate to follow Anka.

Had the brew really begun to work that fast? Or was it Anka's charming manner at work? Either way, this was a better outcome than Cressi had dared hope.

"Thank you for the offer," Cressi replied. "But we can't spare the time."

"We decide when we go, not you," Boz snapped before turning to Anka and smiling.

And with that, the two guards jumped off the wagon and followed Anka to the barracks, two oversized ducklings fighting to keep up with their mother.

Anka locked the kitchen door and smiled sweetly at Keb and Boz. "I'll cut you both a nice slice of apple cake, but first, would you mind going out back and bringing me more wood for the fire?"

"Whatever you need!" Boz moved faster than Cressi had ever seen, and Keb was right on his heels.

"What did I do wrong?" Cressi asked as soon as the guards had gone. "I expected them to disavow the Manor, to start talking of liberation, not apple cake."

"It's working perfectly," Anka replied. "I just inserted myself, so they felt loyalty to me. It's better they stay here.

Redosing them will only slow your progress and hamper our allies' trust."

"But how am I to travel? I've never driven a wagon, and even if I did, I might as well ride the whole way shouting 'I'm a runner!'"

"No wagons, no horses, no main roads. You'll have to continue on foot. It's the only safe way to go. Here." Anka handed Cressi a bag fitted with shoulder straps. "I've packed you some food and several vials of each of your brews. Blue bottles are your fever remedy, yellow the truth, clear is loyalty, and green is your memories potion. I also stitched your packets of loose herbs into the lining; you never know what you might need. And here's a blade. It's not large, but it's sharp."

"But I don't understand, how am I to find Beau on foot? I only have a day and a half before Barger comes after us." Cressi paused to let Anka strap a sheath for the knife around her waist. "And what of Nate? You still haven't told me anything I can use."

"I've told you all I know. Fledge, me, and a few others know only part of the story. It's safer for everyone that way. It's for you, Beau, and Nate to put it all together. As for going on foot, that's the only way you're going to find them. Here, cover your uniform—it makes you quite the mark." Anka wrapped a shawl around Cressi's shoulders before opening a small hatch positioned next to the hearth. "This leads down into the cellar. Go all the way to the back and behind the pickling barrels, you'll find a door into a tunnel. Follow through that and out onto a path in the woods. Keep to it, no matter what. It will lead you to Gerta before nightfall. A friend and trusted ally, she knows everything that happens south of here."

"Gerta," Cressi repeated. "How will I find her?"

"You won't. She'll find you." Anka kissed Cressi on the forehead and handed her a lantern. "Travel safely and bring back good news."

There was every possibility that Cressi was walking into a trap, but there were pitfalls aplenty no matter which direction she went. She might as well die trying.

Unlike the tunnels Cressi had traversed at the Manor, those with solid walls shored up by large wooden beams, she now found herself in something that more closely resembled a burrow. Cut straight through the earth as if by some magnificently oversized mole rat, the sides and ceiling of the tunnel were nothing more than tightly packed dirt. A tangled web of roots, bulbs, and rocks were all exposed as if intended for display. Like someone out of a fairy story, Cressi felt transported to another world where anything was possible— animals could talk, mountains could walk, and the monsters were always defeated.

Where there was always hope.

But as in most fairy stories, there were unknown enemies

lurking just out of sight. Doubt, distrust, and the ever-present possibility of failure.

Even if she did find Beau and Nate safe and well, that didn't mean Beau would be willing to return to the Manor to face down the greatest monster of them all—Himself. As for Nate, well . . . she had no real idea. He'd always hated the heir, vowed to see him brought down. Was it even possible for him to recognize the promise in Beau? Proud and unpracticed in admitting his mistakes, Nate would sooner charge into a fight blind than admit he'd been wrong.

But there was the pawn, gently purring in her pocket, spurring her along. *Keep walking,* it seemed to whisper, *the truth lies just ahead.*

As Cressi continued on, the confines of the burrow soon began expanding, opening out farther and farther, until finally she realized the tunnel had indeed given way to the woods, a solid path unrolling ahead, clearly marking her course.

Cressi shuttered the lantern, leaving the flame just enough air to survive, for who knew how long it would be before Gerta came to find her.

Chapter Twenty-Five
A Swollen Head

Doone might have defeated Beau at Fist, but for the moment Beau was still a few moves ahead of him. Now all he had to do was make certain it stayed that way long enough for him to get back to the Manor before Doone could find Cressi.

After making up an excuse about wanting to get back to making slings, Beau set out to look for Nate.

He looked in the cookhouse, but the only person there was Trout, still tending to his roast and fire. Nate wasn't out by the wood pile either. Nor was he in the workshop or upstairs. He couldn't have made it back inside already—they'd have crossed each other.

So where was he?

Beau raced around the house and was about to head out into the field when he spotted Nate by the barn, half a load of wood balanced in his arms, the rest scattered at his feet next to an overturned jug, cider slowly filtering from the mouth.

"There you are!" Beau tried to sound cheery and open. "I've been looking for you."

"Why? So you could gloat about what a clever Fist player you are?" Nate was fighting to keep his armful of wood balanced as he slowly squatted to try and retrieve the rest.

"I told him you should play first. You heard me, didn't you?" Beau asked. "And besides, I lost."

"Am I supposed to feel bad for you, while I'm out here doing scut work?" Nate managed to add one more stick of wood to his pile, but there were still many more to retrieve.

"No," Beau said. "But you can't be mad at me for it either. I wasn't trying to show you up, I—"

"Couldn't help it," Nate grumbled in disgust. "You apprentices are all alike. Think you're so clever because you've got a trade."

"That's not fair." Beau recoiled from the sting. "I don't think that."

"You did everything you could to show me up." Even obscured by anger, Nate's pain was clear to see.

"I didn't mean to do any of that, I promise."

"Sure, whatever." Nate was still angry, but there was a softening. "If you're so sorry, help me pick up this wood."

Beau added a few logs to the pile in Nate's arms, then gathered some in his own. "I've been thinking. I think we should go."

"You mean with Doone to the Manor?" Nate asked. "He told us to stay here."

"No." Beau fixed his shoulders. "Away, to be free."

"What are you talking about?" The softness vanished. "We'll never be freer than we are with Doone. Stop talking and get the rest of the wood."

"Fetching wood and carrying cider for someone else—that's your idea of freedom?"

"That's just for now," Nate said. "He'll see my worth soon enough. Probably put me in charge of the raid on Mastery House."

This was going to be harder than Beau thought.

"Look." Beau lowered his voice to a whisper. "You should know, if your friend proves to be a charmer, Doone means to use her to charm the heir and make himself regent. Rule the Land from the Manor."

"As he should!" Nate beamed. "That's brilliant!"

"No, it's not!" Beau fought hard not to shout. "He's no better or different than Himself. Don't you see? He's not who you think he is."

"Really?" Nate's glare was hard enough to crack glass. "Maybe you're not who I thought you were."

"You know exactly who I am." Beau tried to laugh it off.

"Just get out of the way." Nate was as close to done as Beau had seen him. "I've already dropped this load once and kept him waiting longer than I should. You wanna be useful, go fetch more cider."

"Useful? That's all you aspire to be?" It was getting harder by the moment to keep from exploding. "You do know what that means, don't you? Used."

"Don't get all wordy. I'll do whatever Doone wants me to do."

Suddenly there was no more room inside Beau for all he'd been holding in. "Whatever he wants?!" he snapped. "Like forcing your friend to do his bidding? Blowing the Land to bits?"

"Not the Land, the Manor." Nate's face revealed its dark edges and angles. "And if people die, it's for the cause. We have to make sacrifices if we want change."

"How can you say that?"

"How can you not?" Nate shot back. "Which side are you on, Crafty?"

"I'm on the side of what's right!"

Nate shifted the pile of wood in his arms, shaking his head as if taking pity on the ignorant and lost. "You know, I figured you were sheltered, hadn't been around much. But you really are just stupid."

"*I'm* stupid?" A flaming heat shot though Beau. "That's funny, because that's what Doone thinks of you!"

"You lying, rump-faced skunk!" Nate spit at the ground by Beau's feet as he pushed past.

That was it. Before he knew what he was doing, Beau dropped his pile of wood and pushed Nate hard enough to send his burden flying. "Better that than a blind boot-licker!"

"You reeky maggot!" Nate lunged at Beau with the full force of his weight.

Easily toppled, Beau fell flat on his back, an open mark for Nate to land his first punch square on Beau's jaw. The second punch sent Beau's head snapping to the side, the taste of blood seeping into his throat.

"Get off me!" Beau bucked up, throwing Nate off balance. But a life spent scrapping and fighting made Nate fast and flexible. He quickly scrambled back to his feet and was reaching for a piece of firewood when Beau threw a leg out and tripped him, sending Nate to the ground.

"Just stop and listen to m—" Beau began, but Nate flew at him again.

"Rotter!" Nate shouted, his face twisted by rage.

Beau tried to roll out of the way, but Nate was faster. He caught Beau by the hair, easily dragging him back up to his feet. Nate then delivered a swift punch to Beau's ribs, sending him staggering backward as the shriek of a loud whistle broke the air, stopping both boys dead in their tracks.

And there he was, Doone, clapping and cheering on the fight as if he were ringside at a wrestling match.

"Don't stop, I haven't placed my wager yet," he said as he

threw a fistful of coins on the ground at the boys' feet. "Ten on Nate!"

Beau backed away.

How had he let himself go that far? Forget his purpose? His friend?

"I didn't mean for that to happen." Beau threw his hands up. "I'm sorry."

"That's right. Start a fight then walk off before it's done," Nate taunted.

"Crafty started it?" Doone looked impressed. "I'd have put ten more coins on you having thrown the first punch, Nate."

"It was him." Nate stared daggers at Beau. "I asked him to help me with the wood, and he lost his mind, knocked everything out of my hands."

"You'd already dropped the wood and spilled the cider. Don't blame me for that."

"You spilled my cider?" Doone's mood flipped, all traces of amusement evaporated. "Have you any idea what that costs me?"

"I . . . I'm sorry." Nate grabbed the jug, brushing it clean as if it were a priceless heirloom. "Look, it's still half full! I'll fill it up."

He looked so hopeful and yet so lost at the same time. Even as angry as Beau was, he couldn't bear seeing Nate grovel that like.

"Give it here," Beau said. "I'll fill it, you do the wood."

"I don't need or want your help!" Nate cradled the jug as he stepped to Doone's side, his obedience on display like a peacock in full bloom. "I'm sorry. I'll do better."

"I'm sure you will." Doone took a full sweep of Nate before cracking a smile, the signal that Nate was safely back in his good graces. At least for now.

That was all Nate needed for his spirits to be reignited as he took off to the cookhouse.

Beau fought back the urge to follow after him, to make things right, but Nate needed time to cool off. He'd come around. He had to.

"See?" Doone said. "That's why we can't have him coming with us. He's hotheaded, temperamental. I won't have him blowing up our mission."

Beau nodded solemnly as if he were in complete agreement with Doone. But really it was the only way he knew to keep his tongue from taking over and telling Doone exactly what he thought about his deceitful act as the people's champion. As false an ace as ever there was.

Instead Beau simply replied, "I'll get to work on some of those slings."

"Fine," Doone called after him. "But then go get some sleep. We leave with the dawn."

Chapter Twenty-Six
Tastes So Sweet

Beau headed back to the workshop, but it wasn't to craft slings. He was waiting for Nate.

Pig-headed Nate.

Why couldn't he see Doone for who he was? Especially after the way Doone had treated him—shaming him over something as petty as spilled cider.

But he also understood the impulse to refuse to see the truth in front of his face. To stay, to take it, to not fight back. He'd lived it for most of his thirteen years, right up until the moment he met Nate.

Nate, who'd believed in Beau long before he even thought to believe in himself.

No, he wouldn't leave without him. He'd find a way to help Nate come around to the truth whatever it took.

Beau kept to the workshop as time wore on. It might be

late, and Nate might still be steaming mad, but he'd never pass up the chance for a lie-down on that feather-filled mattress upstairs.

He'd be back. It was just a matter of when.

When it got too dark in the workshop to see, Beau went in search of a light for his lantern. He finally found a lit one in the tidy bedroom upstairs. Yet he could hardly force himself over the threshold. Nate had been so excited about the prospect of sleeping in a proper bed. The room was going to be their sanctuary, their home once they'd returned triumphant from freeing the children. From saving Cressi.

But like everything else, appearances had been deceiving.

Beau was lingering in the doorway, too sad to go forward, too angry not to, when Nate came running up the stairs clutching a heavy wool blanket.

"What are you doing?" he snarled, pushing past Beau into the room. "You're in my way. Move."

"I was waiting for you," Beau replied softly, kindly.

"Why?" Nate threw himself facedown onto one of the beds. "I've got nothing to say to you."

"Then I'll talk," Beau said. "I'm sorry I lost my temper. I know you think I tried to take all of Doone's attention. That I showed you up on purpose. I didn't. I told him how brilliant you are. That you're devoted to him, would do anything for him. You have to believe me. He only sees you as a servant, someone to carry his wood and cider. You deserve so much more."

"Just shut your face hole, before I punch you again," Nate growled into his pillow. "And this time things will break."

"You can be angry at me; you can even hate me. But you can't stay here. Everything he's said is a lie."

"You're the lie!" Nate sat up, fuming. "Everything about you is a lie!"

Beau fought to keep himself from falling back, for the truth had come out. "Listen, you don't understand. I thought Doone was—"

"He told me everything."

Beau's throat ran dry. "Everything?"

"You told him I was afraid of fire! And some story about how you had to rescue me from a wild boar! Lies, dirty lies."

"I never said any of that!" Beau vowed.

"And then you know what he did?" Nate pulled back his anger, allowing an eerie calm to overtake him. "He asked me to draw up the plans for freeing Mastery House. Where the doors are, how to divert the doorkeeper and Matron. Me! Not you. He also said next time we fight I should finish you off as if you were the heir himself."

"You'd do that to me?" Beau stood his ground, even as it was crumbling underneath his feet.

"Might be a good time for you to learn to sleep with your ears open."

Beau's head pounded with the thrum of his heartbeat, his throat so tight he could hardly breathe. He wanted to scream, throw something. Cry. Yet none of that would have moved Nate.

Beau may never have known friendship before, but he was all too familiar with the bitter taste of rejection salted with loathing.

It was over.

Beau grabbed a lantern and headed for the door.

"You planning on running? I'll tell Doone. He'll hunt you down!" Nate yelled.

"I'm not leaving," Beau lied. "But I'm not going to sleep here either. I'd rather bed down up a tree than near you."

Not a lie.

"Good." Nate grabbed the quilt off the second bed and threw it, along with the wool blanket he'd carried in, over his head. "I hope you freeze."

"I probably will now." And with that Beau left, the final wisps of what he'd thought was his first real friendship gutted like a candle burned down to the nub.

His lantern turned down low to avoid casting shadows, Beau passed through the workshop and out to the forge. If he was to be on his own, he had to change his thinking. No one—not Nate, not Doone, not even some mythical ace—was going to protect him or do what he had to do. He had to be his own ace now, find his own way to rescue Cressi and protect the children of Mastery House.

Unlike his escape from the Manor, this time he intended to be prepared, for everything. Including defending himself.

There were plenty of sharp objects to choose from in the workshop; everything from an awl to a razor to a sharp billhook—one of those curved blades for cutting wheat. But the very thought of brandishing a blade left Beau twisted up and clammy. He could never imagine pulling a knife on another person, so he opted for the smallest awl he could find. Sharp enough to be a threat, but not to inflict real harm. Or so he hoped.

All that was left to do now was to wait until the lanterns blazing out in the cookhouse were extinguished, until Trout was done with his work.

As he sat hiding out in the shadow of the forge Beau considered taking a couple of grenades with him. One or two would offer him protection, but he'd never get anywhere carrying the weight. Besides, destruction was Doone's way, not his.

Then he remembered something Doone had said—something about how wet powder won't ignite.

It took several trips back and forth to the water barrel, but Beau had soon moved enough water to soak Doone's powder through and through, leaving it completely ruined. He'd always thought of revenge as something petty and base, but knowing he'd left Doone's prized weapon useless sent ripples of satisfaction through Beau.

Not long after that the lamps in the cookhouse were extinguished. The time had come.

Ready and more than resolved, Beau turned his lamp down low and stepped out into the night. The moon was a thin sliver overhead, but there were enough stars out to light his way. He planned to avoid passing the house altogether by ducking behind the cookhouse, but then he spotted Trout's great, hulking shadow hunched over the fire. He was still there!

The only way out now was past the house and behind the barn.

The barn.

He'd been thinking he'd have to travel by foot, at least until he could stow away in a wagon or find a willing ride. But now he had another, far faster option.

Inside the barn Beau found four horses bedded down for the night. Doone's dappled gray stallion and Trout's mare were in the first two stalls, their feed full and hay clean. The thought of stealing Doone's gray was almost too tempting to resist, but it would also be borrowing more trouble than was wise. Someone could easily recognize Doone's horse. A plow horse was stabled in the next stall, but that poor thing looked so tired Beau couldn't even think about taking him.

There was only one more stall. Hoping against hope to find a worthy ride, Beau peered inside. Luck truly must have landed on his shoulder, for not only was this horse healthy and strong looking, the filly bore the Manor brand on her rear flank.

Beau smiled. It wasn't stealing if the horse was already his. He gathered a handful of hay and extended it, quietly coaxing the filly to turn around. It took a couple of calls before she raised her head and looked back at him, her black speckled muzzle full of hay.

Beau nearly fell back with joy.

It was Puzzle! Dear, sweet, patient Puzzle who'd been missing for far too long.

"Hey, girl," he whispered. "Remember me?"

The filly turned and reached for him, tapping him with her beautiful, soft muzzle.

"You do remember me!" Beau sighed happily as he slipped into the stall.

She looked good, if a bit thinner. At least she'd been newly shoed, and her coat was clean. Confident she was healthy enough to be ridden, Beau saddled her up. Just as she always used to, Puzzle playfully nibbled at his boot laces as he worked. How he'd missed her!

"Come on, girl," Beau said as he led Puzzle out of the barn. "We have some work to do."

Moving quietly and stealthily, they headed toward the hill when something on the ground caught Beau's eye, reflecting the thin moonlight like so many polished gemstones.

Beau reached down to pick one up but quickly recoiled, his

hand pulling back as if from a flame. It was the coins Doone had thrown down as a wager during Beau and Nate's fight. Yet just as a flame beckons you with warmth, the coins were calling to him.

Beau gathered them up, their weight feeling solid in his hand. Useful. Familiar. As he pocketed them, he realized he wasn't so very different from those simple pieces of copper. There were those who sought to use Beau to enrich themselves, elevate their position, claim his power. But unlike these pounded pieces of metal that had no say in how the bearer used them, Beau had agency. He had options.

Cressi had been right about him all along—it was for Beau to decide how to use his position as heir, no one else.

His choice at long last accepted, Beau headed up the hill to do what he should have done from the beginning.

Chapter Twenty-Seven
Blade and Branch

W hen every minute of life is filled with duty, toil, and drudgery, there's no time to wander, wonder, or just take in the day. And while Cressi's journey through the woods certainly wasn't for pleasure, walking the path alone felt like a revelation. No one watching her, free to set her own pace— hurrying as she saw fit, slowing down when needed. Breathing deep of the cool damp, she occasionally paused to listen to the trees, to smell what the plants along the pathway had to tell her. If she had time, she would've stopped to talk to every new plant she spotted, learn their secrets, and unlock their powers.

One day she'd be free to be herself, to explore, to learn.

To just be.

But for now, dark was falling around her, and she was running out of time to find Beau before Barger came after her himself.

Cressi opened the lantern just enough to light her way, then pulled the pawn from her pocket.

"Can you help me find Gerta too?"

The pawn didn't move; this was not the reply she was hoping for.

As she traveled farther, the ground became rockier, harder, and ever more riddled with heaving roots. The trees here were thinner, more desperate, their bark shaggier, angrier. A stifling stillness filling the air, broken only by the occasional screech of raptors overhead.

And then there was the smell.

The sweet aroma of woody decay had taken on a bitter tang, becoming something crueler, bloodier. Long shadows bobbed and teased, creating illusions all around her.

Did that tree move? What about that rock?

"Where are you, Gerta?" Cressi whispered.

She thought about reaching for the blade but decided against it. For now.

"Just keep moving," she prompted herself.

And she did, though that didn't stop the mirages. No matter what she told herself, faces seemed to appear in broken tree trunks, rocks whispered. Finally, at the point where she thought her imagination surely had overtaken all reason, Cressi walked straight up to a fallen tree limb she was certain she'd seen move.

For all the world it looked like nothing more than a dead

log up close, but just to be sure Cressi kicked it, sending it rolling down a small embankment. The log landed in a low-lying puddle with a sigh, proof it was nothing more than what it was—a dead tree.

Cressi adjusted her pack and was about to step back onto the path when she heard it. The unmistakable crack of twigs breaking underfoot.

Charged as if by a bolt of lightning, Cressi threw off her bag and pulled the blade. No plan in mind, just pure instinct, she spun on the noise. And there it was, a figure coming toward her through the dim, moving with the speed of a panther.

Or a monster.

Cressi gripped the knife and lunged at the figure, sending it jumping back to evade her blade. Another lunge, another evasion, this one landing them farther out of reach.

There were only two choices now—Cressi could take the moment to flee, or she could face down this . . . whatever it was.

Monsters must be faced.

Cressi grabbed a rock and threw it, hoping to stop the creature's approach. And it worked, if only for a moment. She didn't want to kill it, whatever it was, but with no other choice Cressi launched another rock. This one made contact, sending the creature stumbling back into the mud. The creature lurched at her again, yet no matter how hard it tried, it couldn't get a foothold—it was stuck.

Wary of the trick, Cressi crept closer, arming herself with a splintered-off limb, ready to land a fatal blow if need be.

"What are you!" she demanded.

The creature gave no reply, it just lay still in the mud, the only movement sharp, painful panting heaving in its chest.

What was this thing? And what had she done to it?

Cressi was nearly close enough to reach the creature when the ground began to shift and sway underfoot. Reflexes alight, she jumped back to solid ground. But then there was the poor creature, whimpering, sinking ever deeper into the muck.

"Hang on!" Cressi grabbed a nearby branch and extended it out. She'd nearly gotten the limb close enough when something large and absolutely human-shaped came flying at her. Cressi swung the branch but was no match for the size and speed of this new attacker. Before she could swing again something large hit her from behind, sending her crashing to the ground.

She fought to scramble back to her feet when a heavy-booted foot landed on her back, forcing the breath from her lungs, pinning her facedown to the ground.

"Get off!" Cressi howled as she kicked her legs wildly, trying to make contact with something, anything. "I have nothing worth stealing."

"That's not true," came a woman's voice. "But we're not foes. Relax yourself. Let her up."

And with that, the boot lifted off and a large hand reached down and pulled Cressi to her feet.

It took a moment or two for Cressi to see clearly, for the haze to dissipate. When her captors finally came into focus, Cressi thought it must be another mirage. Three men and a woman surrounded her all dressed in the same uniform of mossy-green leggings and tight-fitting jerkins, three large hunting bows aimed at her, arrows cocked and ready to fly.

Cressi lunged to make a run for it but she was immobilized, held up in midair by a clawlike hand. Try as she might to move, she was stuck as if nailed to a wall.

"I told you I have nothing you want!" Cressi shouted, fighting against her captors.

"I think it's you that wants something of me." The woman gestured for her two companions to lower their bows as she stepped closer to Cressi. "Otherwise why would Anka have sent you?"

"You're Gerta?" Cressi practically spat the name out.

"Who else would I be?" the woman replied as if it were the most obvious answer. "If we were bandits, you'd not have lived to ask who attacked you. Release her, Hugo."

Abruptly freed, Cressi collected herself, fighting to stay calm, shaking off the pain from the boot in her back.

"Take your blade. And your bag." Gerta thrust them back to Cressi. "And don't ever make the mistake of taking them off again."

There was nothing in the least bit kind or even agreeable about Gerta, nothing to lead Cressi to think of her as an ally. But as with Anka, she had a surety about her. A feeling of solidity. But then she leaned in closer and it was as if she'd turned to hot molten rock. "And never, ever push one of my people into a sand pit again."

Cressi forgot her own pain, and melted inside. "It that what it is? I had no idea."

"Obviously," Gerta growled as she stalked off, cutting a path through the trees.

"Wait! Where are you going?" Cressi ran after her. "You're supposed to tell me how to find Be—"

"You want to know what I know, you come with us," Gerta said without turning or stopping.

At that, Hugo and another of Gerta's men stepped up and planted themselves on either side of Cressi. They made no move to control her, but the message was clear: one wrong step and they'd fell her like a rotten tree.

Cressi was bursting with questions as she followed Gerta along a rambling route that led them ever deeper into the woods. Where was Beau? How close was she to finding him? And how had they camouflaged themselves as they did? But the group walked on in a stony silence Cressi dared not try to crack. Around rocky outcroppings, past another sand pit, and up a steep hill they climbed. Gerta and her men lit small lanterns, which they fitted onto their heads with straps, but when Cressi moved to open her own lantern Hugo turned on her, a warning to leave it unlit.

"Are you taking me to Beau?" she whispered, but no one even acknowledged her, let alone answered. They kept walking. Silently.

The farther they traveled, the more Cressi began to wonder if they weren't walking in circles. Or figure eights. They'd already passed this rock face once, hadn't they? And that stand of dying fir trees looked eerily familiar. It was when they climbed over the jagged remains of a once solid stone wall for the third time, Cressi knew it for a fact.

"What's happening?" she demanded. "Why are you leading me nowhere?"

"Silence!" Gerta's warning trailed behind her like a snake through the leaves as she brought the group to a halt under the shelter of a large stone outcropping.

Cressi was certain Gerta was about to turn on her when two men came crashing through the tree line, each brandishing a large machete.

Dressed in ragged jerkins and leg wraps in place of trousers, they were gaunt and rangy. Yet more than their appearance, they had a kind of desperation about them, a hunger clinging to their bones.

Pilfers—the poorest of the poor in the Bottom. Known to be violent and reckless, they were desperate enough to do anything for their next meal.

Cressi moved to run, to shout, to pull her blade when she felt Hugo's hand land on her shoulder, a warning to stay put.

Why just stand still waiting to be attacked? Why weren't they running, or, better yet, stringing their bows in a show of strength?

And that's when it happened—the pair walked right on past. They never broke their stride, never turned their heads; the bandits did nothing to indicate they even saw Cressi, Gerta, and the others standing right there.

Half-elated, half-petrified, Cressi held her breath until the pair disappeared into the woods. "What just happened?"

"What kind of charmer doesn't recognize a charm when she sees one?" Gerta tutted.

"A charm?" Cressi repeated. "Why didn't Anka say you were a charmer?"

Gerta's shoulders heaved in a way that said she had little time or interest in offering explanations. And she didn't. She simply stepped out from under the rock outcropping and walked away, her two companions close at hand.

"Why won't she answer?" Cressi asked Hugo, who was sticking close to her side.

"She's not going to talk out here, and neither should you. Inside."

"Inside where?" There was nothing around, just trees and rocks. But like Gerta, Hugo offered no reply as the group tramped down the same hill once again, across the same dried-up stream, and into the same broken up stand of fir trees.

Cressi was beginning to think she'd stepped into a trap when right before her very eyes Gerta disappeared.

Vanished.

And then so did her two companions.

Cressi checked herself. It had to be a trick of the night.

But then Hugo stopped short of where they disappeared and asked, "You coming or not?"

Cressi could hardly move, for that's when she saw it.

A flash, a spark, a momentary vision of a cluster of small cabins lit up by a large bonfire.

Cressi grappled to understand. This was not her imagination, it was another charm, a powerful and unimaginable charm obscuring the cabins from view.

"How?" she asked.

"You want answers, you follow." Hugo walked into the tree line, his large frame momentarily breaking the illusion as he passed through to the other side.

A shiver ran up Cressi's spine and over the top of her head. But this wasn't a quiver of fear, it was the thrill of recognition as the pawn warmed and jumped in her pocket, pressing her to step through the veil.

Chapter Twenty-Eight
Found and Lost

After racing away from Doone's, Beau and Puzzle finally slowed to a walk. As far as Beau could tell no one had followed them. Yet. At this rate, he'd be back in the Lower Middlelands before sunrise. Almost halfway to the Manor.

Almost halfway to Cressi.

But every good plan needs to leave room for luck, both good and bad. There were too many pitfalls in the Bottom, dangers lurking around every turn. He had to stay vigilant.

At least for now, though, the woods were quiet. Beau urged his mind to do the same, but he couldn't keep thoughts of Nate and their broken bond from pushing in.

During all those years sitting alone in his apartments, Beau had been certain friendship was the key to finding happiness. An end to loneliness, a call to adventure. And that's exactly what it looked and felt like when he met Nate. But apparently Himself had been right when he said friendship was useful only if it served a purpose. No one sought to make a friend of anyone unless they had something to gain from it. The sooner Beau understood that, the happier he'd be.

Standing on the backside of a failed alliance, Beau did have to admit he'd used Nate too. Without him, he'd never have gotten off the Manor. Even so, that hadn't stopped Beau from caring about Nate or feeling like their bond was real.

As Beau pushed on, he entered the part of the forest where the tree cover grew thinner, where the dark of the night yielded to the stars above. Free from the clutches of predatory brambles, Beau let his guard down for a moment. But just as his shoulders began to unwind, he heard the snap and crackle of someone, something making an approach from the north.

Beau quickly backed Puzzle into the shadows, his heart racing along with his mind, trying to reckon what was approaching. A bear? Doone? Thieves?

Why hadn't he taken a real weapon?

But it was too late to wonder now as two people came pushing through the brush, each hauling a sack over one shoulder. The first to step out onto the road was a woman who carried herself as if her bundle contained all the weight of the world. Beau's throat ached at the sight of her burden. But the girl with a long braid falling down her back who followed her made his pounding heart almost stop.

"Cressi?" slipped out of his mouth like a wish or a prayer.

The woman, who'd been moving so slowly, sprang to action as she pushed the girl into the brush hissing, "Run!"

The girl froze for a moment, just long enough for Beau to catch sight of her hollowed out cheekbones, and to realize she was a stranger to him. Then she took off into the tree line, lithe as a rabbit, leaving no sound or scent in her wake. The woman watched until she'd disappeared, then turned to scuttle off in the opposite direction. Although she tried, she couldn't move very fast, her hurrying less a run and more a hobble. It was only then that Beau recognized the hunch to her shoulders, the downcast way she held her squared-off jaw.

It was the woman they'd passed on their way to Doone's.

"Wait!" Beau called. "Hold on!"

At the sound of his voice the woman froze, every muscle and sinew taut. Slowly she dropped her sack to the ground and raised her hands in surrender.

"Please, sir," she said, her voice trembling and thin. "I meant no offense."

"Offense?" Beau tied Puzzle's reins off and approached the woman. Although he moved slowly, with care, she cowered, shrinking back into herself.

"It's only a squirrel and some ground nuts." She sounded close to breaking. "Just trying to feed my family."

"With a squirrel?" Beau couldn't contain his disgust. That would hardly be enough to feed a child, let alone an entire family.

"We didn't trap it or anything. Found it already dead. We'd never hunt without your say-so. And I'd never have taken it if your other man left us anything, even onions. But he took it all. Said we had to pay next season's custom now. He said it would be enough. Here, take it!" The woman thrust the sack at Beau. "I've got nothing else to give you!"

"I don't want anything, I promise." Beau waved off the sack and took a few steps closer. "Don't you recognize me?"

"Yes, sir," she said. But rather than being calmed, her fear intensified. "You're one of Doone's. You have to tell him it's all we have, nothing more. I've paid with all I have, down to my last piglet. Please!"

A chill gripped Beau's neck. The screech that had filled the woods while Doone taught Beau and Nate about the runner's code was this woman's pig! Her only pig—the same one Trout had been roasting all day long out in the cookhouse. He'd stolen it.

"I'm not one of Doone's," Beau vowed. "I was with him yesterday, but I have nothing to do with that villain."

The woman eyed Beau cautiously.

"I've run from his house," he confided. "Believe me, I'm frightened of him too. And repulsed. He's not who people think he is, who I thought he was. Please, let me help you somehow. Try to make it right."

"No one can make it right." The woman's voice took on a bitter edge. "Life down here is what it is. And if you've run from Doone, you best keep running."

"I will. But first let me help you somehow, to prove I'm not who you think I am."

The woman shifted. "What do you care what I think?"

She was right. What did it matter what anyone thought about him? The only important thing was what he did.

"What's he done to you is terrible, unimaginable. I want to help."

The woman gathered her thin shawl closer around her. She was fighting to keep her gaze pinned to Beau, but she kept stealing quick little glances off into the woods. He realized then the girl was hiding behind a scraggly thorn bush.

Beau had no real idea what maternal love looked like, but the way she softened every time her eyes skipped past her daughter was as close to anything he'd ever imagined.

"I promise you, you're safe with me. I can help if you let me."

The thick rod of fear that had been keeping the woman upright and ready to flee softened. "You really want to help?"

Beau nodded. "I do."

"Come on then. Can't talk out here." The woman threw the sack over her shoulder, wrapped a protective arm around her daughter, and led the way to their tiny hovel in the burned-out village.

The woman's cabin, which from afar had looked solid enough, was the saddest place Beau could ever imagine. Tiny, drafty, and barely standing, it leaned to one side and looked as if even the smallest breeze could topple it. The woman was clearly doing the best she could to keep it clean, to keep a fire burning, to keep the rodents at bay, but it was a losing battle. She insisted Beau make himself comfortable, offering him the thin pile of rags they called a bed, but instead he chose to get to work.

While the woman set to skinning and cooking the squirrel, Beau hauled in wood, collected water from a nearby stream, and turned Puzzle's saddle pad into a covering for the drafty window. And all the while he gently pressed the woman for details about how she managed to survive.

She told him about losing her husband to an illness that settled in his chest and never left. That her two oldest children had been sent to Mastery House, a price that covered her tax for ten seasons. They were strong and healthy babies, she said. She could only hope they'd survived. But when the time came, she refused to make her youngest daughter's birth known. The child had been sickly from birth. She'd not have survived half a season in Mastery House.

"But defying the law means keeping her hidden," the woman said.

"From the Manor's tax collectors you mean?" Beau asked.

"And other folks around here. We all hate the Manor the same, but coin can feed you. There's not many who'll pass that up, even if it costs someone else."

"People do that to each other? Turn their neighbors in?"

"Survival turns the unimaginable into the unavoidable. I can't blame them. Most of them are in the same exact position I am, some even worse."

Beau's anger ignited, but he tamped it down. It would do the woman no good. "And that's why you're paying Doone."

"He offered protection. Promised he'd never let anyone take her from me."

"As long as you paid with everything you have!" No longer able to contain his ire, Beau started pacing, but stopped as soon as he realized he'd become a mirror of Himself's own thinking posture. He shoved his hands into his pockets as a way to settle himself, and that's when it hit him. The answer was right there. It was so simple, so obvious. All Beau could do was start laughing.

The woman and her daughter retreated to the back wall of the cabin, worry creasing the corners of their eyes.

"I'm sorry!" Beau said, trying to wave off his behavior. "It's all right. I didn't mean to scare you. It's just that, I'm so stupid. I've had the answer all along! I can't believe I didn't think of it sooner."

While the woman and her daughter watched, eyes wide with caution, Beau pulled his fist out of his pocket. And then, with his face lit with a smile bright enough to illuminate the dim hovel, he poured a fistful of coins into the woman's hand.

"I . . . I . . ." The woman fumbled for words as she watched the shower of copper filling her palm.

"I know it's not much," Beau said. "But it will help for now."

"Not much?" The woman's thin voice was on the verge of breaking. "It's more than I've seen since I was a girl. My family once owned land, a good working farm. I don't remember much of that life, but I know before the last war we had coin to pay for what we needed."

Beau's throat tightened; the depth of her loss was far greater than anything he'd ever known.

Since leaving the Manor, Beau thought he'd come to understand how very different people's lives were from his. Seeing Mastery House had hit him like an anvil on the head. Hearing how the people in the Lower Middlelands scratched to survive pulled at his heart. Even those who had the means to live well in the Upper Middlelands lived in fear. But like the children of Mastery House, this woman and her daughter in the Bottom were beyond vulnerable. They'd been wholly abandoned. And it was all because of the cruelty perpetuated by the Manor, by Beau's father. By Beau's own blindness.

Beau took his riding jacket off and draped it around the young girl's shoulders. "I'm sorry I haven't done enough for you."

"But you have!" The woman wrapped the coins in a ragged piece of cloth as if they were the very miracle of life itself before turning back to her stew pot. "Please, sit. Food will be ready soon."

"Thank you," Beau said. "But I've got to be going."

"No, you should wait here for the dawn," the woman insisted. "It's not safe out there, especially at night."

"I'll be all right," Beau said.

"I hope you will." The woman took Beau's hand in hers. As thin and cold as she was, her hand generated a warmth and kindness such as Beau had never felt. The touch of trust.

He turned to leave when she called after him, "Wait, what do they call you?"

The answer he wanted to give got stuck in his throat, pulled at his very core. A cough cleared it enough for him to reply, "Crafty."

Chapter Twenty-Nine
Charming the Charmer

As soon as Cressi stepped through the veil, the pawn began shaking and quaking so hard she was certain Beau would be on the other side waiting for her.

But he wasn't. The only person on the other side of the veil was Gerta, looking less than pleased.

"Where is he?" Cressi asked. "He is here, right?"

Gerta gave no reply, instead only signaled for Cressi to follow her.

Certain she was about to come face-to-face with Beau, Cressi pulled the pawn out of her pocket. It was hard to discern if the excitement she felt was hers alone. What would the pawn do when she and Beau finally met? Jump from her hand to his? Go silent? Disintegrate?

But the cabin Gerta led Cressi to was empty, save for a bed, a table, and a cold, unlit hearth. No Beau.

"Where is—"

Gerta cut her off with a flat palm.

"Sit."

"Why won't you let me see him?" Cressi pushed. And then it struck her. "Is he hurt? Did something happen? What about Na—"

"Stop. Sit. Listen." Gerta pointed to the chair and waited.

That was the last thing Cressi wanted to do, but Gerta was a wall. The only way around was to wait for her to open up. Cressi sat.

"He's not here," Gerta said. "Never was."

"But the paw—" Cressi stopped herself. She'd not told anyone about the pawn yet. Why would she begin with Gerta?

"What of the pawn?" Gerta asked. "It's all right, I know you have it. I imagine it's been leading you, like a dog wagging its tail whenever it picks up its master's scent. But it's not a perfect charm, especially in your hands."

"What does that mean?" Cressi balked.

"Annina charmed it and left it for Beau to use one day. She knew her time was coming and wanted to leave something for her son, a trail to follow to find his own mage and his ace when the time came. She didn't want him to make the same mistakes she'd made. Nonetheless you can trust the pawn to lead you to him. Eventually."

"I don't have until eventually."

"Then you'll go to Doone's." Gerta sounded as if this

were the most obvious answer, one Cressi should already have known.

"Wait, he's with Doone? What about Nate?"

"He's there too."

"And they're safe? Doone hasn't . . . Nate hasn't . . ." She couldn't say what she thought Doone or Nate would do if they knew Beau was the heir.

"Both boys looked more than pleased to be in Doone's company. It's not far from here. Hugo will take you."

Cressi jumped to her feet. "I'm ready. Let's go."

"A warning for you first. Doone's only interest in people is how he can use them. You'd be a particularly appealing tool to hang in his shed. I'd suggest you play like you're on his side. You think you can do that?"

"I've already played that game. That's how I got away from the Manor." Cressi fixed her bag and headed for the door. "I can't thank you enough."

"Yes you can." Gerta, for her part, showed no signs of getting up or moving. "You'll thank us by healing Veda, my sentry. The one we pulled out of the sand."

Veda.

Cressi had been so consumed with finding Beau and Nate, she'd forgotten all about the person she'd sent sinking into the pit. How could she have forgotten?

"How is she? Is she very hurt?"

"From what I'm told, burns cover her legs, her side, and

one entire arm. Then there's the blow to the head you gave her. It's a miracle she's not dead."

Cressi melted into the chair, the weight of guilt cutting her legs out from underneath her. "I'm so sorry."

"Don't be sorry," Gerta corrected. "Heal her."

"I'll try." Cressi brightened a bit at the thought. "Where is she?"

"Next door. Then once she's healed, you'll fix our veil."

"Your veil?" Cressi laughed, the idea too ridiculous to believe. "That I can't do. I wouldn't even know how to."

"Then you'll learn."

Cressi stood stunned. "How can I learn something I barely understand?"

"What's there to understand? It's simple magic," Gerta replied. "We diffuse the charm in the firepit outside, the vapor shrouds us from view. For smaller areas, like a rock face, a log, or a hedgerow, we paint the area with the brew. If we are to remain safe and hidden, we need more, and you're going to make it for us."

"I've never done anything like that. And I . . . I have to find Beau."

"And you will. As soon as you're done."

"I thought you were a friend," Cressi countered. "An ally."

"I'd say what we share is more a strategic alliance," Gerta corrected. "We're united in our fight against the Manor, but we don't want the same outcome from the war."

"How can we not? A benevolent Manor can only make us all stronger, safer."

"Again, we differ in our definition. We've had to forge certain agreements, make deals that protect our right to never submit to be ruled by anyone else ever again. We've a treaty with Doone just to that end. He leaves us alone. We leave him alone. But make no mistake—our allegiance is only to ourselves."

Gerta was unlike any woman Cressi had ever met before. It wasn't that she was the chosen leader of her people. Although that was unheard of under Manor rule, stories told of many female leaders in times past. Rather, it was her bearing, her sense of confident, calm command. Certainly, Cressi had suffered at the hand of countless cruel women, Matron first among them, but Gerta was different. She wasn't looking for compliance to feed her pride. She embodied her power and authority without conceit. Had Gerta not made herself an obstacle, she would have been an inspiration. But right now, she was a barrier Cressi had no good way around.

"We agree on our terms then?" Gerta asked.

It was irresponsible and plain stupid to make an agreement Cressi didn't know how to fulfill. But there was no other choice.

Gerta led Cressi into one of the larger cabins where Veda was laid out on a bed. Her legs were covered in moist linens, the smell of burned flesh hanging heavy in the air. A girl not much older than Cressi was attending her, mopping her forehead with a cool compress.

"You need anything, Lula will help. She's got a healing touch. Perhaps she can learn from you." And with that Gerta left, the sound of a lock engaging in her wake.

"Don't expect too much from me, please." Cressi smiled weakly at Lula as she took off her bag.

After laying her brews out on the table, Cressi inhaled of each deeply. Truth. Loyalty. A cure for the fever. Each brew was perfectly balanced for its intended purpose, not for healing burns. The closest thing she had was the pot of salve she'd used to heal the guard's hand and Beau's nose, but it was nearly spent. She'd need at least thrice the amount to tend to Veda's legs, and it still might not work. Yet coming up with a new brew would take all night. She didn't have all night.

Then again, she also didn't have a choice.

Cressi asked Lula to bring her a couple of bowls, a mortar and pestle, and a kettle of hot water, and then she began mixing and muddling. She added a bit of one brew to a bowl, then stirred in a dash of another, hoping together they'd make something new and useful. But every attempt resulted only in the brews battling each other for domination, a fight that wound up canceling them both out.

Cressi then tried adding new ingredients to the brews. She added in bits of roots and leaves, pushing the mixtures to expand their use, yet nothing she did produced the results she needed.

By the time she'd tried every possible combination she could think of, the candle clock had burned down two pegs. The night was speeding past and signs of infection were beginning to set in. There was only a short window of time before Veda would begin to fade.

"You will be able to heal her, won't you?" Lula asked. The girl had hardly spoken all night. Cressi had nearly forgotten she was there.

"I hope so," Cressi said.

"I knew this would happen one day when she was out scouting," Lula said. "I told her. But then she'd look sad, tuck me back into bed, and remind me to be brave. So I stopped telling her."

"Oh," Cressi said, understanding finally dawning. "Veda is your mother."

Lula nodded. She was a stoic little thing who showed no emotion on her face. Although that didn't stop Cressi from seeing straight through her, all the way to her dear, loving heart and beyond.

"Why did you say you knew this would happen?" Cressi pressed.

"I'd see it when I'd go to sleep at night. Smell it in my dreams."

"What else do you smell?"

"Besides food, fire, and farts?" Lula laughed. "Not much I don't think. I mean, I can smell fear and fury. But everyone can do that, right?"

"No." Cressi had been thinking all along that charming meant only one thing, but perhaps there were other talents and abilities that had been lost to time. Talents like Lula's.

Cressi pulled the bottle of blue-green liquid from her stocking and set it on the table. She wasn't sure what to expect, if anything. But she certainly wasn't expecting Lula to lurch away from her mother's side and make a beeline for the bottle. Her eyes glazed and her lips agape, she looked as if she wanted to swallow it.

Cressi quickly pulled the bottle away and shoved it into her boot.

Her suspicions more than confirmed, she turned to Lula. "What do you smell from me?"

"Right now? Hesitation," Lula replied.

Smart girl.

All the while Cressi had been mixing and muddling, trying to listen to her brews, there'd been something itching at the base of her spine. Something pushing her, goading her further. But Cressi shoved it back, tried to ignore it. Whatever it was, it was unstable, murky. Dangerous.

But what if it was the answer?

Cressi turned back to her brews and started again.

Instead of falling into that lovely, almost trancelike state she'd found in Anka's kitchen, Cressi was now twisting, turning, pushing the plants where she wanted them to go. Instead of listening, she was telling, demanded the plants follow her command, submit to her will.

And soon after, she found it: a brew that smelled of a cooling compress and healthy skin. Wholeness.

Cressi doused a linen in the new concoction and tested it on a small burn on Veda's hand. Lula held the lamp higher, casting a bright light for the experiment to either bloom or wither under.

Moments passed. Cressi caught wind of the scent of lavender. Or was it skunk? The smell kept turning and changing, never once settling long enough to be defined. And then the healthy skin around the burn began to look burned too. First it looked gray, then blue, and finally black as soot.

"What's happening? The burns are spreading!" Lula was inching toward panic. "Should I get Gerta? I need to get Gerta."

Cressi held fast. The plants wouldn't betray her. "Give it time."

And still the skin kept blackening until it began to smolder, a haze of smoke rising just above the wound. Lula was about to bolt for the door when Cressi stopped her. "Watch."

And that's when it happened. The ashy curls of smoke began dispersing as if blown apart by a cooling breeze, leaving behind perfectly healed, unblemished skin.

Relieved right down to her bones, Cressi exhaled as if for the first time ever. Somehow, she felt older and wiser.

As Lula grabbed her mother's hand, relief pinking up her cheeks, Cressi set the bowl and linen down next to her.

"You can apply it now. Go slow. Do only small sections at a time. Wait for the healing to take hold before moving on. Understand?"

Lula nodded, wiping her eyes clear as she set to work on her mother.

Now came an even bigger challenge—figuring out how to charm the very air itself.

Cressi thought about how the rock hid them from the thieves. It wasn't that they'd disappeared as much as the veil obscured them from view. So, in theory, charming an object or the air wasn't very different than charming a person. She'd simply have to figure out what its essential nature was.

Once again, she had to dig deep in that place hidden between her bones to find a brew that would work. Trying, failing, then trying again, she finally landed on something, a brew that could render anything capable of creating an echo of itself.

Cressi spilled a few well-considered drops on the table, then stepped back.

At first, she worried it was her tired eyes showing her what she wanted to see, but the look on Lula's face said it all.

It worked! The table was gone—at least to the eye, although her hand knew different.

"Call for Gerta," Cressi said, nearly collapsing from joy and exhaustion. "Tell her I've figured it out."

Lula called out the window to a sentry to send for Gerta. She arrived a few moments later.

Implacable and unmoving as always, Gerta stood in stony silence while Cressi showed off both Veda's newly healed skin and the veil she'd drawn around the table. Gerta took her time inspecting both, testing the resiliency of the veil and examining Veda's legs.

"You've done it," she said, finally. "And you've made enough to last us?"

"Yes, there's plenty of both the burn remedy and the charm for the veil to keep you safe for a long time. I hope the day comes when you won't need it."

"There will always be a need to keep ourselves protected. Isolation is the only way we will thrive. Very well. Hugo will take you as far as he can. You'll be on your own to enter Doone's. We will not violate the agreement we have with him."

"Thank you," Cressi said. "I would never have come to understand so much without you."

"Probably not," Gerta said, then added, "Be careful out there."

"I will. I've a blade and my charms."

"I don't mean that. Don't follow the same path that swallowed up Annina."

"Don't worry, I won't be marrying Himself," Cressi laughed.

"You're thinking too simply again. Annina made too many mistakes. Miscalculated who the ace was. She was convinced it was Himself and wouldn't listen to reason when she was told why it couldn't be him. Then she pushed her power too far, abused it. In turn it cost her everything, and the rest of us as well. Be smarter."

Cressi nodded. "I'll try, I promise."

Chapter Thirty
Fixing and Sinking

Beau mounted Puzzle feeling refreshed, even though it was late into the night. Carrying the woman's trust fueled him for the journey ahead.

He knew giving her those coins hadn't been some great feat of benevolence or even a real solution to her problems. He'd only offered her a brief reprieve. She was still vulnerable, had no proper home to call her own, no way to raise her daughter safely. Her life, and all the others like hers, couldn't be fixed by a few coins. But as he headed north, Beau finally knew what he had to do—the exact opposite of everything he had been doing.

From the moment he left the Manor, he'd been certain he was running toward something: finding his ace, getting Doone to help liberate the children of Mastery House, even heading north to free Cressi on his own. But in truth it was no different than what he'd been doing all his life—trying to escape the inescapable and reject the life fate had chosen for him.

"No more and never again," he whispered to Puzzle. "This is my tainted inheritance. It's mine to fix."

Puzzle replied with a nicker and a toss of her head.

As they pressed on the pathway was getting more difficult to navigate. Clouds had blown in masking the moon and stars, forcing Beau to open his lantern wider, holding it out front like a beacon.

Then it began to rain hard enough to turn the dusty pathway to a muddy slick. Fearing for Puzzle's safety Beau slipped off her back. As long as the storm got no worse, they would push on. They had to.

But soon the winds picked up and Beau had to shutter the lamp in order to protect the precious flame. If not for the light from periodic lightning strikes, he'd have completely lost his bearings. During one of these momentary ignitions, Beau spotted the fallen tree, sharpened like an arrow pointing the way to the runner's code stump.

He'd been so full of hope and trust when Doone told him and Nate about the code. He'd seen the signs pointing toward Doone's as proof they were on the path to safety. But time and experience now exposed them as part of an intricate trap to steer innocents into Doone's web of deceit.

Not for much longer though.

Beau tethered Puzzle to a tree and headed for the stump. At least the woods offered some shelter from the winds, allowing him to open the lamp up more. He soon found the stump, set the lantern down, and got to work. The small awl he'd taken was the perfect tool for the job.

The runner's code marking on the south-facing side was a series of five hash marks—the sign for a safe road. Somehow Beau would have to change that to the cockeyed *T*, the code for beware. The only way he could figure to do that was to carve straight through the five hash marks, turning them into a single line, and cross them on an angle.

But before Beau could finish, the winds began to shift again. Even under the cover of trees, the rain hit hard. He could hear Puzzle nervously snorting and pawing at the ground. He quickly finished up his work, heartened that he'd done enough to warn any future travelers to stay away from Doone's, then took his first muddy steps toward what awaited him next. But before he reached Puzzle's side, he felt a strange heat coming through the bottom of his boot. He shifted his weight to change direction but found his foot stuck to the ground. He tried again, this time pulling harder. But instead of releasing, Beau's foot sunk deeper. More confused than afraid, he tried again only to feel the heat inching up past his ankle.

No, it couldn't be.

Not a sand pit.

Beau tried to scramble onto solid ground, using his one free leg and hands to pull him out. But the more he fought the sand, the harder it pulled him back. He looked for something solid to grab, but the stump was out of reach, and there were no overhanging branches.

This couldn't be!

But it was. He was sinking into a sand pit, with no chance of climbing back out.

Confusion turned into full-out panic as he heard Puzzle whinnying and whining, straining at her tether.

"No!" he begged. "Stay there! Do not come any closer!"

Puzzle's cries filled the air as Beau slowly succumbed to the searing pain, to the pull of the sand, and finally to the dark.

Chapter Thirty-One
Fevered

The journey to Doone's took Hugo and Cressi through forests thick with tangled trees and riddled with pockets of deadly sand. When a rainstorm blew in from the west, Hugo found a small cave for them to wait it out in. Although Cressi tried to sleep, the mounting anticipation of finally finding Beau and Nate along with the pawn jumping in her pocket made sleep hard to find. It was shortly before dawn when they finally emerged from the woods on the edge of a large, open field.

If she didn't know better, Cressi would've mistaken the homestead laying at the far end for the picture of the ideal family farm, a dream left over from a time long ago.

"You'd best get in and out without Doone finding you," Hugo counseled. "When you find the others, you come straight back to us. We'll help you get where you need to go from there."

"Really?" Cressi was more than surprised. "I thought Gerta would never want to see me again."

"If that were true, you wouldn't be here now. Good luck, charmer." And with that Hugo turned and melted back into the woods.

With her bag strapped tightly to her back and her resolve fixed even tighter, Cressi stepped out into the field. The morning sun had not yet risen, giving her time to find a good hiding spot, but it also made her passage treacherous, for the field was riddled with shallow craters and clumps of soil, rocks, and debris. But more than that, the ground reeked of a smell she couldn't put a name to. The feelings of devastation it evoked, however, were crystal clear.

This was nowhere she wanted to be for very long.

She finally made her way to the closest outbuilding—a two-story stone structure—just as the sun began to rise. The spot afforded her a view of the rest of the compound and a convenient corner to hide behind. She was peering out to survey the area when the sound of footsteps sent her back into hiding, waiting for them to move on. But when the sound didn't recede, she cautiously eased forward to get a better look.

That's when she saw him standing there, wobbling on unsteady legs. She knew it was him before she could see his face, for she knew his shadow as well as her own.

Cressi raced out of hiding to his side, catching Nate just

as he was about to pitch forward into the dirt.

"What happened?" she whispered, helping him to the ground.

But Nate had no answer. Though he looked in her direction, his eyes were glazed over, and his skin was electric to the touch.

"You're fevered. You should be in a bed, wrapped up warm," she said. "Not out in the night air."

Nate flinched at the sound of her voice, as if he knew it yet couldn't place it. He licked his dry, cracked lips, trying to form a word.

"Shh," Cressi counseled. "Where can you lie down?"

Nate managed to raise a hand and feebly pointed to the second floor of the stone building.

He wasn't completely lost to the fever yet. "Lean on me. I'll get you there."

All thoughts of her original plan and her own safety vanished as Cressi managed to pull Nate up the stairs into a cozy bedroom. She laid Nate out on the unmade bed and covered him over with the blankets, for the fire in the hearth had burned down to cinders leaving the room colder than the predawn air.

"Why were you outside?" she pressed, yet Nate only mumbled incoherently. "Where's Beau? Why isn't he tending to you?"

"Beau!" Nate spat the word out like a bite of rotten food.

Cressi turned the lamp up and examined Nate, almost hoping to find a wound or festering puncture to explain his condition. But the telltale grayish cast to his skin, the red blotches, and the signs of dehydration confirmed it.

It was the fever.

If Nate had it this bad, what of Beau? Had he already succumbed? Who else had it, and how far had it spread?

No, first things first.

Focus.

If Beau were dead the pawn would have told her.

Fighting to keep her hands steady and her mind still, Cressi pulled her bag off and fished the fever brew out. Gently cradling Nate in her arms, she poured a small measure of the charm into his mouth, but he was so parched he could barely swallow it. It took some doing, but she finally managed to get a fair dose into him, then she laid him back against the pillow and waited for him to pink up.

"You'll feel better soon," she whispered, as much a promise to herself as to him. She hadn't come this far only to lose him or Beau to the fever. She would not let that happen.

"Nate." She gently nudged him. "Where is Beau?"

Nate turned and looked at Cressi, recognition finally sparking in his eyes behind the fever.

"Cressi?"

She smiled, the better choice than crying. "You'll be fine, very soon."

"You charming me?" Nate could barely speak above a whisper.

Cressi shrugged. "I'm trying to."

"He was right," Nate said. "The rat-mucker."

"Who was right about what?" Cressi urged. "Where's Beau? Is he all right? What's happened?"

But it was no good; Nate slipped back into the deep, dark sleep of the very ill.

"Please work fast," she implored the brew.

While Nate slept, Cressi pulled a chair up to his bedside and waited, fighting to stay awake and watchful for the moment the brew would bring him back to full health. Yet no matter how hard she tried, she couldn't stop herself from bobbing and weaving into a restless kind of sleep.

When the rustling began it wasn't loud enough to wake her, though it did infiltrate her dreams, filling her head with visions of bedclothes being tossed off and leaves flying. Then came the scratching at her ankle. A bug? A rodent? Cressi shooed it away without waking.

It was only the telltale clink and clank of bottles being jostled that finally sent Cressi swimming back up to consciousness. Weighed down by exhaustion and her bearings off-balance, it took more than a few moments for her eyes to refocus, to remember where she was. To see him.

He stood right before her, her bag at his feet and several

of her vials open in his hand. He was tall with a thick mop of hair and eyes so blue they nearly glowed. At first glance, he was handsome, smiling, but Cressi quickly saw him for what he really was—a foul and twisted monster.

Judging from the expression on his face as he sniffed at her various brews, he clearly saw Cressi for what she truly was too—a charmer.

Doone corked the vials and dropped them back in her bag. "And here I was about to ride off to find you. The famous Cressi. Crafty was right about you, wasn't he?"

"Crafty?" she repeated. "Who's that?"

But instead of answering, Doone kicked the foot of Nate's bed. "Wake up! Where is he?"

Cressi jumped to her feet and planted herself between Doone and the bed. "He can't answer you—he's got the fever." She spoke with absolute authority, as if there were nothing strange about her being there.

"Serves him right." Doone slipped the straps of Cressi's bag over his shoulders. "Shouldn't have taken what wasn't his."

Choosing to ignore the obvious irony, Cressi smoothed back the fringe of hair plastered to Nate's forehead. "I've already given him something for the fever. He should come around soon."

"We'll leave him to rest then. You and I need to get to know each other better."

As Doone pulled the covers up closer to Nate's face, Cressi

winced at the nauseating funk of fever filling the air.

"I need to stay until he's well," she said, masking her revulsion behind a smile.

"Devoted, aren't you?" Doone ran his hands along his shirtsleeves before clasping them together at his chest. "A worthy attribute. I like it. We'll find Crafty and have him keep an eye. They could use some time together."

"I'll wait for his arrival then." Though half Doone's size, Cressi refused to budge.

It was a dangerous play. She could see the anger sparking inside him, a bonfire on the edge of combusting. He might just as soon cut her down where she stood than let her live another minute. But he needed her, that much was clear. Even though he had her brews strapped to his back, if he was half as smart as he thought he was, he'd know they were useless without her. As long as she didn't overplay her hand, she might be able to run the board.

"All right, charmer," Doone relented. "You wait here. I'll be back shortly, Crafty in tow."

As soon as he'd gone, Cressi peeled back the two blankets covering Nate. She smelled the quilt first. Other than must and a bit of mold, it was without secrets. But one whiff of the wool blanket was all it took to recognize that it was riddled with disease, as if the fever had been woven into the very fibers.

No wonder the charm hadn't yet begun to work.

Were the fire still lit Cressi would've burned the vile thing, but with no other choice she dropped the infested blanket in the farthest corner of the room.

She turned to go back to Nate's side, but something about the blanket was bothering her. Why? There was nothing particularly special about it. Every guard in the Land had been issued the same one. Cressi remembered when the shipment arrived at the Manor, it was right after she'd been put into service. The guards lauded it over the other servants that they'd be warm at night while the others would be left shivering under thin tattered coverings.

New blankets that only the guards received.

The same guards who were falling to the fever.

Cressi burst with hope at the revelation. Not only had she found a cure, but she'd very well found the source of the fever and who was behind it!

A short time later, Nate awoke.

"Is it really you?" he whispered.

"Fully and completely," Cressi said, relief raising goosebumps on her skin.

"You got tired of wiping the heir's chin, did you?" Nate pulled himself up. "Finally realized I've been right all this time. Did you bring any others with you? Pervis?"

"Just me."

"That's all right. We're going to free them. All of them.

Doone asked me to help with the plans. He has these amazing things called grenades. You've got to see them, they're magic!"

Cressi could see the color returning to his cheeks as he spoke. "I can't believe you're here. That rat was actually right about you."

"Who was right about me?"

"No one you need to know," Nate grumbled. "Just a lying ground-snipe who tried to tell me Doone wasn't who I thought he was. He's the one who wasn't who I thought he was. I bet he's not even the cordwainer's apprentice."

So Crafty, the lying ground-snipe, was Beau. Cressi thought about playing the innocent, not letting on the truth. But there was no time for that.

"You're right," she said. "He wasn't who you thought he was."

"I knew it!" Nate crowed. "Wait . . . how do you know?"

"Because . . ." Cressi shifted in her seat. "He's the heir, Nate."

"What?" Nate turned bright red, his lips curling and eyes narrowing. He tried to lever himself out of bed but was still too weak. "Where is he? I'll run him throu—"

"Listen to me. You've got it all wrong." Cressi gently pushed Nate back into his pillows. "I did too. Believe me, he's not his father. He's honest to a fault, and the best chance we have."

Nate recoiled from her touch as if she were a viper winding up to strike. "Do you even hear yourself? Defending that lying sack. Doone is our only future, Cressi!"

"He is not." Cressi fought to hold his gaze. "*We* are. You, me, Beau, the people of this Land. With our support, Beau can make change possible. If I didn't believe it with all I have, I wouldn't have convinced Barger to let me try to bring you both back."

Nate went from red to white and back to red. "You told them I'd run?"

"I had to. It was the only way Barger would let me come find you. Here, I'll show you." Cressi pulled the pawn from her pocket and held it out to Nate. "This pawn tells me where Beau is. It's some kind of connection to him. It's been helping me, guiding me. Look, take it, maybe you'll feel it too."

Nate looked from the pawn back to Cressi. With his hair plastered to his forehead with sweat and his eyes still glazed and bleary, he remained still for a number of very uncomfortable moments.

"You . . . you sold me out for him," he finally said, the words sticking in his throat.

"Never would I." Cressi reached for Nate's forehead. "Are you still fevered?"

Nate shook off her hold as he pulled himself up to sitting. "I'll give you twenty minutes before I tell Doone you've run. That'll give you time to get up into the woods." His voice was cool and even, no emotion at all. "After that you're on your own."

"What's happened to you?" Cressi reached for him again, but he pushed her away, his strength clearly returning.

"I've found what I've been looking for! You've never understood, never saw it." Nate shook his head in pity. "You're just like him, aren't you? Too blind to see the future for what it is."

"*I'm* blind?" Cressi laughed.

"You're on the losing side. A choice that you'll pay for with all you have." Nate drilled each word deep into her core. "Don't say I didn't try to warn you."

If she didn't know better Cressi might've thought Nate had been charmed, but the only magic at play was blind loyalty. And pride. He'd spent his entire life believing one day Doone would save them all. Of course he couldn't see the monster hiding in plain sight. That would mean he'd have to admit everything he'd built his life on was wrong.

Serving Doone was the only thing Nate had ever wanted, maybe it was time to let him be. Leave him to learn the truth for himself.

"I'll take the twenty minutes." Cressi gathered her wrap around her shoulders. "I hope you're still good for your word."

"I'm not the one who ratted out a friend to Barger," Nate shot back. "Now go, before I change my mind!"

Chapter Thirty-Two
The Arrival

Beau fought to throw the dark off, but no matter how hard he tried he couldn't summon the strength to resist its stifling pull.

And yet, even as he was immobilized, gone was the searing pain, the heat, the burn. The ground, which had been so hot, was cooler now. Even the stink of the sand somehow smelled more like jasmine and honey. Shadows and light played against his closed lids, teasing him with the promise of safety waiting for him somewhere above the surface. If only he could reach it.

Then came the sound. A whine? A call?

Puzzle?

He tried to call her, but his tongue lay heavy in his mouth. Trying to piece his thoughts together was like doing one of those riddle games he had when he was young. Nothing fit.

No matter how hard he'd tried, a square peg would never fit inside a round hole.

Unless, as Fledge once suggested, Beau shaved off the sides. Changed the rules.

With that thought, an anger as hot as the sand began to rise from deep inside Beau. No matter how heavy or murky or unyielding the dark, he wasn't ready to stop fighting. Not when there was so much at stake, so many other lives at risk—Cressi, the children of Mastery House, the people of the Land. Let it try to swallow him whole; he wouldn't surrender.

Pushing, pulling, testing, Beau fought to lift his lids. At first all was a blur. Shapes were formless, shadows everywhere. But slowly, slowly the fog began to dissipate. Lines began to come into focus; colors bled in through the gray.

"He's waking," came a voice.

"About time," another replied.

"Beau." The first voice returned. "Can you see me?"

Several more blinks to clear the fog and a face came into view. A halo of brown hair framing heavy-lidded green eyes hovered inches above his own.

Cressi?

Beau stared at the face in front of him. So much about it was familiar, the shape of the nose, the cut of the jaw. And yet if it was Cressi, she wasn't as he'd remembered. This girl's hair was lighter, and she was smaller. More angular.

"Sit him up. Maybe that will help."

Beau felt a pair of strong hands pull him, snapping the world into focus. A rough-hewn cabin. A bed. His right leg wrapped in a linen cloth.

He looked at the girl again. She definitely wasn't Cressi, although she looked similar. But before he could ask who she was, a new face entered the frame. Long braids flanking sun-worn cheeks. It wasn't an old face, but there was nothing youthful about it either. The lines etched into the forehead carried the weight of the world. The eyes had the look of having seen too much.

"Told you," the world-worn woman said. "Get him up and walking."

The girl who wasn't Cressi hesitated. "I think he needs a few minutes to get his bearings."

She tipped a cup of cool, sweet liquid into Beau's mouth, freeing him to unleash a barrage of questions.

"Who are you?" Beau's voice was tender and cracking. "Where am I? What happened? Where's Puzzle?"

The woman grimaced as if his questions were a burden she was too tired to bear. "I'm Gerta, this is Lula, you're here with us. And the horse is fine. She was smart enough to stay out of the sand. Unlike you."

"I didn't go in on purpose," Beau countered. "It was an accident."

Gerta tipped her chin to Lula and retreated to the hearth.

"The brew has done its work. Go now, send him in."

Beau stiffened. Which him? But before his body could respond to the instinct to flee someone new walked into the cabin. Beau checked his eyes and shook his head to make sure he wasn't dreaming.

Fledge!

"Well, you look awful." Fledge laughed as he perched on the bed next to Beau. "And oddly taller. Could you have grown in these few short days?"

"Is that really you?" Beau asked. "How did you . . . Where did you come from?"

"It is absolutely me. I took a detour away from the North Hills as soon as I could. Most of Himself's private reserves have fallen to the fever. I left under the pretense of finding help for them. I stopped at the Lower Middlelands barracks first, then came straight here." Fledge gathered Beau in a hug. "I can't tell you how relieved I am to see you."

Everything Beau had been feeling and seeing and doing since leaving the Manor bubbled up in a great big tangle of emotion. Safe in Fledge's embrace he let himself run the gamut from relief to joy to surprise to gratitude. Then another emotion arose, strong enough to push the others aside.

Bitter resentment.

Beau shoved Fledge away.

"Why couldn't you have just told me what to do?" he shouted. "Where to go. Who to find to save Cressi! Or about

Mastery House! You let me remain oblivious to truth, to all that pain! Why?"

"I wanted to tell you everything, believe me," Fledge vowed. "But I'd promised to wait until the time was right. I didn't think it had come quite yet. I was wrong. I'm sorry."

Beau couldn't decide if he should laugh or cry. "I don't even know what that means."

"It means he was following orders," Gerta grumbled from her perch by the hearth. "He only knew part of the story That's all any of us know. Putting it all together, that's your job."

Beau really wanted to dislike Gerta. She was sharp, cold, and exceedingly blunt. And she certainly seemed to care little for him. But she was also absolutely honest, an attribute that was far too rare in the Land.

"But I didn't, still haven't," Beau said. "You sent me to find my ace, so I went. I thought I figured it out, knew who it was. Thought I was lucky to find him, only to realize that he is exactly the enemy I've been warned about all my life."

"Doone?" Fledge swallowed back a laugh. "You thought *he* was your ace?"

"Don't say it like that." Beau already felt stupid enough. "The way Nate talked about him, I thought he had to be the ace. Since everything else I'd ever been told turned out to be lies, I figured the stories about Doone probably were too. I had nothing to go on."

"You had everything to go on. Why do you think I'd been teaching you Fist all these years?"

"So you had someone to beat at a stupid game?"

Even Gerta cracked a small smile at that.

"Well, sure." Fledge raised a brow. "But more than that. To train you to think strategically. Fist is more than a game, it's an allegory, directions, coded instructions on how to raise a rebellion. Still, it's my fault. I thought I'd have more time with all of you. Cressi especially. I never thought her powers would come in so quickly. I failed us all, and for that I am beyond sorry. But you didn't need me, that's the point, Beau. You found your mage on your own, as you needed to. And your ace—"

"But that's just it! There is no ace! And if I were any kind of Fist player, I'd never have let Barger take her away. What kind of idiot gets their mage captured by the enemy? And now I've wasted so much time trying to get back to her. For all I know Barger already had her executed."

"Executed?" Gerta scoffed. "Who do you think made the brew that healed your burns? Last I saw her she was more than alive."

"You saw her?" Beau pulled himself up. "When? Where is she?"

"Out looking for you," Gerta said. "Hugo took her to Doone's. Left her there before morning light."

"No!" Beau tried to get to his feet, but he was still too

woozy to stand. "She can't go there. He means to use her to gain control of me so he can rule in my stead!"

"Good luck to anyone who tries to use that girl," Gerta quipped.

"It's true," Fledge added. "If Cressi could get around Barger the way she did, she can handle Doone."

"What do you mean 'get around Barger'?" Beau asked.

Fledge told Beau about Anka, that he'd stopped to see her, and all that she'd told him about Cressi's journey to the Bottom. What a strong charmer she'd become in a few short days.

"She's been growing more powerful than I ever thought possible," Fledge said. "She's too smart for Doone to outwit her. You both are."

Beau looked down at his salve-covered legs.

"That's not what I mean," Fledge said. "The bond you share, the connection is powerful. You're like the sides of a triangle, supporting each other, making the others stronger."

"First off, Cressi can barely stand the sight of me. She probably came to find me so she could kill me herself," Beau said. "And second, triangles have three sides, not two."

"Thank you for the math lesson, but I know that." Fledge smiled. "The third side is your ace."

"Well, then we're bound to topple over."

"That's it." Gerta pushed off from her perch, retrieved Beau's boots. "I've heard enough of this. You're healed. Time for you to go. Get back to Doone's, collect your mage and your ace, and go do what you have to do. But me and my people have played our part. It's time you leave here."

"What Gerta means is—" Fledge began when she cut him off.

"Exactly what I said." Gerta dropped Beau's boots on the bed and left the cabin.

"Guess we've overstayed our welcome," Fledge said.

After Fledge helped Beau to get up and dressed, and then made certain he ate and drank his fill, Beau began to feel more like himself.

"So how do we do this?" Beau asked. "Wait until dark, steal Cressi away from there?"

"We?" Fledge repeated. "No, that's for you to do. I need to ride north. Himself and what's left of his regiment are due back at the Manor by morning. I need to try to find a way to turn Torin and his men back before they reach our borders."

Fledge threw this information out as if it were old news, but it hit Beau like a gale-force wind.

"So the rumors are true. My father is truly willing to unleash them on the Land again. How can he do that?"

"Desperation."

Beau pushed back the instinct to look to someone else for help, to follow rather than lead. Instead he pulled himself up, steeling his jaw. "Then we have to stop them."

"I'm working to foil their approach. See if I can't offer them a better deal. We've got some allies in the east that are ready to help, and Gerta's sending some of her best scouts with me. But she's refusing to help you. You're going to have to change that, for even if we foil Himself now and spare the Land Torin's assault, we'll be no better off. The problem is much larger and far older. The pain in the Land will only end when the Manor's rule ends."

"That's what my mother tried to do, wasn't it?" Beau said. "By leaving an heir to both sides."

Fledge looked at once both surprised and pleased. "That's an interesting idea, but no. She was trying to do nothing short of bringing the entire Manor system down from the inside. But she misjudged who her ace was. She was certain it was your father. No one could convince her otherwise. Not even Gerta."

"So who was it?" Beau pressed.

"I have my ideas . . . It doesn't matter anymore. She realized she wasn't the right player. You are. That's why she charmed the pawn, to make certain it led its protectors to each other. She didn't want you to make the same mistakes she did."

"But if I'm the ace, why did you tell me to find myself?"

Fledge looked at Beau with a mixture of love, pity, and amusement. "You are not the ace, Beau. You're the pawn."

"Me?" Beau couldn't decide if he should laugh or cry. "I'm prepared to do whatever it takes to change my father's mind, find a way to work with him. I think I can get him to protect the children from Doone and possibly even free them, but . . . replace him? I don't have that in me. I don't want to rule anyone. He's been right all this time, I'm too much like my mother."

"You've got much of her in you, that's true. You're kind and gentle. You want the best for everyone and are willing to do what it takes. Yet you also have much of Himself. You've been handed two legacies. It's for you to find the way to make them work together." Fledge set the collar of Beau's shirt straight and tipped his chin up. "Go back to Doone's and collect your friends. Play to win."

"Friend," Beau corrected. "Certainly not friends."

Fledge pinned Beau with an all-too-familiar look, the one that said, "We both know you know the right answer."

No.

It couldn't be.

"But he's impulsive, short tempered, and so, so stubborn! He'll do anything for what he thinks is right. He's completely blinded by loyalty and . . ."

Beau sank into the chair. He'd just described the ace.

All this time and it was Nate?

"Why couldn't you have told me before you left?"

"I've had my suspicions. But only the pawn will know for sure," Fledge said. "Though I'm willing to bet my life, yours, and everyone else's on Nate. Besides, even if I had told you, you might not have believed me."

"I barely believe you now."

And yet it made so much sense.

"I've wasted so much time," he sighed.

"There's no such thing when you're searching for the truth." Fledge held the door open, leading the way out. "Come now, we both have work ahead of us. I'll be riding out, but you need to convince Gerta to stop hiding in the shadows and stand with us."

Chapter Thirty-Three
Left to Smolder

L eaving Nate behind and her brews in Doone's possession
was not a choice Cressi would have ever wanted to make,
but it was the only one she had.

She flew down the stairs, determined to find Beau and
get them both out of there, but just as she reached the door
Doone stepped up, blocking her way.

"Our friend is feeling better, I take it. Hungry?" He took
hold of her elbow and steered her to the house. "Of course
you are, you're from the Manor. You've never known any different."

"You find the other boy you were looking for?" Cressi
asked as casually as she could.

"Trout's got him."

While Doone still exuded the same outward confidence,
there was a tension there that she hadn't seen in him before.

An agitation. A wobble that just might show a lie.

Doone led Cressi inside and sat her down at a table piled high with platters of brightly colored fruit, freshly baked bread, and a large, meaty joint of ham. The smells were intoxicating, though the last thing she'd ever do was eat from his table. Yet no sooner had she sat down than the pawn started quaking and quivering. Beau had been here, maybe in this very chair.

"Eat. Don't be shy," Doone said, filling a plate for himself.

"I'm not hungry, thank you," Cressi replied, even as her growling stomach betrayed her.

"I needn't be a charmer to see through that falsity." Doone bit into a bright red berry, letting the juice run down his chin before wiping it with a linen. "My mother was a charmer, you know. I learned at her feet, until she was slaughtered by the Manor. I was about your age. Too young to lose her and old enough to know exactly what I'd lost. What about you? What have you lost that you want found?"

Beau.

"Wait, let me guess." Doone was clearly enjoying himself. "What would the only charmer in the Land want that I can provide. Protection? Certainly. The promise of freedom? Absolutely."

Cressi remained silent.

"But there's really only one thing you want." Doone leaned in close and whispered, "Power."

Cressi fought the urge to laugh. Only people who don't

understand the power of power hunger for it. But Doone misread her silence.

"Good, we have a deal," he said. "But you'll have to prove your worth first. What can you show me?"

"I've already healed Nate," she countered. "That's as good a proof of my powers as any."

"I've not seen him up and about yet. And besides, healing is boring. A talented apothecary could do nearly the same." Doone pulled Cressi's brews out of her bag and uncorked them one by one, taking the time to smell each in succession. "No, I want to see something spectacular. Something that speaks to the depths of your talents. Something like this."

Doone set the truth brew down in front of Cressi.

"I told you, I learned from my mother," Doone replied unprompted. "I can't make charms of my own, but I can smell their properties, know what they can do. This is a very fine truth brew you've made."

There went any chance of charming him.

"The question is, whose truth do I most want to hear?" Doone began rattling off names, none of which Cressi recognized, until he got to the last on his list.

"Crafty. That's who I want to hear from. Trout!" he shouted. "Bring our young cobbler in!"

No more than two, three seconds later, the door flew open, and so did Cressi's heart. But it was Nate, not Beau who came barreling in.

He looked awful. Pale, pasty, and covered in sweat, he had the deadly wool blanket wrapped around his shoulders. "Doone! I figured it out. I have the perfect strategy for storming Mas . . ." Nate let his words trail off as his bleary gaze landed on Cressi.

Silently, they exchanged a dare—she challenging him not tell Doone about Beau, while he defied her not to try and expose Doone as a liar ever again. Eyes locked together, Cressi was certain he'd honor their bond, not betray her or Beau. But then he looked away.

"Crafty is the heir," Nate crowed. "She told me; did she tell you yet?"

He did it, he actually broke their bond.

Cressi girded herself, waiting for Doone to explode. But instead he calmly rose and stepped around behind her chair. She could feel the heat rising as he took hold of her shoulders, his hands a vise.

"We hadn't gotten to that part." Doone's voice remained calm, too calm. "Nate, I need you to get Trout for me. But first, burn that blanket."

"But I'm so cold," Nate countered. "It's the only thing keeping me warm."

"You'll do better without it, I promise. I need my chief strategist healthy."

Nate's ashen complexion brightened. "That's how you think of me?"

"Why wouldn't I?" Doone tightened his hold on Cressi. "Looks like he could use a bit more of your fever brew."

"Of course." Doone let up the pressure just enough for Cressi to lean forward and pour some of her brew into a mug of cider.

Nate dropped the blanket and downed the mug, the haze quickly clearing from his eyes.

"I have the perfect plan!" he exploded with energy as he pulled a scrap of parchment from up his sleeve. "I drew it all out. Not one child will get hurt if we do it right. Then we can return them all to their families after. Those we can't, can live here. There's plenty of room. I've planned that out too. Look, you'll see."

As Doone released his hold on Cressi to retrieve the parchment, she tried to catch Nate's eye. But he was consumed, waiting on Doone's response. Bouncing from one foot to the other, he looked like a five or a six waiting for their turn for a once-a-season swim.

"Does Crafty know you know about him?" Doone asked, letting the parchment flutter to the table.

"Of course not," Nate replied. "I wanted you to know first. So what do you think of my pla—"

"Then why are you still here?" Doone snarled. "Go find him!"

Cressi recognized that expression blooming on Nate's face. It was the same one he'd wear when Matron would shame him in front of all the other children. He was thinking, trying to see how hard he could push back. His mind not quite made up, he was teetering on the edge of uncertainty.

Then Doone barked, "GO!" loud enough to send Nate running out the door.

Watching him go, Cressi could only hope he'd land on the side of what's right. •

"Rehoming the children?" Doone laughed as he tossed the parchment into the hearth. "What good would they be to me then? They're useful only as workers, fighters maybe. What a fool. Although fools, like charmers, have their uses. Depending on what kind they are."

Doone pulled a chair up and planted himself inches from Cressi's face. "There are the smart and the smug. My mother, Rana, was among the very smartest. She understood where her loyalties should lie—the bloodline through which she got her powers. Then there were others, like Annina. Vainglorious power mongers who didn't understand their responsibilities to the Badem, to their people. Which kind are you?"

"I have no interest in power, only fairness." Somehow Cressi managed to remain expressionless. "I'll do all I can to help those who also seek equity for all."

"Then I'm your man!" Doone crowed. "You think anyone with Manor blood in their veins cares for the people of this Land? Never. Besides, your little heir has no power, never will, at least not without me. And you."

She could have played along, pretended like she was on his side, but the charms she'd made wouldn't allow her to lie. Her deceit would be laid plain.

"I'll never see him harmed or used." Cressi spoke slowly, clearly, so he'd hear every word. "Not for the Manor, not for anyone. Especially you."

That was it—she'd pushed him too far. Like a burst of lightning, Doone grabbed her by the neck as he reached for his blade. But the object he pushed in her face wasn't a knife, it was one of her own vials. The one she'd hidden in her boot. The charmer's brew.

"Never say never, charmer." Doone turned the vial of swirling blue-green brew so that it caught the rays of sunshine streaming in through the windows.

Cressi felt the blood drain from her head, leaving it cold and spinning. That was the tug she'd felt when she was asleep at Nate's bedside. A rodent had been pawing at the top of her boot, a tall, blue-eyed rat.

She tried to pull away, but Doone held her too tight as he uncorked the vial with his teeth. As the nauseating fog filled the air Cressi immediately became lightheaded and weak. She could feel her resolve melting away like a spring snow in the sun, her will surrendering itself to Doone.

But just as she was about to succumb fully, the door burst open, startling them both. Doone pulled away, taking the vial with him.

"He's gone!" Nate erupted into the room. "And one of the horse stalls is empty too!"

"Curse the day he was born!" Doone recorked the bottle, tucked it into his pocket, and headed for the door. "Guard her with your life, Nate, your actual life. Understand?"

Nate nodded and locked the door behind Doone. But he didn't advance into the room, instead he just stood there, cautious and watchful.

For her part, Cressi collapsed back into the chair, grateful her mind was once again her own and that Beau had managed to escape. As for Nate, she'd have to wait for his next move.

Finally, after too long a silence, Nate spoke. "What did he put in his pocket?"

"A brew."

"For what?"

"You sure you want to know?" A hesitant nod was Nate's only response, so Cressi continued. "It's a charmer's brew. Only charm that can work on the likes of me."

"To do what?"

"Control me, make me do his bidding."

"But that's because you refused to help the cause of liberation." Even as Nate laid the blame at her feet, the bitter edge in his voice had softened. Nate had softened.

"No," Cressi countered. "It's because I refused to help *him*."

"So you'd rather help Craf . . . the heir become the next Himself than the one person who can take down the Manor?

Who's willing, right now, to go free Mastery House!"

Cressi couldn't help but let a small laugh escape. "He might be planning to free them from Mastery House, but there'd be no freedom for them. They'd go from serving the Manor to serving Doone."

"That's a lie!" Nate fired back. "Those plans I made to free them, he asked for them."

"I'm sure he did. And then he threw them in the fire. See there? They're still smoldering."

"He did not! He . . ." But as Nate pulled his parchment out from among the dying coals, the fire behind his eyes dimmed. "I . . . That can't be true. He's not like that. He's kind and generous. You saw that room he gave us. Why would he . . . ?" Nate stared at his singed plans.

"I suppose you could call him generous," Cressi agreed. "After all, he sent all those brand-new blankets to the guards, masked as a gift for Himself from an admirer in a foreign land. But not without first adding a healthy dose of a deadly disease to kill most of them off. You should ask yourself why he let you keep that blanket up until now."

"He told me to burn it—you heard him," Nate countered, but then he took a step back. "Why are you doing this? Siding with the heir over me! What has he promised you?"

"Nothing. He's made no promises. But unlike Doone, who would go on using the children of Mastery House for his own ends, Beau wants to see them returned home. See that the taxes, the cruelty, our entire awful way of life is changed."

Cressi reached out and laid a hand on Nate's back. He allowed it to linger for a moment before pushing her off, the sadness overwhelmed by a return of his bitterness and rage. "Don't you dare talk to me about the heir! He's no different than Himself. He's a liar and—"

"He doesn't want to be Himself, Nate," Cressi broke in. "If anything, he only wants to be himself and let everyone be as they are too. You must have seen this in him."

Nate started to answer then stopped. He looked lost, heartbroken, as close to tears as she'd ever seen him. He turned away and stared into the fire for several, long minutes before he spoke again.

"He hit me; did you know that?" He was clearly not ready to let it all go.

"I'm sure you deserved it." Cressi joined him by the hearth and brushed his hair out of his eyes as she always did. This time he didn't push her away. "Come with me to find him before Doone can. I promise, together with Beau we have a better chance of doing some good than Doone ever would."

"I don't know." Nate hesitated. "I don't know who to believe anymore."

"Then believe only yourself. You're a born leader. I know it, everyone in Mastery House knew it, and Matron knew it better than anyone. Why do you think she refused to place you? The Manor couldn't afford to have you anywhere but beaten

303

down. You're needed, Nate. I can't promise you won't regret it, but it's the right thing to do."

"The last time someone said that to me, I wound up getting thirteen lashes and a week with quarter water rations for putting a family of possums under Matron's bed."

"Well, you should've known better."

"I never do," Nate said. "Why would I start now?"

Chapter Thirty-Four
Gather Your Army

Beau found Gerta in her cabin finishing up her morning meal. She almost looked at ease sitting there with her hair down and her boots off. But then she took one look at Beau and stiffened.

"I already told Fledge, I have no intention of storming the Manor, nor will I face off against Doone." Gerta waved him off. "Our treaty with him ensures he doesn't bother us and we don't bother him. It took us years to build this haven, and with our veil newly fixed, we'll be safe for a long time to come."

"I'm glad you've found a way to make a life for yourselves." Beau planted himself in the chair opposite Gerta. "Fledge told me how you lost everything and nearly everyone during the last battle for the Bottom. He also told me how angry you were at my mother for marrying my father, that you knew he wasn't her ace but she wouldn't listen. I also know you asked Cressi to help you and she did."

"And?" Gerta was cutting her food into tiny pieces yet eating none of it. Himself used to do something similar, stirring and stirring his tea, a signal his patience was running thin.

"And while you should be protected, not everyone in the Land has a veil. Don't you think that unless everyone is safe, no one is?"

"What do I care about anyone else?" Gerta kept cutting. "I have my family with me, trusted friends, and a few wanderers who found their way to us all who understand what we're doing here."

"What is that exactly?"

"You trying to be clever?" Gerta dropped the pretense of eating and began plaiting her hair—tightly. "We're living. Surviving. Protecting what's ours."

"Funny, that's what my father says too." Beau dropped his voice taking on his father's intonation. "'It's our duty to protect what we've fought so long and hard for.'"

"Comparing me to Himself will win you no favors."

"I don't need you to like me," Beau countered. "But I do need you to help stop Doone from merely replacing Himself. I need you to help me protect the children of Mastery House from him. Reclaim the Land. Restore liberty, choice. Life."

Gerta looked him over as if seeing him with new eyes. "You're not who they say you are."

"I don't know what they say, and I don't care anymore. I just want to do what's right. And you know better than most that even if we manage to keep Doone at bay, or hold off Torin this time, nothing else will change in the Land. Not as long as the Manor rules. You'll still be living in hiding, your safety perched on a precarious deal made with Doone. Just because your prison is more comfortable, doesn't make it any safer. Believe me, I know all about that."

Gerta stopped braiding her hair. "If this is an audition to prove yourself a worthy leader, you can stop. We're not looking to be ruled."

"Hardly," Beau laughed. "Despite my father's wishes, I have never once in my life wanted to rule and that will never change. The Land belongs to those who live in it."

"Then what's your plan, exactly? Who will rule?"

"No one," Beau replied. "Everyone."

Gerta grimaced. "That sounds like pure pandemonium."

"I mean that the different parts of the Land should choose for themselves. Even *The Histories* say that's how it was before the Manor rose. We should go back to that."

"There's no such thing as going back, only forward."

"Or, in your case, standing still." Beau waited for her to reply or throw something at him, but Gerta simply gathered the rest of her hair and began plaiting it into a second braid.

Only once she'd finished did she speak again. "We'll escort you north to the Manor. Don't expect us to fight for you."

"I'm not looking for a battle," Beau replied. "That's not how we'll defeat Doone. And I won't take up arms against my father. We'd never win anyway. Have you seen his elite guard? They're the strongest in the Land, even with half of them sick with fever. But we do need a show of unity, proof that there's another way forward. Besides, as much as I hate to admit it, Doone was right. There are better ways to defeat your opponents than combat."

Gerta let out a heavy sigh. "At least he remembered something of value from his youth."

"What?" Beau was certain he'd misheard her. "Were you his teacher?"

"How old do you think I am?" Gerta growled.

Nothing could tempt Beau to answer that.

"We were raised together, he, Fledge, Anka, and me," Gerta continued. "I thought Fledge told you everything."

"So did I."

"He likes to forget the part about Doone. They were inseparable when they were young, until the rift." Gerta sounded as if she'd just as soon forget it too.

"So will you help me then?" Beau pressed.

"Just as you won't fight your father, I won't fight my own people either." Gerta rose from her chair and pulled on her mossy-green jerkin. "I've already sent out a delegation to convince Doone to abandon his plans, to respect our treaty and you as one of our own."

Her certainty would have once been enough to convince Beau, but he'd since learned to question everything. "And you think your ties with him are strong enough that he'll listen?"

"We'll find out, won't we?"

A short while later, Gerta had her entire camp assembled around the firepit. There must have been at least fifty people—not including the twenty children—and each and every one stood ready to do their part to help get Beau back to the Manor safely. As Gerta laid out her plans, never once did she try to incite fear, condescend, or belittle. To Beau's mind, she was the model of true leadership—a commander who appreciates each member of her company for the talents and abilities they bring to the fight. But as she finished up, Beau realized something was missing in her planning.

"What about finding Cressi and Nate?" Beau pressed. "I won't go without them."

"You entrusted me with a job. Let me do it," Gerta replied as she and her second-in-command, Hugo, led the way out through the veil.

With no other choice, Beau took hold of Puzzle's reins and followed them out. He expected to feel touched by something magical as he passed through the veil, but it felt more like a shiver or a whisper than anything mystical.

Everyday magic.

^ ^ ^

As they traveled through the forest, Beau led Puzzle rather than riding her, knowing that dangerous terrain lay ahead. And yet somehow the Bottom no longer felt quite as perilous. All those sharp edges and pitfalls took on an almost protective feel now, as if the Bottom were an ally one only needed to make peace with. Even the sight of Gerta's scouts appearing as if out of nowhere from among the trees, brush, and rocks was no longer startling. He quickly got used to scouts emerging from behind veils to deliver news and information. Her responses were always the same, a calm nod, a quiet reply, or a thoughtful "Hmmm."

Until the last one came in.

Beau watched as the lines that drew the corners of Gerta's mouth downward deepened, the furrow in her brow widened. A sinking feeling told him to prepare for the worst as she stopped to address the group.

Please, don't let it be Cressi and Nate.

"We have a change of plans," Gerta announced. "Lula, head back and take whoever you need with you to prepare for the arrival of two wounded."

Lula sprang to action, taking two others with her back to the settlement. Among the rest of the party there was no murmuring, no panic, just focused attention waiting for Gerta to continue.

"Hugo, take a team of eight and try to get ahead of Doone. Word is he's riding north to the Manor with Trout and a full load of those infernal grenades in tow. But don't engage him yet. Wait for us."

With just a nod, Hugo peeled off with eight other scouts, disappearing into the forest.

"I don't understand," Beau said. "I thought you had an agreement with him."

"We did," Gerta replied. "But he claims we broke it when we aided your escape from him."

"But you didn't," Beau insisted.

"It doesn't matter. He learned we were harboring you, and that was enough for him to justify attacking my messengers, leaving them for dead along with any peace we've enjoyed."

"How did he find out?"

"We all have our spies, Beau. Some are willing, others are coerced. Either way, information is better than gold down here."

"I'm sorry. I didn't mean for it to go this way."

"Keep your apologies and focus on what we need to do next."

"You're right." Beau pushed aside the rising tide of guilt. "The only thing I need to think about now is getting to Cressi and Nate."

He moved to scramble into his saddle, but Gerta stopped him with a firm hand. "That won't be necessary."

Beau's stomach turned in on itself. "Why not?"

"You'll see soon enough," Gerta replied as she stepped

away to speak with yet another scout.

"No!" Beau insisted, following her. "Enough secrets, enough lies! Tell me right now! Where are they?"

Gerta surrendered a small smile. But rather than dripping with judgment, there was something almost kind as she nodded toward the pathway. "Why don't you ask that pair of wanderers there."

Long before he could see their faces, Beau knew them. It was the way they carried themselves, the cock of his head, the regal thrust of her chin. These weren't just any two wanderers; they were the very wanderers he'd been searching for.

Never before had Beau been happier to see two people who despised him as much as Cressi and Nate did.

Chapter Thirty-Five
United Front

Beau thought he'd know how to handle this moment. That he'd say the exact right thing. He'd tell both Cressi and Nate how sorry he was, how he'd done them both so wrong. But seeing Cressi running toward him now and Nate hanging back, his expression fixed in a glower, Beau was too overwhelmed to do anything but stand there.

Then Cressi hugged him.

In that brief moment when her arms were thrown around his neck, Beau understood what he was feeling was bigger than relief, wider than guilt or regret. It was deeper than sadness, anger, or unbounded joy. It was as if a part of himself had been restored.

Cressi fell back and punched him playfully on the arm.

"You're an idiot," she said. "I hope you know that."

"It's the only thing I do know," Beau said, rubbing his

shoulder. "And I definitely didn't know you could land such a blow."

Cressi raised a brow then opened her palm, revealing the power behind her punch.

"My pawn!" Beau exclaimed as she pressed it into his hand.

"It's happy to be back with you. It's almost like it's purring. You feel that?"

He did. It was warm and comforting, but it was also a reminder of all he'd almost lost.

"I'm so sorry, Cressi, I—" Beau began when she stopped him.

"We're not doing that now. There are too many other things to talk about." Cressi cast a glance behind her where Nate had stopped on the pathway.

With his eyes downcast and a scowl planted on his face, Nate looked no more approachable than a pacing panther.

"I'm not apologizing," Beau whispered. "He hit me."

"And you hit him back."

"He deserved it!"

"He wouldn't be Nate otherwise."

Beau looked over at Nate just as he was sneaking a look up at Beau. They were sizing each other up like a couple of predators, each waiting for the other to pounce. Or to yield.

How is it possible to both despise and miss someone at the same time?

"You don't have to like each other," Cressi announced,

"but you do have to make your peace."

Judging by the look on Nate's face, there was no peace to be had.

"You lied to me," he snarled.

"I did," Beau agreed. "I thought if you knew who I was you'd run me through with your blade."

Nate shrugged. "I probably would've."

"Nate!" Cressi scolded.

"No, it's fine," Beau said. "It's honest. Which is more than I was. I hid the truth from him, just as it's been hidden from me my whole life. It wasn't right."

"Yeah, well, you can't trust anyone, can you?" Nate clearly wasn't ready to let it go yet, and Beau wasn't about to push him. He was here and that was enough.

"Can we move this reunion along?" Gerta called. Her usual gruff impatience had returned, although there might have been a tiny hitch of relief hiding in the back of her throat.

The three walked on in silence, Beau and Cressi side by side, Nate still maintaining his distance. And even though she'd told him not to, Beau couldn't hold back all the things he wanted to say to her.

"I need to tell you, you were right about me, about everything," Beau began. "I should have listened to you, but I didn't know how to, I didn't understand any of it. I don't even understand it now, but I do know I have to go stand up to my father, demand he put an end to Mastery House, return the children to their families. Ensure everyone in the Land has food to eat and homes to live in. Lives of meaning. But I already put you through way too much. You both should go back to Gerta's settlement. Between my father and Doone and Torin, you won't be safe anywhere else."

Cressi gave Beau a knowing look, the same one she'd hit him with when they first met. "I didn't come to find you only to make sure you were safe. I came to help you do what you need to do. We're going with you. You need us."

"No, it's—" Beau began.

"Not really your choice." Cressi took the pawn from Beau and placed it in Nate's hand, watching with satisfaction as he jumped with recognition.

"I guess none of us have a choice, do we?" Nate muttered.

As the party traveled north, Cressi told Beau how she and Nate managed to escape Doone's and how they met two of Gerta's scouts in the woods who were on the way to rescue them.

"They didn't seem pleased to be spared the heroics," Cressi laughed. "So we let them think we needed them to lead us back to you. But really, it was the pawn. The closer we got, the more it jumped. It was almost making me woozy with the heat."

Even though Fledge and Gerta had already told Beau most of what Cressi had gone through since leaving the Manor, he asked her to tell him herself. Hearing her voice, her story, calmed him and energized him too.

When she'd finished, Beau couldn't help but laugh. "I wonder how Barger would feel knowing he and Doone both hatched the same plot against me?"

"I'm sure they'd both be flattered," Cressi said. "Thinking like the enemy and all that."

"Well, too bad for them," Beau said. "No one is going to use me."

"As it should be." Cressi hooked one arm through Beau's and the other through Nate's. "Now, I don't care how you do it, but you two are going to have to forgive each other before we get back to the Manor. We'll never make it if you don't."

Nate scoffed and kicked at the ground. Clearly it was up to Beau to break the deadlock.

"I'm sorry I didn't know it was you," he said. "It's just that the way you talked about Doone I thought it had to be him. I should've known it was you. What a pillock, right?"

"I don't know." Nate gave a begrudging shrug. "I would've thought it was Doone too."

"Then you're both pillocks," Cressi said. "All right, so now that's out of the way, we can get on to the barracks."

That feeling of warm comfort abandoned Beau, leaving him chilled to the bone. "Why would we go there?"

"There's an entire battalion of guards at the barracks in the Lower Middlelands," Cressi explained. "I left a brew to heal them, but if they've kept covering themselves over with Doone's blankets, they won't have healed."

"Wait, your grand plan is to heal a bunch of guards?" Nate interrupted. "They'll escort us back to the Manor all right—in shackles!"

"I've thought well past that," Cressi said. "I also left a loyalty brew. If Keb and Boz are any indication, it works like a . . . well, like a charm. They'll help us."

"Ooh." Nate lit up with a wide grin. "I know exactly how to use them to our best advantage too."

"Hold up." Beau stopped, loosening his hold on Puzzle's reins, leaving her room to feed on some nearby moss. "We're not going to use other people like Doone and Barger do. We're not looking to inflict harm, not even on those who would rather see us dead. We'll fix this ourselves and without starting a war."

"We're already in a war," Nate said.

"And we can't simply walk into the Manor and expect Himself to greet you with open arms," Cressi added. "The loyalty brew will do them no harm. Once it wears off, they'll be free to choose for themselves. Although I warrant they'll not want to return to the days of Manor rule. In the meantime we have to be prepared, ready for anything."

Cressi had been right all along, but Beau really hoped this might be the one time she'd be wrong.

^∨^

Soon after they'd reached the border between the Bottom and the Lower Middlelands, one of Gerta's scouts arrived with the news that the two messengers Doone had attacked were doing well under Lula's care. They would both make a full recovery.

"She's a charmer, you know," Cressi said. "Lula's got the gift."

"If she's a charmer and you're a charmer, how many more are there?" Nate asked.

Cressi shrugged. "There's no knowing until it's safe to be one again. But the art is not nearly as dead as the Manor would like people to think."

A short while later, Gerta brought the small company to a halt at the mouth of the tunnel leading into the barracks.

"My scouts tell me it's safe to go in," she announced. "But I think it best if you three proceed alone. No sense in over-whelming Anka."

After assuring Gerta they'd be safe, swift, and above all, successful, Cressi led the boys to the barracks' kitchen where Anka was awaiting their arrival.

Anka hugged each of them as if they were her own long-lost children before sending Cressi and Nate off with a large cauldron of soup to begin healing and making loyal champions out of the guards.

"But Beau," she added, "if you'd stay with me for a moment, I have something for you."

The thought of being separated from Cressi and Nate,

even by a few rooms, raised a sweat on Beau's brow. He didn't want to do it; it felt wrong in every possible way. Only after Cressi assured him that she and Nate would be more than safe did Beau agree.

Anka locked the door, then pulled a small salt box down from a high shelf. It was a plain, dusty old thing, but she set it down on the table before Beau like it was cast out of gold.

"Open it."

Before the lid was even all the way off, Beau smelled it. Her. That heady mix of apples and lily that permeated everything in his mother's apartments. He'd once taken a small hand linen from her rooms that carried the scent and tucked it under his pillow. The sweet, earthy smell became a calming balm, lulling him to sleep. But one night after Beau had crawled into bed, he found it gone. The next day her apartments were shuttered, leaving the Fist set he'd found in her wardrobe the only tangible reminder of her.

Whatever else the box contained, Beau was sure it couldn't be as precious as the chance to breathe in her perfume once again.

But he was wrong, for the box revealed two small canvases wrapped in scraps of dark green velvet. One canvas was a portrait of a young man, handsome with an open smile. Beau recognized parts of the face in his own, but otherwise the subject was a stranger. The man appeared in the second painting as well. There he stood at ease, his hand lovingly draped on the shoulder of a woman cradling a tiny infant. Beau had never seen the woman before either, but he knew her. He knew that look in her eye. He'd seen it every time the woman in the Bottom looked at her daughter.

"Are these my . . . parents?" Beau looked up to ask Anka, but she was gone, the back door hanging open in her wake.

Beau stared at the paintings, torn between tears and fury. They looked so happy. Himself was a different man. There was nothing in the images to foreshadow all the pain and anger to come.

Why would anyone want Beau to have this? So he knew all he was missing in life? Beau dropped the paintings on the table like a pair of red-hot coals just as Cressi appeared at the back door.

"Can you come outside?" she asked. "There's something you need to see."

Grateful for the distraction, Beau started to follow her out then doubled back to slip the pair of small canvases into his pocket instead.

As torn up as the paintings made him feel, he wasn't ready to let them go yet.

Cressi led Beau outside through the large kitchen garden, where off in the back corner Keb and Boz were following Anka around like calves after their mother.

"That's what you wanted to show me?" Beau asked.

"It's not, although it is a satisfying sight," Cressi laughed. "This way."

They continued on through the garden and around to the front of the barracks.

At first, Beau thought there was a stand of trees or pillars planted in the middle of the drive, but then he realized there was a constant, orderly movement. As he got closer his hands began to shake, and his blood began to quiver. It was Nate leading an entire column of guards through a drill in the middle of the drive.

Cressi had done exactly as she'd promised—she'd delivered Beau his own private army.

Now it was up to him to lead them all safely to freedom.

Chapter Thirty-Six
A Battle of Wills

By afternoon of the next day, the boy who'd never wanted to lead anyone found himself leading a company of some eighty souls onto the Manor lands. Cloaked by a charm, Beau guided the brigade—which included forty of Gerta's fellows, thirty-three guards from the Lower Middlelands, twenty horses, and thirteen wagons—through the peddler's gate, up the hill, and on to the outer pasturelands.

How strange it was to be returning to the Manor along the same route he had taken out. Except of course, nothing was the same. A pall of silence hung over the estate. The gatehouse and fields stood empty, not a single guard or worker in sight. Even the Manor looked different to Beau now. Smaller, diminished. The seven turrets that had stood glowering over the land for generations had somehow been blunted, robbing them of their power to intimidate.

Beau brought the company to a halt and watched as they all stepped out from behind the veils they'd been traveling under. All these people assembled in a common cause was an inspiration, their bravery bolstering his own. They had a plan—a good one—designed by Nate to protect the children of Mastery House from Doone, and they were ready to employ it. But confronting Himself, convincing him to send Torin back and liberate the people of the Land was Beau's burden to bear alone.

"Listen, I've been saying the whole time, I don't like it," Nate said as he, Cressi, and Gerta stepped up to Beau's side. "I say we send a few guards with you and Cressi."

"No." Beau was adamant. "We stick to our plans. The guards will wait behind the veil in the hedgerow until you, Gerta, and the others have gotten the children out of Mastery House. We need all the guards there to load them into the wagons and get them clear of here as fast as they can."

"I wish I'd known that Cressi and I had cut our path in the hedgerow right through one of those veils," Nate said. "The things I could have gotten away with!"

Gerta raised an eyebrow. "And that's exactly why we made sure you didn't know."

She'd been impressed with the strategy Nate devised and had asked him to join her ranks once this was all over. But Nate refused, saying, "I'm not looking to follow anyone anymore."

"Once you've gotten all the children out and secreted away," Beau continued, "send a scout to get word to me so I know everyone is safe."

"Wish you'd do the same," Nate said. "I can't be worrying about you, you know."

Try as he might to come off calm, confident, even cocky, Nate couldn't mask his emotions. Neither could Beau. Before Nate could try to dodge the attempt, Beau gathered him in a hug.

"Be smart," Beau said.

"Be bold," Nate countered.

"And crafty," Cressi added, throwing her arms around them both.

A shiver ran through Beau, but it was borne of anticipation, not foreboding.

"Then we're ready," Beau said, breaking the embrace. "Aren't we?"

"I've been ready my whole life," Nate said.

At Beau's command, the guards moved off to take up their position while Nate, Gerta, and her scouts took off toward Mastery House.

Beau and Cressi entered the Manor through the kitchen yard and continued down into the servants' hallway. They'd prepared a story in case they ran into anyone, but the halls were as empty as the yards had been.

Cressi sniffed the air as they passed all the empty work-rooms. "It's the fever. Servants must've been taking the blankets for themselves."

Beau shivered at the thought. "Imagine being so desperate for warmth to be driven to steal from the dead."

"I've plenty of the fever brew. We'll tend to all of them soon enough." Cressi patted the bag slung over her shoulders.

They continued on in silence until they reached the servants' entrance to Barger's office.

"This is it," Beau said. "Are you ready?"

"I am." Cressi nodded. "And so are you. Now go."

While Cressi crept up the stairs to Barger's office, Beau raced up to the first floor. He'd always hated this part of the Manor. The entire hall was done up in gold fittings and marble details, and heavily armed guards were usually posted outside every door, footmen stationed at every corner. But now there was no one. The Manor was empty, a thunderous silence echoing through the halls.

It was only when Beau approached the mahogany door inlaid with golden scrollwork that he heard the first signs of life—that all-too-familiar rhythmic clicking of heels striking marble.

With one deep breath for courage, Beau eased the door open.

He thought he knew what to expect as he stepped inside, but the library was in complete disarray. Books lay strewn about the floor, chairs upholstered in the finest silks and brocades had been thrown aside, many twisted and broken. Paintings and ceremonial weapons, the pride of Himself's collections, sat crooked on the walls, many hanging as if by a thread. Yet the strangest thing of all was the large fire roaring in the hearth, filling the air with a stifling heat as if fed by the very chaos in the room. This was not the frigid chamber of command and control Beau had always known as his father's library. Nor was the man at the far end of the room, his folded hands pressing down upon his bowed head, anyone that resembled Himself.

"Put the tray down, touch nothing, and leave," Himself growled. He was pale and drawn. Thin. Almost fragile. Had he always looked that tired? Old?

"You needn't worry," Beau said, his voice clear and strong. "I don't have the fever."

"Everyone has the fever," Himself muttered. "Everyone."

Beau stepped farther into the room.

He'd always felt so small in here, dwarfed by the furnishings, tapestries, his father's anger. Yet now he planted himself in the center of the room, as sturdy as a hundred-year-old oak.

"Father, it's me," he said. "Beau."

Himself raised his head, squinting at Beau as if trying to remember him from a life long forgotten.

"Have you grown? Why do you look different?" Himself

spoke as if it were a betrayal, a mockery of his power. "Why are you not in your apartments? Barger assured me you were safely locked inside, fever-free."

"What else has Barger told you?" Beau challenged.

"Get back to your apartments and do not leave until you are instructed," Himself ordered.

"I haven't been there for days." Beau spoke boldly, confidently, even as his heart was racing inside. "I've come to tell you some things and demand others. You need to know—"

"You have nothing to tell me. Get out of my sight!" Himself picked up a vase and threw it at Beau.

But Beau easily dodged the porcelain projectile, letting it shatter at his feet. "I can tell you I know the cause of the fever and how to cure it."

"What are you talking about?" Himself snarled. "There is no cure for a charmer's curse."

"It's not a curse," Beau said. "The blankets that you received as a gift from over the seas, the very ones you distributed to guards throughout the Land, are what's making people sick. Your so-called foreign admirer was Doone. But there is a cure. I've seen it work. It healed the entire battalion of Lower Middlelands guards."

"Lower Middlelands guards?" Himself's mouth puckered as if he'd bitten into bitter fruit. "That battalion couldn't fight their way out of a pig barn. They're the weakest of the weak, a waste of food. Why do you think they're posted there?"

"They are neither weak nor useless. They are strong and assembled here at the Manor."

"Send them back!" Himself gestured wildly. "Or put them to work in the fields. I have no need of them. Torin will be arriving by nightfall. His army will see that order is restored. Properly."

Beau fixed his stance. This was his moment.

"Call him off," he said. "Break your pact or pay him off, but you cannot set him loose on the Land again. He'll kill countless innocents, just as he did before."

"As he should! Clear the scourge of the disloyal, the weak, the useless!"

Once Himself's rage would have sent Beau scurrying for the solace of his apartments or the relief of Fledge's comforting words. Now his words rang as empty as the halls of the Manor.

"None of this is necessary," Beau calmly countered. "We've found the cause of the fever, and we've a charmer who has a cure."

"A charmer?" Himself looked at Beau almost as if he were seeing him with new eyes. "Where? Bring them to me. Now!"

"Not until you vow to keep her and all those like her safe, to call off—"

"Who do you think you are, boy?" Himself seethed.

"I'm the person with the answers and solutions," Beau said. "And I haven't finished with my demands. Call off Torin's approach, set the children of Mastery House free, and put an end to that terrible place. Stop the exorbitant taxes and all the other cruelties the Manor imposes on the people of the Land."

Himself started to reply, then stopped. Beau couldn't tell if he was about to laugh or explode as he rose to his full height. "Well, look at you, finally playing the role of the worthy heir. Except you still understand nothing of how the Land works. 'Free the people,' you say? How can you have any of my blood flowing through your feeble veins? How can you—"

"I've got her, the charmer!" Barger shouted as he rushed into the library, Cressi in tow. "She's confessed everything to me. She's . . . What are you doing here, boy? You're supposed to be in your apartments. She said she'd locked you back in . . ."

"In my apartments," Beau repeated. "That's what we planned for her to say. But as you well know, it's been days since I was last there. That's why you sent Cressi to find me."

"That's absurd." Barger tightened his grip on Cressi. "He's deluded. He's lying."

Barger looked to Himself like a puppy waiting to be rewarded, but Beau's father turned away in disgust.

"Release her." Himself waved Barger off.

"Sir—" Barger began.

"I'd cut you down right now if you weren't one of the last left standing. You have one chance to make yourself useful.

Go prepare for Torin's arrival or I'll feed you to his army myself!" Himself's order rang through the room like a bell.

Barger tried to fight it, but Himself shriveled him with a look. "Go."

Barger shoved Cressi toward Beau, then turned to stalk out, a warning he'd have his revenge.

But Beau knew better. Barger's days were over.

"Young, aren't you?" Himself smoothed out the wrinkles on his coat as he looked Cressi over. "I knew a charmer once. Thought we'd change the Land together."

"We can do that now." Cressi lifted her chin, matching his stance.

Himself laughed, his power renewed. "You're as stupid as he is, aren't you? I'd sooner use you to extend my own life and double the length of my reign than let this boy rule with his ridiculous notions of peace and equality. So noble, so naive."

"Much as you were once," Cressi replied. "Until you let others poison you with their lies. But you still have that in you. Why else would you have continued to protect Fledge, Anka, and the others all these years?"

"You know nothing!" Himself raged. In one smooth move he reached up and pulled a ceremonial sword from the wall. He lunged at Cressi, missing her by a hair's length. She jumped back, forcing him to reset his balance before trying again. In that split moment, Beau grabbed up a broken chair and hurled it toward his father. The chair caught Himself at

331

the shoulder, sending him faltering backward.

"Run!" Beau shouted.

He turned and raced for the exit, assuming Cressi was behind him, but when he reached the door, he saw her dashing in the other direction—straight for Himself.

"What are you doing?!" Beau tried to catch her, but she pulled away just as Himself got back to his feet.

"Too stupid to even try to survive." Himself fixed his grip on the sword.

Beau ran to put himself between his father and Cressi, but Himself easily threw him off, sending Beau flying over a broken settee.

While Beau scrambled to find his feet, Himself closed in on Cressi, his sword cutting the air between them. Beau saw Cressi dodge the blow, then throw something into the fire. With a snap and pop of shattering glass, thick, yellow smoke began pouring out of the hearth, sending both Beau and Himself reeling back, coughing and gagging.

Lungs too heavy to breathe, his head woozy and suddenly filled with strange memories of a time long ago, Beau buried his face in his elbow. He tried to push on but couldn't tell reality from the pictures playing before his eyes. He saw a room, much like this one, only warmer, softer. Filled with light and laughter. A place for a family perched on the edge of a new life. Faces, like the ones in the paintings, taunted him with all he never had.

He could feel himself slipping away, drawn into the dream, unable to stop it when a hand grabbed him.

It was her; he knew it without seeing.

Their hands intertwined, Cressi and Beau charged out of the study and went racing for the door toward freedom. They'd just cleared the marble verandah, clean air filling Beau's lungs, when a loud explosion rocked the ground underneath their feet.

Beau caught himself midstumble and moved to race on when he saw it—a cloud of smoke, debris, and destruction raining down over the hedgerow.

His feet unable to move, his mind unwilling to believe, Beau cleared his eyes, hoping it was another vision, an illusion. But then the smell of smoke and the sounds of screams filled the air. This was no dream, it was nightmare.

Mastery House had been blown to pieces.

Chapter Thirty-Seven
All Fall Down

Beau raced toward the hedgerow, the faces of the children—
Bea, Rory, and all the others—the only thing he could see.
He'd nearly made it through the laundry yard when another
blast exploded from the south side. Undaunted, he tried to
keep going through the storm of dirt and debris, but Cressi
pulled him to the ground, shouting to cover his head. Ears
numbed by the blast, he waited just long enough for the shower
of destruction to stop before racing on.

"This way!" Cressi called as she headed for the veiled passageway in the hedgerow.

Beau barreled through and made to head straight into the
rubble, but Cressi pulled him up short, stopping to assess the
damage. Smoke was pouring out the back side of the building
while the east end was nothing more than a pile of rubble. A
line of Gerta's scouts were streaming out the front door of

Mastery House carrying children of all ages.

"How many more are inside?" Beau called to two scouts racing past with children in tow.

"We don't know!" one answered. "There might still be a few upstairs, maybe none!"

"Just get those you can to the guards and the wagons!" Cressi ordered. "We'll do another sweep through to make sure."

Beau darted for the door, but Cressi pushed past. "Follow me. I know the way."

Cressi slowed them to a walk as they made their way down the dark and ash-filled hallway toward the stairs. But any hopes of reaching the second floor were quickly dashed. The stairwell was leaning precariously and looked as if it would collapse any moment.

"There's another way," Cressi said. "Through Matron's rooms."

Carefully picking her way past debris and around gaping holes in the floor, Cressi led Beau around to another dark and narrow corridor. Beau fought to remain focused on putting one foot in front of the other—for if he let any other thoughts in, he'd ignite in an explosion of his own.

When they reached the end of the hall, Cressi threw open the door. But rather than exposing Matron's fine set of rooms, they came face-to-face with a gaping hole blown into the side of the building. Velvet curtains flapped in the breeze, overhanging a window that was no longer there, while bricks and mortar lay scattered, covering the fine furnishings.

The outside wall had been decimated, but the inside wall was still intact, along with the stairwell.

"Some of them won't trust anyone but me or Nate, not even Gerta and her scouts," Cressi said as she headed for the stairs. "You check outside. If you find anyone shout for me."

Beau waited until he heard her footsteps arrive safely overhead before climbing over the rubble to the outside. He moved carefully through the ruins, searching, hoping to find someone still alive. Bea's sweet face, Rory's sharp elbow teased at his memory, but he found no one, living nor dead. Choosing to take it as a good sign, he headed for the side yard, but just as he was about to round the corner of the building the sound of shuffling feet and the clatter of metal on metal hit his ears.

"I told you to guard her with your actual life, traitor," Doone jeered.

"Better a traitor than a fraud," Nate taunted in return.

Beau reached for the awl he'd taken from Doone's, but it was too small to be useful now. Desperate for something, anything, he grabbed a large fallen tree branch. After testing the weight in his hands, Beau raced around the corner just in time to see Doone, armed with both dagger and cutlass, lunging at Nate.

Quick as ever, Nate jumped back, forcing Doone to miss his mark.

Beau pressed himself back against what remained of the corner of Mastery House and peered out just far enough for Nate to spot him. In that flash of a moment their eyes met, and they silently agreed on a plan.

"You're not very quick, are you?" Nate taunted as he raced atop a pile of rubble.

Doone followed fast on his heels, but not before Nate started firing broken bricks at Doone, forcing him to duck.

The time was now.

Beau cocked the branch over his shoulder and raced into the fray aiming for the back of Doone's head. But the moment he got within striking distance, Doone spun on him. His pursuit of Nate quickly abandoned, Doone lunged for Beau. But Beau was ready. Swinging the branch wildly, he held Doone off just out of reach as Nate scrambled down from his perch atop the ruins. His blade grasped tight, Nate came tearing at Doone's back.

But before Nate could get close enough, Doone turned and threw his dagger.

Time stopped; the very air froze as Beau watched Doone's blade hit Nate in the thigh. As if in slow motion, Nate's face lit up in a laugh only to melt slowly into a cry of anguish as he collapsed to the ground.

The sound that escaped Beau's mouth then was like nothing he'd ever made before—it was a cry, a roar, loud and fierce enough to startle even the deadliest beast. Without another thought he went tearing toward Doone, brandishing the tree limb like a saber. Back and back he forced Doone into a corner. His moment had come. Beau pulled the branch back, primed and ready to land a crushing blow. Then one misstep on a pile of rubble and he lost his footing. Fight as he might he couldn't keep from landing hard on broken glass and bricks.

Throwing off the pain, Beau scrambled to get back up. But Doone was right there, the point of his cutlass inches from Beau's heart.

"I knew threatening Mastery House would flush you out," Doone crowed.

"That wasn't very hard to guess." Beau gasped against the pressure of the blade. "But the real problem is, how do you plan to force me to do your bidding?"

"I have a charmer," Doone said. "Yours."

"Really? Are you certain you—" Beau began when the sound of glass breaking underfoot announced a new arrival.

"Absolutely certain," Doone said, his eyes lit up with delight.

He pulled his blade back just enough so that Beau could turn his head and see what Doone was seeing—Cressi stepping out through the blasted wall, walking slowly and calmly.

Too calmly.

Beau started to call her name, to warn her away, when Trout appeared behind her, the tip of his sword pressed to her back. Beau lunged for her, but Doone caught him just as

Trout stopped dead in his tracks.

"Why are you stopping, you idiot? Bring her here!" Doone shouted as the strangest look bloomed on Trout's face. And that's when Beau saw it; the point of a sword emerging through the front of his bloated belly. With a sigh and soft cry Trout collapsed in a pile just as another figure darted out from amidst the ruins.

Moving with the speed and grace of a hawk on the hunt, Himself pulled his sword from Trout's back with one hand and grabbed Cressi with the other.

Pinned to the ground by Doone's blade, Beau screamed for him to release her, but it was too late. Himself shoved Cressi through the gaping hole back inside. Beau watched helplessly as her arms pinwheeled to try and stop herself from falling. But it was no use. Cressi lost her footing and stumbled forward, her head slamming against an overturned table.

Ignited by rage, Beau grabbed the closest thing at hand, a large brick, and threw it at Doone's head. The brick missed, but Doone faltered long enough for Beau to scrabble away. He went running for Cressi's side, but before he could reach her, Doone grabbed him by the neck, spun him around, and landed his fist straight into Beau's nose.

As Beau's neck snapped back, daylight turned to black, filling his mouth with the taste of copper and grass. He tried to fight through the pain, through the haze. But it was too much. The world around him was spinning too fast. Beau's stomach came up to meet his throat as he staggered and crumbled to the ground.

The sounds of shouting and the *shush*ing of swords slicing through the air teased at his mind. Somewhere he heard Cressi's voice, either real or imagined, urging him to wake up, to fight back. Slowly, painfully, as if crawling through mud, Beau clawed his way back to the world. One eye opened, then the other, looking for which of the two villains—Doone or his father—would have their blade to his throat now.

But no one was there.

As Beau scrambled back to his feet he realized Doone and Himself were going at it, their swords dancing through the air, each trying to gut the other.

Squinting through the pulsing pain, Beau found Cressi in the blown-out remains of Matron's salon exactly where she'd fallen—still. Lifeless.

"Please, please," he whispered, pleading for her to be alive. He waited motionless, hope trying to ignite until at last he spotted it. Though shallow and ragged, her chest was rising and falling.

Beau was struggling to pick her up and carry her away when one of Gerta's scouts emerged from down the darkened hallway and scooped Cressi from his arms.

"This way," the scout whispered, beckoning Beau as he melted back into the corridor. Beau started to follow when he was pulled up short by a clawlike grip.

"You don't get it," Doone cooed as he locked his arm around Beau's neck. "You are mine."

Beau was fighting to push him off with all he had when Himself came hurtling toward them through the blown-out wall.

"Run!" Himself commanded as he threw his weight into Doone, knocking Beau free.

All that happened next passed in a blur that Beau would only be able to fully reconstruct after many days.

While Beau sprang to escape, Doone swept his cutlass through the air. Beau saw Himself jump back, his face lit up in surprise, at the very same moment as Gerta and a swarm of her scouts appeared. Shouts and orders filled the air as the scouts brandished their blades, all descending on Doone. Beau had nearly made it outside when he saw Himself stumble and fall.

"Get up!" Beau shouted, but Himself only smiled and raising a hand, reached out through the chaos for his son.

Without another thought, Beau rushed to his side. He tried to pull Himself to his feet, but that's when he saw it—a river of crimson seeping through his father's velvet cloak. He'd been struck straight through the chest.

"Lean on me," Beau counseled. "I'll get you help."

"It'll heal," Himself said.

"We have to go, get out of here," Beau pushed.

"I think your friends have us covered." Himself tipped his

chin, forcing Beau to look behind him.

Gerta had Doone pinned down, her scouts surrounding him on every side.

"I didn't understand. Didn't know why you came out here," Beau began, his words catching in his throat. "I thought you came to . . . to—"

"Kill you," Himself said. "Collect your charmer?"

Beau nodded.

"I would have," Himself said. "But your charmer . . . Whatever she threw into the fire, it showed me what I'd buried long ago. What I forced myself to forget. I saw her as if she were standing right there."

"Saw who?" Beau pressed.

"Your mother."

He'd seen her too. Those images of happiness that had filled his head—his parents standing in the library, Beau as an infant cradled between them—weren't regrets of a life he never knew. Nor were they just echoes of the paintings. They were memory. Truth.

Beau tried to prop his father up, but Himself was growing heavier, stiller by the moment.

"She loved you," Himself said. "Loved me."

"I know," Beau whispered.

"I didn't." Himself paused to swallow, to find more strength. "I couldn't let myself. I listened to the wrong people. Forgot who I was, who I could have been. Who I wanted to be."

Himself took Beau's hand. He was so cold, Beau tried to will some warmth into him.

"Don't forget yourself." Himself's voice was nothing more than a whisper now.

"I won't," Beau vowed. "But you'll help me remember. Remind me, tell me. Right?"

Himself sank back against Beau. Where he'd been so heavy moments earlier, now he was light. Too light.

"Right?" Beau repeated, desperation bleeding through. "Right?"

Yet the only answer Himself gave was the thinnest smile followed by a sigh, a whisper of breath.

Chapter Thirty-Eight
After

Beau sat at the desk, staring out the window, wondering when the first snows would fall. He should have been writing—finishing what he started. But he just couldn't do it.

It wasn't a matter of finding the right words. Those would come, they always did. Nor was it some deeply buried wish for the work to be ongoing, for his task to never end. All he'd wanted since he began was to get to the end. To put down the final period.

The problem was, he was beginning to doubt there ever could be such a thing.

When Beau set out to rewrite *The Histories*, it seemed a clear and straightforward task. All he had to do was tell the truth, chronicle events as they'd really happened. And for a long time, he thought he was succeeding. He faithfully spoke with people all over the Land to hear their perspectives, to collect their stories. He worked hard to reconcile conflicting accounts. He thought he'd be able to weave it all together into a kind of tapestry of truths so that future generations could know exactly how and why the Manor had fallen. And how to prevent it from ever rising again.

Yet the deeper he dove, the murkier it all became.

Not even Cressi and Nate always agreed with Beau's memory of how things happened. Facts, it seemed, were always colored by point of view. And that's why he was dreading finishing the work. No matter how clear and thorough he tried to be, he'd never be able to control how readers perceived the tale he was unwinding. Even after he was long dead, history would keep rewriting the story. Time distorts all truths.

Still, it hadn't kept him from trying. Until now.

Maybe it was just the day weighing especially heavy on him. Cressi had told him to take some time. He had enough on his mind without trying to finish the book too. He thought the distraction would do him good.

Yet once again, and as always, Cressi was right.

Beau wiped the nib of his pen clean and blotted the still-wet ink on the page, allowing himself to sink into the dread of the news they were awaiting.

It was possible the rumors were wrong, gossip. But his gut, and Cressi's dreams, warned him away from optimism.

Beau banked the fire in the hearth and headed for the door, stopping as he always did to look at the two paintings his mother had left him. It had become a kind of ritual, a way to say hello every time he entered the room and goodbye when he left. It was silly, he knew that, but it always made him feel loved and gave him strength.

Beau stepped out into the corridor to find Cressi waiting for him.

"She's coming," she said. "Are you ready?"

"As much as I'll ever be."

"Where's your—"

"I left it downstairs." Beau filled in the thought. "We'll get it on the way. How is he today?"

"Faring very well. I tried a new brew and it gave him more relief. I think this one will do it."

"Good. I can't bear to see him in pain."

"Me neither," Cressi agreed.

They continued the rest of the way down to the first floor in silence. But as soon as they landed in the marble entryway it was hard not to get caught up in the lively mood.

Morning lessons had just ended, and the halls were filled with children racing outside to play, but Bea stopped as she always did whenever she saw Beau. Some mornings she brought him a flower or a piece of her morning bun, but today she wore a serious look on her face.

"I want you to know something," she declared.

"I'm listening," Beau replied.

"I like my name now, and I'm going to keep it!" And with

that, Bea went running to catch up with the others.

"I'm glad it's no longer a burden to any of us," Beau said as Cressi stopped one of the taller boys zooming past.

"Have you seen Nate yet, Pervis?" she asked.

"No, sorry, not this morning," Pervis panted, eager to be on his way.

"All right, well, thank you." Cressi brushed back the boy's messy fringe of hair. "Have fun but stay away from the veils!"

"Sure, sure!" Pervis laughed as he raced out the door.

"So, are you ready then?" Cressi asked Beau.

"I need to stop in the library first, get my robe."

"You know, you don't have to wear it. Just because the others decided to maintain the tradition doesn't mean you have to as well."

"I want to." Beau was adamant as he headed into the library. "I need to. I feel like it's been the only way to change the story attached to it."

Beau stepped into the library, a place he'd avoided for a very long time. Unlike his mother's rooms, ripe with the scent of lilies and apples, which gave him solace, the very scent of cloves made his stomach lurch. He hadn't even allowed anyone inside the library to clean up for a long while. But then the time came to expel the ghosts of the past. The Manor's new residents deserved access to the wealth of knowledge kept there.

Beau found his father's council robes hanging on a hook

next to the children's painting smocks. The walls, which had once been draped in tapestries depicting bloody battles and adorned with swords and weapons, were now covered in maps, colorful paintings of the alphabet, and math formulas. Transforming the library into a classroom seemed the most fitting purpose Beau could ever think of.

Cressi offered to help Beau, but he waved her off. The robes weren't nearly as heavy or ornate as they'd once been; he'd had the heavy gold buttons and fur trim removed and repurposed for more practical uses. After they'd established the new order of the Land, he'd thought long and hard about never putting on his father's robes. He found them too intimidating. But then the others convinced him there was something to be said for maintaining some of the old rituals—changing them to fit new ideals. And so Beau agreed, as long as all the council members designed and wore their own robes as well. Never again would one person dictate the choices others could make.

Together, Beau and Cressi headed to the council chambers. The rooms in the back hallway were the last remaining vestiges of the old Manor system. It had been decided by unanimous consent that the Leadership Council, the members of which had been elected by the people of their districts, along with their trusted advisors, should still meet at the Manor. For what better reminder could there be of who they were serving than having their offices in the new Academy of Letters and Learning.

Beau and Cressi entered the council chambers, where four of the other members were already gathered. Woolever, the representative from the Upper Middlelands, greeted Beau with a broad and friendly smile, while Topend's Parvenue nodded solemnly. Jakers, a farmer from the Lower Middlelands elected to represent that district, still had a hard time looking Beau in the eye. But it was the cordwainer who gave Beau the heartiest greeting. He still couldn't believe that he'd been elected by all the craftsmen in the Land to represent them. He celebrated his good fortune by vowing to supply every child at the Academy with a new pair of boots every year they were in attendance.

"Not arrived yet?" Beau asked.

"They say any minute now," Woolever replied.

"We should all take our seats," Parvenue intoned. "The moment demands formality."

"The moment demands patience," the cordwainer replied. "I could no more sit while we wait than dance a jig."

"Highly irregular!" Parvenue puffed. "The old Himself would never have stood for such a break with protocol."

Parvenue was having a hard time letting go of the old ways, which caused tension with the others. But Beau took a different view. At least Parvenue was changing, if slowly, and was taking the rest of the Topenders along with him.

"The model of my family's rule is gone," Beau reminded him. "The only thing that matters now is the work we're all doing for the people of the Land."

"Has no one seen Nate this morning?" Cressi asked.

"I heard he rode out to meet the messenger," Jakers said. "He couldn't stand the waiting for her arrival any more."

"Sounds about right. Think I'll go join hi—" Beau began when the door flew open.

It was Nate, hot and sweaty from his ride, followed by Hugo.

"It's as we feared." Nate shook with disgust. "Tell them, Hugo. Even saying it makes my stomach lurch."

"The rumors are true," Hugo reported. "Our scout confirmed it with her own eyes. Doone's gone and pledged loyalty to Torin."

Beau let the news wash over him. He kept waiting for it to hit him hard, scare him, turn him inside out. But he'd known this was coming ever since the day some of Doone's loyal followers from the Lower Middlelands blasted a hole in the side of the dungeons, allowing Doone to escape. They had taken Barger and Cook along with them, presumably as hostages, which was the only small solace Beau could find. He'd no sooner pay to see Barger released than grant him immunity for his countless crimes against the people of the Land.

Cressi lay a comforting hand on Beau's shoulder.

"I say we go and fight them!" Nate declared. "The both of them! We have the weapons, the fighters. We can—"

"Do no such thing," Woolever counseled. "That would

break the truce Fledge negotiated with Torin. We cannot risk it. Doone's not worth it."

"Not worth it!" Nate exploded. "He's a murderer. He'll stop at nothing to get Beau and Cressi and take over the Land!"

"Not if he has power where he is," Parvenue replied.

"That's true," Hugo agreed. "And our scout did report that Torin has given Doone an entire village to rule."

"I agree. Our pact with Torin means too much to him," Beau added. "I can't see what makes it worthwhile for Torin to forfeit the steady supply of Cressi's healing charms we're providing them. I don't like it any more than you do, but I do think we are safe from them both."

"For now," Cressi added.

"I want Doone punished," Nate said. "I want him to pay!"

"We do too. But the people of the Land deserve some peace," the cordwainer said. "The fever victims are all well mended now. We have our lives, our families, and our safety back. He's gone. We have to let that be good enough."

Nate threw his hands up in resignation. "I'll wait for you outside," he said to Beau and Cressi. "I need some air."

Beau waited until Nate had gone before he turned to the other council members. "Even given this news, I think we continue as planned. Please know I have the utmost faith in my surrogate. He will serve the Land well and faithfully. He always has."

"It doesn't seem right for you to go," Jakers said.

"I think it's more than right," Beau replied. "Given Doone and Torin's alliance, it's past time we find new allies beyond our borders, discover new ways to protect ourselves, new weapons before our enemies do and use them against us. And it's time I go too."

"You'll take some of our scouts with you. Gerta insists." Hugo moved for the door. "I'll get them ready."

"No," Cressi said. "We'll be fine. Leave them here where they're needed the most."

"Gerta won't like that," Hugo warned.

"She'll get used to it," Beau laughed. "Look at everything else she's grown accustomed to."

"You'll send word as often as you can?" the cordwainer asked.

"Of course," Cressi replied. "Beau will be recording every moment, I can guarantee you that."

"Very well then." Woolever nodded a small bow. "By the Goodness of All, safe travels to you."

After a hearty round of handshakes and even a few hugs, Beau and Cressi left the council room.

Two steps out the door and Beau already felt lighter, easier. Younger. Who knew what waited for them on the other side of the sea, but he couldn't wait to find out.

"There's only one last thing to do then," Cressi said.

Beau nodded.

Of all the goodbyes he had to make, this one would be the hardest.

They found Nate waiting for them by the front door, whispering conspiratorially into Pervis's ear before sending him running off.

"You weren't telling him where to find other veils, were you?" Cressi scolded. "He already scared the life out of Lula when she couldn't find him yesterday."

Nate shrugged innocently as the three friends headed out to the front lawns.

"You're a terrible influence," Cressi continued. "You know that?"

"Of course I do." Nate smiled. "It's my job."

Cressi and Nate continued teasing and taunting each other all the way to the stables but stopped short of the entrance.

"Do you want to go in alone?" Cressi asked Beau.

"Of course not."

Keb and Boz were posted outside the door, as they always were these days. Even though Fledge told them daily they didn't have to be there, they refused to stand down. Beau and everyone else knew their loyalty wasn't actually directed at Fledge, but as long as Anka and Fledge were together, Keb and Boz would be nearby.

Beau had been coming to see Fledge every day since the master of the stables returned home to a hero's welcome after forging the treaty with Torin. But Fledge had been in such terrible condition he barely had the strength to enjoy it. How unfair it was that after walking straight into the enemy camp and boldly striking a deal, it was a panther attack on the way home that had almost cost Fledge his life.

Almost. But thanks to Cressi's brews, he'd been slowly regaining his strength, and he was beginning to walk with the help of a cane. He still had some bad days, but today, it appeared, was not one of them.

"You look good," Beau exclaimed, rushing to his friend's side.

"And you look like a poor excuse for a liar, all three of you do." Fledge smiled. "Sit down and tell me the news."

Anka brought in a tray of strawberry hand-pies and some tea while Beau told Fledge about Doone.

"Are you certain that leaving now is the right choice?" Fledge asked.

"We are," Beau said. "He won't be expecting it, and we'll be long gone before word of our departure ever reaches him."

Beau shrugged out of the heavy velvet robes and laid them across the back of a chair. "These are yours now."

"Only until your return." Fledge looked at Beau, Cressi, and Nate, his lips pursed tight. But his look wasn't one of hesitation or fear. It was contentment, pure and simple, woven through with pride.

After several rounds of long, warm hugs the trio left Fledge's quarters and headed back to the Manor to pack for their journey.

It was only once he was back in his mother's room to gather his things that Beau finally knew how to end *The Histories*.

It couldn't end in a period—it needed something less definite. It needed a question, a prompt, a dare to those who one day might read his account.

"If there's one thing I've learned by living through this piece of history," Beau wrote, "it's that in order to live, to thrive, to win the day, you have to be willing to follow fate where it leads, trusting you are exactly who and where you need to be.

"So then the only question left to ask is: Where will you let the truth take you?"

Acknowledgments

Like many books, this one took a long time to make its way out into the world. Writing, rewriting, editing, and then doing it all over again took long enough for some readers of this book to have gone from kindergarten into middle school. But in a lot of ways this book took even longer still. Don't ask me why, but I ran away from writing for a long time. It was hard. It was lonely. And mostly I wasn't as good as I wanted to be. So I left it. Found other outlets. I had a couple of interesting careers, started a family. But writing was always there, sitting on my shoulder, reminding me I had stories to tell. A move out of the city and into the country, where it was quiet, sometimes too quiet, left me with far fewer distractions and the wherewithal to finally sit down and get to work.

With this work now done, I am so grateful to be able to

thank those who've guided, inspired, and bolstered me along the way.

I don't even want to think about what would've happened if I hadn't met Christine Heppermann, and then hadn't been pushy enough to make her my friend. Thank you for the chance to thank you.

Rebecca Ansari and Phoebe North are immensely talented writers who I'm lucky enough to call my friends, support system, and part-time therapists. Thank you for holding my hand when I need it. I couldn't have asked for two better guides through this new and wonderous terrain.

Thank you so much to the brilliant HV writers Ann Burg, Julie Chibarro, Lesa Cline-Ransome, Jocelyn Johnson-Kearney, Stephanie Tolan, and Virginia Ewer Wolff, who welcomed me into their ranks and make me feel at home.

Nan Gatewood Satter has been generously sharing her wisdom with me for a long time now. There are not enough cups of coffee in the world to thank her properly.

Although in very different arenas, both Peter Lerangis and Peter Nathan gave me the encouragement and confidence to keep going, for that I am incredibly grateful.

Thank you to the remarkable writer friends I'm so fortunate to be surrounded by: Erika Ely Lewis, Leah Glennon, Jennifer Mazi, Gail Upchurch, Janna Wallack-Cohen Kowan, and my 21der pals. You inspire me.

To Linda Oehler-Marx, Jane Dunkel Hernandez, and June

Wheeler, thank you for always cheering me on.

Maia Rossini has been my friend, endless source of culinary inspiration, and generous sounding board for a long time—I can't wait to see what we cook up next.

To my brilliant Atlantic Theater Company family who've been inspiring me since those summers in Vermont so, so long ago. I love you all.

David and Shirley aren't here to read any of this, but they're here in every page of this book.

Thank you to my sisters, Dara and Kari Wishingrad, and to my sister of the heart Kate Blumberg, who told me to write that none of this would have been possible without her. She's probably right.

To Laura Ruby, a remarkable writer and teacher, thank you for your guidance and faith.

To Anne Ursu, weaver of beautiful tales, generous cheerleader, and fairy godmother, thank you for believing.

So much gratitude to Laura Mock, whose beautiful design has brought the world of the book to life. To Laura Harshberger for wrangling my over-exuberant use of commas and em dashes, and Alison Brown for ushering this book into the world. Infinite thanks to Emily Zhu and Lauren Levite for their work promoting and marketing this book. I am so grateful to you both. Júlia Sardà is a genius, and I am incredibly honored to have her gorgeous artwork adorning the cover.

To Victoria Marini, as fierce and brilliant an agent as there could ever be. I'm as lucky as they come to have her in my corner.

I am forever grateful to my magnificent editors, both charmers in their own right. Megan Ilnitzki believed in this book from the start. And Toni Markiet, whose wisdom and insight cut straight to the heart of this story, knew what it could become and exactly how to help me get there. Thank you for sharing your magic with me!

Owen and Oona are the brilliant humans who own my heart, who keep me honest, and always learning. And lucky for me, they're both fantastic sounding boards who have helped me fill in many plot holes.

And finally, nothing would have been possible without Dan, who has held the gates open all this time, while I followed this long and sometimes twisting path. Thank you for your ever-faithful trust. Here's to continuing to follow winding paths and seeing where they lead.